Betrayal of the Court

The Other Realm Series, Book 6

Heather G. Harris

Huge thanks to my Patrons, my advance reader team and my beta reader team. I am blessed to have such an amazing support network around me. With special mention to Mel, Beba and Kass.

Chapter 1

'You pissed someone off,' I murmured to the mangled corpse in front of me. I'd seen my fair share of death, but this body had anger written all over it. The poor chap had been whaled on, probably with a baseball bat or something similar. His features had been thoroughly destroyed to the point that it was hard for my brain to recognise that I was looking at a human body.

My phone rang and I grimaced internally. I pulled it out and saw that it was Lucy. My best friend had recently managed to swipe the title of Queen of the Werewolves and I worried that she might need my advice. Dead body or not, I needed to answer.

'Sorry,' I said to the pathologist and held up a finger. 'Just give me a minute.'

I gathered my magic within me, focusing my intention, intending to draw a sphere of privacy around me so I could talk to Lucy without anyone else hearing. The conversation could be about important werewolf matters or a fashion faux pas – with Lucy, I could never be too sure. 'Privacy,' I uttered, the release word, letting my magic sweep out. A wizard's magic – the Intention and Release aka the IR – sure was handy.

I swiped to answer the call. 'Hey, Queen of the Bitches!' I answered, stepping back from the battered body in front of me.

There was a beat of silence during which I suspected that Lucy was sighing internally. 'Now I'll have to explain to Esme why that is *not* an appropriate title.'

I sniggered. 'Sorry not sorry. How are you doing?'

'I'm okay. The mansion is overrun with snooty werewolves.'

'And you're hiding in your office?' I guessed.

'I'm not *hiding,* I'm seeking solitude,' she said snottily.

'Potato, tomato,' I teased.

'Actually, I'm ringing to check on you. You and Emory flew out of here like bats out of hell and I feel so

responsible. I've made a complete mess of things for you.'
True.

'Don't be silly, it'll be fine.' *Lie.* I winced. Stupid radar.

'Have you told the Court yet?' Lucy asked archly.

'About Emory making true brethren for the first time in centuries and accidentally enslaving a whole race to his will?'

'Yeah.'

'Nope,' I said cheerfully. 'It hasn't come up yet.'

'Jess! I don't think this is something you can ignore. Emory broke dragon law.' She said the last few words in a hushed whisper, like saying it louder would get us in *more* trouble. We were already screwed; admitting it out loud couldn't make it any worse.

'We just need some time to find some loopholes,' I said optimistically. 'You know me; I can always find a loophole. It'll be fine.' *Lie.* Dammit, even *I* didn't think it was going to be okay. 'The wedding preparations are distracting everyone.'

'The *wedding* preparations?'

'Oh.' I cleared my throat. She was going to squeal. 'I forgot to mention before ... we've set a date.' I pulled the phone away from my ear just before she let out an ear-splitting shriek of excitement. 'In two months.'

'In two months?' The words exploded out of her. 'Are you kidding me? That's not enough time to plan a fricking wedding!'

'When you're rich, you can do a lot in two months. Hell, we could probably do a lot in two weeks if we really needed to. We're using the wedding to keep the Court busy and occupied – Elizabeth is positively salivating over the guest list. I just need them to focus on that, then I can find a missing jewel for Emory and sort out this whole gargoyle situation.'

'Situation isn't really the word for it. Emory turned the gargoyles human again and then he bound them to himself. He has an adoring army at his command – a *forbidden* adoring army.'

'It makes it sound bad when you say it like that,' I admitted. 'Anyway, they're not human – they're something else. They have wings now. Besides, he saved their lives. If he hadn't made the gargoyles into true brethren, they would have all died.'

'I get it – you're preaching to the choir – but Greg told me that making true brethren has been outlawed for a good couple of centuries. Dragons have very long memories.'

'You'd think immortality would make them forgetful, but they always remember the crap that you wish they'd let slide,' I complained.

Leonard could remember every penny of the hoard that I spent, including the money I'd used to pay for lunch for the younglings on an outing. You'd think he'd be happy that I was bonding with the kids but no; he was grumpy that I hadn't completed Form 238. He'd only mentioned it five times this week, so maybe he was letting it go.

Lucy blew out a breath. 'So, when do we get a hen do, then?' she asked, blatantly changing the subject to happier matters. There was a beat, then she muttered to Esme, 'No, you don't *eat* the hens.'

'I don't know when exactly, but I promise it's on the cards. It'll be great. You and I will have a blast—'

'It's not just going to be you and me,' she scoffed. 'I'll organise it! It'll be amazing.'

'You have other stuff on your plate—' Queenly stuff.

'Don't you dare take this away from me! I've been dreaming of this moment since we were six years old. Amber will be up for it, I'm sure. Who else?'

My thoughts immediately flashed to my sole employee. Hes and I had been good friends prior to her little hiccup, and thankfully our trial by phoenix fire had set us back firmly on track. 'Hes.'

'Hes?' Lucy sounded surprised. 'Did you guys make up?'

'It'd be hard not to after she got kidnapped and held hostage by the great fire chicken.'

'Dare you to call the phoenix that to her face,' she sniggered.

'Erm ... no.' The phoenix was hellish scary and just a smidge insane.

'Okay, so Hes. Who else?'

I racked my brains. My circle of friends had increased a lot in the last few months, but most of them were men like Nate, Bastion and Shirdal. I was scraping the barrel for female friends. 'Elvira and Summer?' I suggested weakly. They mostly liked me, right? 'Oh, and maybe Emory's mum Audrey?' That was it. You could almost count my female friends on one hand; I'm much more of guy-friend type of girl.

'Now we're cooking.' I could picture Lucy rubbing her hands together in glee. 'This will be great. Leave it all to me. It's exactly what I needed, something to look forward to. I'd best go and get stuck in. And Jess?'

'Yeah?'

'Erm...' She cleared her throat and sounded awkward, something rare for her. 'You're excited to marry Emory, right? This isn't political manoeuvring to cover up the gargoyle thing and buy you time?'

I smiled as I thought of my fiancé. 'I'm *so* excited to marry Emory. Nothing has ever felt more right.'

'Great. So we're good?' Relief coloured her tone.

'We're good,' I agreed firmly. 'I love you, Luce.'

'I love you too, Jess. Speak soon.' She made kissy noises and hung up.

I released the privacy bubble that I'd created and let the magic fizzle away, then pocketed my phone and turned my attention to the twisted body in front of me on the pathologist's metal table. I wasn't quite sure why I was looking at the destroyed flesh. The body certainly wasn't recognisable; the face had been pulverised until it looked like so much meat and bone.

'Sorry,' I said to Noah, the pathologist. 'I wasn't sure if it was an important call or not.' It had turned out not to be, but with Lucy you could never be sure.

'No problem,' Noah said genially. He gestured to the mangled corpse. 'He's not going anywhere.' Ugh, dead-body humour. Great.

Chapter 2

'Why am I here?' I asked the room at large. 'Not existentially,' I clarified. 'Why am I here in this morgue?'

'The Prime Elite wants you briefed on the deaths,' Mike Carter said firmly. I noted that he said 'deaths', plural. There was only one corpse laid out for me to see, so I waited for him to get to the point. He'd get there eventually.

Mike was brethren and he was usually part of the castle personnel, but he'd been seconded to look after me. Protect me. Babysit me. Lucky Mike, and lucky me; there's nothing I like more than having my every step dogged by guards.

I had argued with Emory good and hard about having a protection detail because, let's face it, I can protect myself. He had explained patiently that appearances were important in the dragon court and I needed to visibly admit the brethren into my life. It was another step of acceptance after I'd passed the Court's stupid challenges. If I was going to be their Prima, I had to play by their rules. It was restricting and annoying, but I was trying to be understanding and accommodating. Once I was Prima – if I ever got to be Prima – there would be lifestyle changes. Luckily, I liked Mike so that helped a lot.

'Why didn't the Prime Elite brief me himself?' I queried, hands on my hips. I was only half-joking. Since the challenges, it had been really difficult to get some time alone with Emory. Elizabeth seemed to be making it her duty to keep us apart until we were formally bound. If she said 'absence makes the heart grow fonder' one more time, her shoulders were going to be minus a head. Okay, not really – but I'd definitely bitch to Gato about her. I didn't need to be any fonder of Emory. I loved him.

'He's very busy negotiating a company purchase,' Mike explained. 'Otherwise I'm sure he'd tell you himself.'

'Which company is it this time? Harrods?' I asked drily.

'Linkage LLP.'

I frowned. That name tickled something in my brain. 'Wait – isn't that the company that Gilligan Stone used to own?'

Mike nodded. 'The one and the same.'

'What happened to it when Stone Senior died?'

'It passed to Stone Junior. The shareholders voted him chief executive.'

'And when Stone Junior died?' I queried.

'The shareholders put the company up for sale.'

'Two dead chief execs made them twitchy?'

'Something like that.' Mike shrugged.

I frowned. 'Didn't the Connection use that company to carry out its nefarious work?'

'Black ops work. Yeah.'

'So if Emory owned the company... ' My voice trailed away.

'He'd get access to some very helpful information.'

'Nice.' I relaxed. 'Okay, that's a good reason to be busy.'

'I'll tell him you approve,' Mike said drily. I liked that we'd reached a place in our relationship where he felt comfortable to give me sass rather than non-stop 'ma'aming' me. When we'd first met it had been 'ma'am' this and 'ma'am' that. Let me tell you, the 'ma'ams' grew old fast.

'So why does that bring me to our lovely pathologist here? And John Doe?' I gestured to the pulverised corpse in front of us.

'John Doe is not John Doe, his name is Derek Ives,' responded Noah. 'He's been identified by a custom tattoo on his calf. Obviously dental records couldn't be used in this case.' Derek had got the stuffing knocked out of him – and his teeth, too. Even after Noah had cleaned him up, he was still in a state. Broken bones and broken skin. There had been hatred here.

'It looks like he got whacked with a baseball bat or something,' I observed.

'Exactly.' Noah leaned forward. 'There's nothing magical about this murder.'

'So why are we here?' I asked, raising my eyebrows.

'Derek Ives was a satyr,' Mike stated.

'Half-man, half-goat?'

'That's the one,' Noah confirmed.

Jack had once said that he was hung like a satyr but I'd thought it was a joke; I hadn't realised that satyrs were real. 'Huh. I haven't seen any of those walking around Liverpool.'

'You wouldn't – they're mainly rural,' Mike explained.

'So are we looking at Derek the satyr's death because he's Other?' I asked. 'Or is there more to it than that?'

'We're looking at his death for a couple of reasons. There's been a rash of Anti-Crea sentiment lately and a lot more attacks on innocent creatures. We need to determine if this death is an escalation of that or something else entirely because, on the surface, it looks like he was killed by someone from the Common realm.'

'I'm not following,' I said flatly.

'Death by baseball bat,' Noah explained. 'It wouldn't have raised a flag if his housemate hadn't also been bludgeoned to death about two days earlier.' He opened the door of the cold cabinet, pulled out another body and removed the sheet. 'Arlo Hardman.'

I grimaced; this body was as ruined as poor Derek Ives'. The flesh looked like something you would see on the butcher's table, not at the morgue. 'Let me guess,' I said cynically. 'Arlo was also a satyr?'

'Bingo,' Noah pointed both forefingers at me like guns.

I studied Arlo – what was left of him. Like Derek's, his face had been destroyed. 'Neither of them look ... goaty. Were they in the Common realm when they died?'

'No, they were in satyr form. Their bodies shifted back to human on their deaths,' Mike said.

'Like a werewolf's does?'

'Exactly. All of the creatures do that when they die, with the exception of dragons. If they die in dragon form, they stay in dragon form even in death,' he explained.

I sighed. 'And I'm looking into these deaths because...?'

'Because Emory was their Prime Elite. Two dead satyrs are making the satyr community anxious. He needs to be seen to be taking action, and who better to investigate the crimes than his Prima?' Mike asked with fake innocence.

Who indeed? 'Okay, so what's the plan? I propose we hit the crime scenes first, question any friends and relatives of Derek and Arlo and see what we turn up.'

'I agree with that course of action.' Mike cleared his throat. 'There's just one more thing.'

'Yes?' I bit back a sigh.

'Because we're going into an Other hotspot, I won't be able to protect you all the time.' His voice morphed into lecturing mode.

'I don't need—' I started.

'Let's agree to disagree on that, Prima,' he said firmly. 'The Prime has ordered in more back-up.'

'Who?' I asked resignedly.

'Shirdal.'

Why was I not surprised? When death and destruction were involved, a griffin was never far behind.

Chapter 3

Gato, Mike and I had a great car journey to the crime scene where Shirdal was meeting us. Mike is a fan of nineties' rock and we had the music loud while we drove. I sang and Gato tapped his tail to the beat. It was a party.

'So where exactly are we going to?' I asked belatedly.

'Portmeirion.'

I waited a beat to see if he was going to elaborate. When he didn't, I asked, 'Where's that then?'

'It's a town in Wales. It's … unique. It was designed and built between the 1920s and the 1970s in the style of an Italian village. It's been adopted by the Other realm because it's quirky and weird – like us,' he said with rueful self-deprecation.

'Why on earth would it be designed to look Italian? In Wales?' It seemed a bizarre choice.

'You'd have to ask the guy who built it. It's a tourist trap, but its eccentricities appealed to the Other community straight away. When the tourists are away, the Other come out to play.'

'And Derek and Arlo lived there?'

'Lived and worked there. You have to work there to get accommodation in the village itself. They both worked part time for the charity that runs the place. It's quiet and sleepy, so the whole community has been rocked by their deaths. It's spilled over into the Common realm. The police are all over it.'

'Have we already got the crossovers in place there?'

'You bet. Emory pulled some strings and the case landed on Elvira's desk. He thought you'd appreciate that.'

Mike wasn't wrong. Elvira and I have a decent working relationship that is tottering slowly towards friendship. I would rather have her than some other Connection badge that I don't know from Adam. 'I appreciate it,' I agreed. 'But I bet Elvira is less than sunny about it.'

Someone else had pulled strings last time to get her to work on the break-in at my office. At times, she must feel like she works solely on Jinx-related mysteries. Lucky me.

I refocused. 'You said that Arlo was killed two days ago? When was Derek killed?'

'Last night,' Mike said grimly.

'In the same place?' I asked, surprised. That seemed somewhat short-sighted on the killer's part. Surely they realised the police would grasp pretty quickly that the incidents were connected? Same MO, same location. It made me lower my estimation of the killer's intelligence. I suspected he or she was rowing with only one oar.

'Not the *exact* same location but in Portmeirion, yes. The village has been closed to tourists for now. The only ones allowed in there are the residents.'

'Are they all Other residents?'

'Yes. It just so happens that everyone there is Other,' Mike said.

Of course they were.

It was an April day, but we'd avoided the showers that are characteristic of the month. The sun was beating down on us, warming the day. Lilac skies hung above us, clear and bright. If death hadn't been on the agenda, I'd have been feeling upbeat.

We parked in a public car park and got out of the car. I looked around at the surrounding trees. 'Where's the village?' I asked.

'This way.' Mike nodded to the right.

'You know the area well?'

He coloured slightly. 'I've spent some time here in the past.'

'Oh yeah? And that made you blush because…?' I teased.

'Best you find out for yourself.' He smiled awkwardly. 'I don't want to cloud your judgement or anything.'

Ha! He just didn't want to talk about his shenanigans, but that made me want to dig them out all the more. I have a nosy problem. I brightened; this village looked like it was going to be more fun than just ice cream and cake.

Gato trotted happily at my heels before stopping to pee to mark his territory. 'We've literally just arrived,' I bitched. 'You can't claim this place as yours.' He gave some happy wags, blithely ignored me and from then on peed on every single tree to spite me. The joke was on him, though; his jets would run out before we reached buildings for him to piddle on. Heh-heh.

The entrance to Portmeirion was a beautiful, dramatic arch – though it was marred by the blue-and-white police tape all around it. A bored looking policeman was sitting by the tape, his head buried in a book.

'I'm sorry, no entrance today,' he intoned without looking up. I could relate to that; if I'm reading a good book, I hate being interrupted too. In fact, death might follow – all right, probably not death but maybe some minor mutilation.

Mike clearly wasn't a reader. He frowned prissily at the police officer, pulled out a law-and-order-style badge and dumped it on the open book. 'We're with Elvira Garcia,' he ground out.

The badge slid onto the policeman's lap. He fumbled with it, shut the book and leapt to his feet. I resisted the urge to tell him he was shutting the barn door after the centaur had bolted.

'Right you are, sir,' he snapped out. 'I'll radio Inspector Garcia right away to let her know to expect you.'

'Thank you,' I responded, despite the fact that he was bowing and scraping to Mike and not to me. 'Please tell her Jinx is here, too.'

'Yes ma'am.' He pulled out his radio.

Ah: 'ma'am'. Well, surprise, surprise; I had actually missed being 'ma'amed' a little.

The officer lifted up the striped tape to let us in and we ducked under it. While the bookworm radioed ahead, Mike and I walked into the village.

As we entered it, my eyes were bigger than a centaur's bollocks. It was something else, and it was difficult to do it justice in words. It was full of buildings painted in bright colours, with Roman-looking columns, statues and manicured lawns. If I hadn't known better I'd have thought I really was in Italy, but I knew I wasn't so it made me feel a bit like I'd taken some sort of hallucinogen. I felt trippy.

This village was completely at odds with the Welsh landscape. Whoever had designed this crazy-ass place had done a great job, though ultimately the cold and dreary weather would give it away as being somewhere other than Italy. I imagined it was hugely popular with tourists looking for a spot of foreign holiday in their life without the hassle of a flight.

It wasn't hard to pinpoint where we needed to go; another property up ahead was also surrounded by blue-and-white police tape. Mike, Gato and I headed there.

'What was the badge you showed the policeman?' I asked curiously. The police officer had reacted like it was a decree from the king himself.

'An MI5 badge.' Mike smirked a little.

'MI5 have badges?'

'Yes, though I imagine they don't wave them about.' MI5 are spies; having a badge to proclaim their identity might not be the best policy.

'Couldn't you get into trouble for waving around a fake badge?' I queried.

'Who said anything about it being fake?'

Huh. 'Do you have any idea where we'll meet Shirdal?'

'He'll be about. At one of the cafés, I expect,' Mike said.

I frowned. 'I thought you said everything was shut?'

'To tourists, not to residents.'

Another policeman was outside the house we were heading for. This one was standing to attention, no book in sight, and he held up a hand in a 'stop' gesture. I recognised him instantly, but today he was wearing a frown rather than his usual smile. 'As I have said over and over again, no one can gain access to the property until... Oh! Hi, Jinx!' said Inspector Gordon Bland, Elvira's ginger-haired partner.

'Officer Tasty,' I greeted him before my brain caught up. 'Oh shit! Erm ... Officer Bland.'

He laughed. 'I wish El had been here to witness someone calling me Officer Tasty.'

I blushed. It had slipped out – how embarrassing. 'I'm so sorry.' I had the IR, so conceivably I could get the ground to open and swallow me up. It's always good to have options.

Gordon Bland winked at me while still grinning broadly. I might have been mortified, but I'd made his day – possibly even his week. 'No problem. Honestly, it's funny. You can go in. Elvira will want to see you. She's with the surviving roommate.'

'Name?' I asked, trying to get back to a business-like footing.

'Shane Brown.'

'He must be feeling nervous if he's the only one left alive,' I noted.

'I don't think he's made the connection yet. You head on in.' Bland opened the door for us.

'I'll stay out here,' Mike said. Bland raised an eyebrow in surprise; he didn't know that Mike was here as a guard rather than in an investigatory capacity. Mike had many hats; I hoped he had a good hatstand at home.

Gato and I strolled into the property. It was a terraced house painted an entirely too cheerful yellow that felt at odds with the murder of two of its residents. The house was small but was spread across three floors. We went into the main room, which had been converted into an open-plan area with the kitchen and dining area all in one space. Even so, it didn't feel especially spacious. If I'd been an estate agent, I'd have called the house cosy and full of character, but I wasn't an estate agent so I thought it was small and poky. It wasn't for me, not even with the Italian vibes.

Elvira stood as Gato and I entered; she had assumed her professional demeanour. She gave us both a brief inclination of her head. 'This is Civilian Consultant Sharp and her hellhound.'

'Hello, Mr Brown. I'm sorry to make your acquaintance under such circumstances.' I offered with a sympathetic smile.

'I appreciate that.' Mr Brown kept his eyes lowered and fiddled with his hands.

I had met quite a few people who had suffered loss, and grief was something that came off them in waves. Not so for Shane Brown; if anything, his body language said he was anxious. I guessed having both your roommates murdered might be a cause for concern. I wanted to see if he was right to be worried.

Chapter 4

Shane Brown had mousy-brown hair, a big nose – and two very goatish legs. Weirdly, he had human-type knee joints so he could sit comfortably on a chair. He was wearing a striped, white-and-red shirt with a badge on it that proclaimed his name and also said 'Izzy's Ices'. He was wearing black slacks; the evidence of his goatish legs were the cloven hooves at the end of them and the tufts of fur sticking out from the slacks. Presumably it was tough to get shoes to fit cloven hooves, and besides he didn't need them – he could clip-clop all over the place without worrying about standing on stray stinging nettles.

I tried hard not to stare. His hooves weren't the only goatish addition to his appearance. Instead of human ears, he had furry, goat-pointed ears, and two medium-sized horns curved backwards on the top of his head. Apart from that – the fur, hooves and horns – he looked completely human.

Mr Brown appeared to be agitated but not upset. He went from wringing his hands to setting them firmly on his knees, then he'd forget and start rubbing his neck before determinedly stilling his fingers in his lap again.

I wanted to get a better read from him so I moved closer. In the Other realm, we're supposed to greet each other by touching a hand to our heart and bowing slightly. When I was a babe in the woods, I'd thought that was a respectful tradition but I knew now that people didn't shake hands because Others like me could use it to get information from them.

Technically speaking, I was still relatively new to the Other realm, and now and again I found I could use my supposed ignorance. I held out my hand and said, 'Jessica Sharp, nice to meet you.'

He blinked in surprise but took my hand. He was British; it wouldn't do to appear rude.

In preparation for the physical touch, I had pushed away the sound of the ocean in my mind ready to receive any impressions from him. I was braced to feel a wash of grief and loss rush over me, but instead I felt an overwhelming sense of relief. He was glad that Arlo and Derek were dead. Huh.

'Sorry about Miss Sharp's manners,' Elvira apologised, glaring at me. 'She's new to the Other realm.'

'Oh!' I said, eyes wide. 'I'm so sorry. We do it like this, don't we?' I put my hand to my heart and gave a little bow. 'My honour to meet you, Shane Brown.'

It didn't matter; I'd got what I needed from him. Shane Brown was officially a person of interest in the case.

He copied me, touching his hand to his heart and giving a little bob. That gave me a better view of the jet-black horns curling back from his head. Cool. 'My honour to meet you, Jessica Sharp,' he intoned with the appropriate degree of pomp and reverence.

Elvira had already had her chance to interview him so I stepped right in. I'd do good cop first, then see if bad cop needed to be pulled out. 'I'm sorry for your loss,' I started, with another sympathetic smile.

'Thank you,' he responded stiffly.

'Were you close to your housemates?'

'Not really.' *True.* 'We kept ourselves to ourselves.' *Lie.* Not best buds then, but not the strangers he wished to project. Interesting.

'And what do you do for a job?' I asked, like I couldn't see his uniform and ice cream nametag clear as day. Most people aren't terribly observant and they expect others to be the same. I'm not most people, but he didn't know that yet.

'I work here in the village, in the ice-cream parlour,' he explained. His shoulders were rigid and his arms were folded across his chest. Shane was too tense; I needed to get him to relax.

'What a cool job!' Literally. 'I love ice cream. What flavour would you recommend?' I gushed.

'The truffle chocolate is divine – if you like chocolate.' His shoulders dropped a little.

'I love chocolate, though mint-choc-chip is a close second.'

'We have that one too,' he assured me with a small smile. His shoulders relaxed a little more.

'Did Derek and Arlo work in the village too?'

'No, not really. On paper they work for the charity but the reality is that they don't work. *Didn't* work. Derek won the lottery a few years ago and he used his winnings to cover his spends.'

'And to bribe people to keep him on the payroll,' I guessed.

He shrugged uncomfortably. 'That's what I always figured.'

'And Arlo?'

Shane snorted and his mouth twisted in distaste. 'He's a freeloader. He lives off Derek. *Lived.* Has done since the win. They were peas in a pod.' Bitterness had crept into his voice.

'Not nice peas?' I said sympathetically.

He froze and his tongue darted out to wet his lips. Involuntarily, one of his hands reached up to tug at the neck of his shirt. I peeked to see if there was more fur, but no: all he exposed was more human skin. Just the goaty legs, then. I find the Other fascinating.

'It's okay,' I assured him. 'You can be frank with me. Your roommates are gone now and we're going to find out about every aspect of their lives. It's one of the best ways to find their killer – first know the victim. It's rare for a murder to be truly random, though not impossible, but since *both* of them were targeted it's unlikely these killings were random. It's more likely that someone knew the two of them and took them out.' I paused then added, 'Quite violently. I assume they had enemies?'

Shane chewed his lip anxiously as he wondered what to say. I had to resist the urge to lean on him, to compel him, which would be so much easier and quicker than straight questioning. But I bit back the urge; I was better than that and I could get the information without using magic.

'They lived a carefree life.' Shane was picking his words with care. 'Not just with their money – they didn't give a damn about the consequences of their actions. Derek's cash bailed them out of trouble more than once. There were no consequences for them.' The bitterness was back.

I leaned forward. 'What sort of trouble?'

'Derek and Arlo were the type of satyr that give the rest of us our bad reputation.'

'What sort of bad reputation?' I asked baldly. 'Sorry, I'm still new to the Other realm.'

'Right.' Shane cleared his throat. 'We have a reputation for being drinkers and brawlers,' he admitted unhappily.

'And womanisers,' Elvira added, her tone caustic.

Shane winced, then seemed to collapse in on himself. 'Yes, that too,' he agreed.

Now we were getting to the heart of the matter.

'Derek and Arlo liked to drink and they liked to spend time in the company of women,' I clarified.

Shane shifted in his seat, gave a noncommittal shrug and studied his nails. I lowered my mental shields and focused on him. I gave him a sympathetic look then reached out and touched his arm; by doing that, I could feel how uncomfortable he was. His skin was almost crawling with revulsion and there was fear, too. In spades.

There were three questions in my mind: had he killed Derek and Arlo; was he afraid of being killed like Derek and Arlo, or had he been afraid of them?

'They cared about money and women. Did they care about consent?' I probed.

Shane's lips flattened into a tight line and his jaw clenched. 'No,' he muttered. 'They didn't.'

Rapists, then. If Shane was right, then all my sympathy at their deaths would disappear. I had my own moral compass and rape didn't figure on any of its points. No means no; if you're man, woman or non-binary, drunk, tipsy or sober, naked, dressed as a slut or a nun – no means no.

If Shane knew what the two men were doing and hadn't tried to stop them, then it was bad-cop time.

Chapter 5

'Do you have names of any of their victims?' I asked.

Shane flinched when I used the word 'victims', but if Arlo and Derek didn't care about consent then victims were what they were. I wasn't dressing it up as anything else to avoid offending his sensibilities. And if Shane had known about Arlo and Derek's rapes and did nothing about them, then in my view he was almost complicit. An enabler. Maybe enabler was too strong – but he hadn't stopped them. All that it takes for evil to flourish is for good men to stand by and do nothing. Shane had stood by. I had yet to establish if he was a good man or not.

He shook his head. 'No, they never brought them back here. They used hotels and the like. They often went to big cities for ... that sort of thing,' he said delicately.

'Did they use date-rape drugs?' I asked bluntly.

'I think so. Or a compliance potion.'

My eyes narrowed. 'Why didn't you report them?'

'I did! I told the head horn about my suspicions, but Arlo is his second cousin and it got swept under the rug. Besides, I didn't have any real evidence, just the stories they told me.'

'Why didn't you go to the Connection?' I pressed.

He snorted before he caught himself then looked apologetically at Elvira. 'Sorry, but ... we're creatures. Both Arlo and Derek's heads would have been lopped off before we were sure that they were guilty. I didn't want to be responsible for their deaths just because I didn't like them. Men talk big all the time, so it might not have been real, it could have been bullshit. I never saw any evidence either way.'

'But you don't believe it was empty talk?'

'No. I believed that they went out and raped women, but believing and knowing are two different things. I didn't want to condemn two men to death just because of my suspicions. Besides,' he said in a smaller voice, 'they threatened me. They used to laugh about it, how I'd like it if one of them actually tried it with me.'

'They bullied you?'

'Calling it bullying makes it sounds like kids' stuff. It wasn't kids' stuff.'

'Adults can bully as much as kids, and bullying is vile no matter what age you are. What did they do to you? Besides the threats.'

'Aren't the threats enough?' he said angrily. His hands were shaking and he tried once more to still them on his knees. 'I lived in fear. I was stuck here, tied into a rental contract I couldn't wriggle out of without being ruined financially. It took me years to save up enough to put down the money to live here. Portmeirion is so exclusive and it's pricey. From everyone's tales, I thought it would be a hedonist's dream to live here, and for many it is. But not for me. Derek's money brought people's silence left, right and centre. He got away with murder.' He blanched. 'Not actual murder.'

'But actual rape.'

He nodded, studying his hooves. 'I think so.'

'How often?' I asked.

'What?'

'How often do you suspect they went out and raped women?' My question was hard and pointed.

'A few times a year,' he muttered. 'They'd plan it for ages beforehand – they called it their "sowing-seeds shag". They never used protection.'

I was struggling not to show my emotions. If any of this were true, I'd find it hard to work up any sympathy for Derek and Arlo. I was trying to keep an open mind but Shane believed everything he'd said. He thought they were vile and I was struggling to form a different opinion.

I changed tack. 'Why did you stay here?'

'Believe me, I wanted to move out but, as I said, I was financially tied in here. Accommodation is hard to find in the village. There's a bunch of hotels for the tourists, but not so many rooms for residents. I love everything about Portmeirion – except for Arlo and Derek. Everyone else is fun and kind. It's a bohemian village full of good people, but Arlo and Derek were outliers. Besides, Derek said that if I tried to leave he'd plant evidence that I was stealing from my employer and get me fired.' His voice was bitter.

'Why did they need a roommate?' I asked.

'What?'

'If Derek had all of that money, they didn't need someone helping with the bills. So why did they have you as a roommate?' I probed.

'I've thought a lot about that,' Shane said finally. 'I think it was for the same reason that they raped women. To have power over someone else. They were the dregs of society, but in this house, they were lords of the manor, and I was their servant. I know I shouldn't speak ill of the dead, but I'm glad to see the back of them.' *True.*

That innocuous phrase made it seem like they'd popped out somewhere. 'They haven't gone on holiday,' I pointed out. 'They're dead. They've been brutally murdered.'

He flinched when I said 'murdered'.

'Do you know who killed them?' I asked evenly, anticipating the answer.

'No, no idea. But I can't help thinking that whoever it was did the world a favour.' *True.*

Damn. I wasn't getting killer vibes from Shane even though that would have concluded the interview nicely. It would have been too easy if Shane had been the killer although I'd seriously considered, vibe or not, that he might have been pushed too far.

Shane checked his watch anxiously. 'I'm sorry, but my shift is due to start in ten minutes. Can I go?'

'I thought the village was closed?'

'To tourists, yes, but we'll carry on serving the residents. At times of stress, we all need ice cream.' Never had truer words been spoken.

'It's not a problem,' Elvira assured him. 'You can go – assuming we have your permission to continue searching the house in your absence?'

'Yes, of course,' he agreed hastily.

'Who is the property owned by?' I asked before he left.

'I have no idea; I sublet from Derek. He was definitely not the owner. I guess I'll find out who the landlord is now.' Shane stood. 'Look, I've got to go, I'm sorry. I don't want to let Izzy down.'

'Izzy?'

'The water elemental that runs the ice-cream parlour. Just close up after you leave, please.'

'Of course,' Elvira assured him. She stood up to show him out of the house, then returned with Bland in tow. 'Poor Mr Brown. He's a wreck.'

I was glad to see she had some sympathy for Shane, despite him being a creature. She'd been raised near Stone, and his father had been as Anti-Crea as they came. I had, perhaps wrongly, assumed she'd been raised with the same beliefs.

Elvira gave my hellhound a little bow. 'Gato, can you see if you can sniff out any potions or drugs? We've done a quick sweep but we didn't find anything incriminating. I find it hard to believe that they didn't have *something* hidden here, but it may be runed up.'

Gato gave a bark and headed up the stairs.

'I'll go with him.' I left Elvira filling in Bland on the interview and followed Gato up the narrow stairs. On the next floor was a neat, tidy room. I didn't need the ice-cream parlour's uniform hanging in the cupboard to know it was Shane's room; he was neat and tidy to the point of being fastidious. I sifted respectfully through his things while Gato did a cursory sniff around the room. Finding nothing, he went next door.

Shane still had a couple of full cardboard boxes in his wardrobe and I opened them to have a quick look. They were filled with knick-knacks and paintings, the sorts of things you use to make a house a home. It was telling that they were still in their boxes. This house had never been home to Shane; Derek and Arlo had seen to that.

Four extra locks had been installed on the inside of the doorframe, all well used. Shane must have locked himself in to feel safe at night. I felt a pang of regret at the hard tone I'd taken with him. I wasn't unsympathetic about what he'd been through, but a part of me thought he should have done more than simply report his suspicions. Still, fear is a powerful motivator, and Derek and Arlo had known full well what they were doing when they had terrorised their roommate. Perhaps they had progressed beyond mere threats...

I touched the locks and grimaced, put Shane in the victim column in my head and moved on.

I had a quick snoop in the bathroom next door but there was nothing unusual there. The spare room across the hallway was pretty bare – it contained only a TV and two recliner armchairs. There was room enough for three seats but I suspected this room was solely for Derek and Arlo. I doubted Shane would have wanted to spend more time with them than was necessary. There was nothing else in the room, no ornaments, no bookshelves, nothing; it was as barren as Derek and Arlo's souls. Not that I was judging them or anything.

I followed Gato up to the next level. He went into one bedroom and I took the other. I worked out pretty quickly that I was in Arlo's because he had a number of monogrammed things lying around both the room and the small ensuite bathroom. Arlo was pretty slobbish; there was dirty laundry on the floor and dirty plates on every flat surface. No wonder he didn't bring dates back – they'd have run a mile.

And that would have saved them.

I looked in all the places people usually hide things: the back of the wardrobe, under the bed, in the toilet cistern. Nothing stood out at first. There were no drugs and no stash of porn magazines – still, most people source porn on their laptops these days. It's much easier to remove your browser history than a pile of mags.

Arlo had a small desk with a dying plant plonked on top of it. The desk looked largely unused, which caught my attention; the room wasn't large enough to have a desk for no reason, and Arlo didn't seem the type to care about the latest fashion in furnishing. I examined it with a critical eye. At both ends, the wood appeared to be a slightly different colour. I ran my fingers underneath the edge until I felt a depression, pressed it and a drawer slid out from the side of the desk. Bingo. I *love* secret compartments and I dreamed of the day when I'd have stuff that warranted hiding. For now, all I had of worth was my car, my house, and Glimmer. The latter of which would follow me, no matter how secret its drawer was.

I slid the drawer fully open and grimaced. It was filled with pairs of knickers crammed into small see-through boxes. Trophies, way too many trophies. Sick bastards. 'Elvira!' I called out grimly. 'You'd better come and see this.'

Moments later, she stomped in. 'What?'

I gestured to the drawer.

'Sick fuck,' she muttered as she looked carefully at the knickers. 'He kept mementos.' Her tone was bleak.

'Yeah, and the fact he kept them in a secret compartment lends some weight to the idea that he was a serial rapist,' I pointed out.

'I agree.' She rubbed a hand over her face. 'This is a mess. No one is going to come forward to try and help me solve his murder once this gets out.' She sighed. 'Vigilante justice is such a pain in the ass. The Connection's punishment for rapists is so much worse than a quick death. You'd think people would use us rather than doling out justice themselves.'

'What do you do to rapists?' I asked curiously.

'First we use a witch's spell to give them erectile dysfunction and a potion that completely eradicates their sex drive – chemical castration, essentially. Then they have good long period in a jail cell to think about what they've done. Magical jail is not for the faint hearted. They're given anti-magic handcuffs to wear 24/7, and when we finally release them we install tracking spells so we can keep a close eye on them.'

'It doesn't sound *that* bad,' I pointed out.

'Men seem to take the permanent erectile dysfunction quite badly.'

'So what do you do for female rapists?' I asked.

'The same, less the erectile dysfunction thing.'

'Rape is often about power rather than sex,' I pointed out, thinking about Shane's words from earlier.

'I know, but there's not much we can do about that.'

I nodded. The Connection's justice did seem reasonable – even a bit heavy-handed – but I could still see why someone had smashed Arlo's face in.

Chapter 6

We searched the whole property thoroughly but we drew a blank. We didn't find any drugs, potions or any other suspicious paraphernalia. If Derek had kept trophies of his crimes like Arlo, he hadn't stored them here.

After I'd finished the search, I filled Mike in about the interview with Shane and what we'd found inside the property. He stayed poker-faced throughout, not reacting to what I told him. I found that surprising because Mike had always come across as someone warm and open. I thought of the MI5 badge that he'd flashed earlier; clearly, there was more to Mike Carter than I'd thought.

He and I went off, leaving Elvira and Bland to do official Connection stuff. They were going to finish off and head back to Liverpool within in the next hour or two; they'd already canvassed the area extensively during the last few days.

Mike and I decided to grab an ice cream. It would give us a chance to observe Shane again and I could also question his employer. Besides, I really did want that ice cream now.

My phone rang as we made our way to the ice-cream parlour. It was Summer, and I wondered if she was sitting in her little office metres away from Emory. Lucky bitch. I swallowed down the jealous side of me that wanted to erupt and swiped to answer her call. Jealousy is no one's friend, and comparison is the poison of life. 'Hi, Summer,' I said evenly.

'Hi, Jinx. I need to get an answer on the flowers.' No 'how are you?' for us. We were friendlier than we had been – after all, she'd dressed me in kick-ass leather – but we weren't quite friends. I hoped we'd get there one day. I also hoped that she'd get laid soon and fall in love with someone other than Emory. In that sense, I suspect our wishes aligned. She knew, and accepted, that Emory was taken and we both wanted her to move on. The heart is a fickle organ; the cock is a much simpler one. I'd seen some light flirtation with Mike Carter and I was keeping my fingers crossed that something developed there.

I drew a blank on the flower issue. 'What was the flower question?' I asked helplessly. 'Give me a clue.'

She huffed audibly. 'Which flowers do you want in your bouquet?' She sounded irritated. There was a pause. 'You haven't read my email, have you?' she asked accusingly.

'Sorry, I've been busy.' My tone wasn't especially apologetic. 'Dealing with dead bodies.' The fact that they were more important than flowers went unsaid.

She huffed again. She obviously thought the flowers were more critical. Some people have weird priorities. 'Have a look now, and I'll stay on the line.'

I obligingly went to my email inbox on my phone and found one of her many emails entitled 'Flowers 1 of 36'.

I put the phone back to my ear. 'Thirty-six emails? You don't seriously expect me to—'

'This is going to be the wedding of the century. How often do you think dragons find their true mate, challenge-tested, no less? Let me tell you, it's not often. Emory deserves every bit of happiness and the big day that he has been dreaming of since he was little, and I will not let you—'

I muted her and went back to the emails. She had sent me not just images of individual flowers but whole bouquets. My mind was strangely blank. How was I supposed to pick a bunch of flowers? I know shit-all about flowers.

The individual ones were out; I couldn't choose every single type of flower to go into my bouquet. It was too much pressure. I thought about what I wanted to achieve with the flowers. I wanted *classy*. I scrolled past images full of beautiful riotous colour; they were stunning and celebratory but I wanted sophistication, not for me but for Emory. He was a guy who exuded elegance and I wanted to aim for that. For one day, I'd give up my jeans and my trainers and try to look bridal.

Then I found a bouquet that made my heart stop. It was beautiful, simple, elegant. The flowers were soft cream and the foliage a dark, forest green. At the start of this wedding planning thing, I'd thought about matching the flowers and décor to Emory's dragon shade of red, but it turned out that was a hard thing to do so I'd swapped to forest green as my accent colour. It was almost the same shade as Emory's emerald eyes. Not that I'd admit to that.

I took a screenshot of the bouquet, sent it to Summer and unmuted her.

'—ultimately this is just—'

'I've picked one,' I interrupted her. 'I've sent it to you.' I hung up. Job done.

Mike looked amused. 'Aren't you the one that's supposed to be a bridezilla?'

'It turns out I've delegated that to Summer.'

He laughed out loud. 'Good call.'

'I thought so. Now, why were you keeping a poker face when I was telling you about Derek and Arlo?' I asked. He raised an eyebrow. 'You know you were. So what gives?'

'I'd heard rumours about Arlo before. As I recall, Emory even had a word with Sean about him.'

'Sean?'

'Sean Hardman, head horn of the satyrs and Connection member of the symposium.'

I frowned. 'I thought most of the creatures were migrating out of the Connection?'

'Some are, but some are staying. Keep your enemies closer and all that,' Mike explained.

'Are the satyrs part of Emory's gang?' I couldn't remember Emory mentioning them; hell, before this morning I'd have said they belonged in *Fantasia*, not the Other.

He nodded. 'They're a small minority. A few years ago they were under the vampyrs' protection but they felt like they needed a bit more clout. They were one of the first to name Emory their Elite.'

'What magic do they have?' I asked curiously.

'Their blood is poison to vampyrs and periodically they threaten to give it to witches to make potions with. As I said, for years the satyrs were under the vampyrs' protection. It was in the vampyrs' best interests to keep them out of Other hands.'

'Or wipe them all out,' I pointed out cynically.

'That would have caused outrage, even back in the day. The vampyrs already get enough flak for drinking blood, so they don't want to bring more attention to themselves. They cling to the shadows.'

Quite literally. I thought of Nate and his phasing. 'Why the change in satyr protection? What happened with the vampyrs?'

Mike shrugged. 'You'd have to ask them.'

'What other powers do they have?'

'They have some – powers of persuasion.'

I didn't like the sound of that. 'Does that mean Arlo and Derek didn't need date-rape drugs?'

'No, the persuasion isn't that strong, not even as strong as coaxing. It's mostly used to encourage people to have fun, to help create a festive atmosphere. That's why satyrs are often welcome at Portmeirion.'

I grimaced. I might not like the sound of persuasion but I could *compel* people, so I shouldn't throw stones. 'Who rules them besides Emory? This Sean?'

'Yeah. They're largely self-governing. Sean is the current head horn. His father was before him, but he died about three years ago in a car accident. There are not many satyrs to choose from to fill the leadership role. As I said, there are not many of them as a species.'

'What's the difference between a satyr and a faun?'

'A satyr is real.' Mike sounded amused. 'Fauns are made up.'

I blushed a little. 'Oh. I thought that a satyr was a male and a faun was a female, or something.'

'No, there are no female satyrs.'

'Right, so how do they...?' I trailed off. I didn't really want to talk about sex with Mike, but how *did* they procreate?

'The usual way, I imagine,' he answered drily. His cheeks reddened. At least I wasn't the only one embarrassed by this exchange. 'They can be very kind and funny. Apparently, they can be quite charming and...' He coloured further.

'What?'

'Rumour is, they're hung like horses rather than goats, even in the Common realm.'

'Oh? So they go to the Common realm for their – you know?'

'The majority of them have sex with Common women,' Mike said evenly.

'Who don't know they're satyrs?' I tried to keep the horror out of my voice.

'Yup. They come across as normal humans, same as anyone else.'

I grimaced. I hoped I hadn't inadvertently had sex with a satyr when I was ignorant of the Other realm. It gave a whole new dimension to the insult 'goatfucker'.

I pulled up that thought and examined it; it was a little bit Anti-Crea. My fiancé is a dragon but obviously our coupling has always been human based. My thoughts about the satyrs were a startling reminder that prejudice can slip in, even when you don't mean it to. The majority of satyrs have relationships with Common women, and why shouldn't they? 'Wait, the majority...?'

'The Other realm has its kinks, the same as the Common realm,' Mike said. 'There are some satyr groupies. Apparently, once you go satyr, you don't go back.' He grimaced.

'There's a story there.' I couldn't help prying.

'One of my ex's got with a satyr after me,' he admitted reluctantly.

'Ouch. Sorry.'

'Yeah. I looked into him, but he seems to be on the up and up.'

'Well, that's something.'

'Yeah.' He paused. 'He seems nice and he makes her happier than I did. But I drunk dialled once and she told me some things about Vickers that I wish I could scrub from my brain.'

'Like what?'

He shuddered. 'Trust me, I'm doing you a favour by not telling you.'

We had arrived at the ice-cream parlour. Shane was behind the counter; his bright, customer-facing smile wobbled when he saw me but he quickly put it back in place. 'Divine Truffle Chocolate?' he asked.

'You bet,' I confirmed.

'The rum and raisin is also divine,' a familiar voice said from behind me.

I whirled around. 'Shirdal! Naturally you'd love the *rum* ice cream.'

He flashed me a cheeky grin. 'Naturally. How are you doing, sweetheart?' He was dressed as a total bum, his usual human-form disguise, and was licking at a waffle cone dipped in chocolate. He wasn't even having the rum-and-raisin ice cream.

If you didn't know Shirdal, you'd think he was innocuous. Mike had tensed; he knew Shirdal and knew he wasn't innocuous. Although they worked on the same team, there didn't seem to be a whole lot of friendship going on.

The two men were having a stare off. Shane interrupted the moment by holding out my ice cream and, as I stepped forward, I broke their eye contact.

My cone was topped with two chocolate scoops and I had a lick. He'd not been kidding – it was divine. Yum.

I stepped back and answered Shirdal between licks. 'I'm good. Are you here to play bodyguard for me again?'

'Sure, why not?' He was back to smiling as if the death stares he'd exchanged with Mike had never happened.

'Are you going to be an asset or a liability?' I teased the deadly griffin assassin, like that was a good idea.

He barked a laugh. 'Oh sweetheart, you wound me. Do you even have to ask? Of course I'm going to be a liability.' *Lie.*

Gato gave a reproving bark.

'I'm kidding, dog. I know you've got this,' Shirdal said to Gato in all seriousness. 'But Emory wanted another man on her.'

'I have Mike and Gato. Any more and it'll turn into a freaking circus,' I complained.

'It's just while someone is bludgeoning Other realmers to death.' Shirdal commented. 'The deaths have been violent.' For Shirdal to call them violent meant they were grisly. I'd once seen Shirdal tear a man apart. Shirdal seemed to have already been briefed about the deaths.

'It's a bit of an over-reaction!' I protested. 'It's just the two satyrs so far. I'm not a satyr, so I should be fine.'

'You didn't tell her?' Shirdal asked Mike, his tone reproving.

'Not yet,' Mike bit back.

'Tell me what?' I folded my arms and glared at Mike for good measure.

'Derek and Arlo weren't the first deaths,' he admitted reluctantly.

'Who else has died?' I demanded.

'A fire elemental and a dryad. Both bludgeoned.'

'And you didn't tell me this because...?'

Mike shrugged. 'They might not be linked.' *Lie.*

'You don't believe that!' I accused.

'No, but it could still be true. I'm trying to keep an open mind.' It was unspoken that I should do the same.

'Keep your mind as open as a field, but don't keep relevant information from me again.' I glared and prodded his chest for emphasis. 'Lies and omissions make me grumpy.'

'Duly noted.' He held his hands up in surrender. Humph.

I re-jigged that extra information into my brain. 'Assuming the deaths are linked, which is a big assumption but we'll roll with it for now, it changes things. The roommate, Shane, confirmed that Derek and Arlo were fans of non-consensual sex. I had assumed that one of their victims had killed them, or a victim's brother or father or lover. But the other two dead people muddy the waters somewhat.'

'Unless they were part of a rapist ring,' Shirdal suggested darkly.

'Yeah, I suppose that's a possibility,' I said thoughtfully. 'We'll need to investigate the fire elemental and the dryad, too, but first, can you get me a meeting with Sean Hardman?'

Mike pulled out his phone. 'I'll see what I can do.' He walked away while he dialled, leaving me with Shirdal and Gato. Gato was making sad, whining noises and puppy-dog eyes at my ice cream.

'I can't give you chocolate ice cream. Sorry, pup, you know chocolate is poison to dogs. I don't know if it's different for hellhounds, but I'm not risking you to find out. Hang on, I'll see if they have a dog ice cream.'

I popped my head back into the ice-cream parlour. 'Shane, do you have any doggy ice cream?' I knew the request sounded ridiculous, but a lot of vendors stocked ice cream to help dogs cool down in hot weather. The only problem was that, it being April, the weather was still decidedly cool.

'Let me check in the back.' Shane disappeared, leaving me alone with the other person in the shop: a blonde with a fierce attitude. She was dressed in the same uniform as Shane and was sitting at one of the tables with a laptop and some paperwork. She was also glaring at me. So this was probably the aforementioned Izzy, the ice-cream shop owner.

'Izzy? I'm Jinx,' I introduced myself.

'I know who you are,' she snapped back. 'Shane told me all about you grilling him this morning. The poor lad,' she said accusingly.

'I don't think Shane has done anything wrong,' I clarified. 'I needed to find out what he knows about Derek and Arlo's deaths.'

'He knows nothing about their deaths,' she said firmly as she closed her laptop and pushed it aside. 'Those pricks got their comeuppance, and frankly I'm struggling to feel anything but satisfaction about that.'

'You didn't like them?' I asked.

'No. Not a single female around here liked them. They thought they were suave and charming, but they were ignorant and sexist.' She raised her chin. 'I petitioned Portmeirion Council a time or two to get rid of them.'

'Unsuccessfully?'

'Sadly, money talks.'

'Who do you think killed Derek and Arlo?' I asked.

'It could be anyone that had met them,' she said drily.

'That's quite a suspect pool.'

'They were vile.' Izzy relaxed slightly; she was opening up. 'I know Derek once had sex with one of the Town Hall café waitresses and she swore she didn't normally find him attractive. I'd bet my ice-cream parlour that he slipped her something. His persuasion magic wasn't strong, but I bet he used something else with it. I could never prove it, and after their disastrous date the waitress moved away. She wouldn't admit it, but the way he came round to the café all the time unnerved her. She felt like she had no choice but to leave. She was scared of him. As I said, I'm not sorry the prick is dead.'

'What was the name of the waitress?' I asked, ready to note it down.

Izzy hesitated. 'It was a long time ago, a couple of years at least.'

'It would still be good to find her and let her know that Derek's no longer an issue,' I pointed out.

That won her over and she nodded decisively. 'True. Her name was Andrea Lyons.'

'What type of Other was she?'

'She was a mermaid,' Izzy replied.

I could see she was uncomfortable talking about Andrea so I pulled the focus back to her. 'It must come in handy being a water elemental and running an ice-cream parlour.'

She brightened. 'It does. I can chill the ice cream to the perfect temperature, both in churning and storage. It's one of the things that makes my ice cream superior,' she said smugly.

I took another lick. 'Your ice cream *is* phenomenal. Thanks for taking the time to talk to me, Izzy.' I paused. 'I'll see if I can find Andrea, just to give her some peace of mind.'

And also to add her to my list of suspects.

Chapter 7

Shane returned triumphantly with a pot of doggy ice cream. 'Sorry that took so long. I knew we had some somewhere but it was right at the back of the old freezer.' He waved the tub at me, looking proud of his find.

'No problem, thanks so much for digging it out.' I paid and took it with a grateful smile, then I pocketed one of Izzy's business cards. I'd put her number in my phone later.

I joined Shirdal and Gato. Gato barked and jumped enthusiastically when he saw I was carrying something. I smiled indulgently, tugged off the lid of the tub and put it on a step so he didn't have to bend down too far to eat the ice cream. He happily chased the tub around the step, licking enthusiastically. He was a happy pup and it made my heart glad.

I met Shirdal's eyes and jerked my head to the right, signifying that we should stroll away from the ice-cream parlour. As we walked, I filled him in on my chat with Izzy. 'Let's go to the café then,' he suggested. 'We can talk to the locals, do some digging about this Andrea.'

'You read my mind.'

'I didn't. Sadly that's not in my skill set.' His voice was wistful.

'You'd like to be able to read people's minds?' I asked.

'It would make it even easier to kill them.' He shrugged.

Yikes. It was comments like that that reminded me who I was dealing with. Shirdal hadn't become leader of the deadly griffin assassins' guild by accident. Griffins are a strange sect of creatures, driven by the need to kill. Early in their history one of their number decided that if they didn't find a successful way to channel their murderous urges, they would happily destroy the whole planet before they then destroyed each other. Consequently, a series of strict rules were put in place to govern them; now the griffins are only supposed to kill to defend themselves, friends or family, or as part of a paid contract.

The griffins are the Other realm's paramount assassins. If you want someone dead, they'll do your dirty work – though the process isn't exactly simple. According to Shirdal, each job is assessed for its moral value before it is passed to one of the griffins to carry out. They have rules, though they have kept them pretty schtum, but I know one of them is not to kill children. There are enough bad people in their crosshairs that they don't need to stoop that low to fulfil their deadly urges. Besides, there aren't many griffins left, a couple of hundred at most.

The griffins don't just murder for the Other realm but for the Common realm too. They run various hitman businesses, killing bad people for good money. It was hard not to be judgemental; in my world killing is a last resort, but if griffins didn't kill then eventually their urges would get out of control and that could be truly disastrous.

I would never forget the scene at Ronan's castle when Shirdal had effortlessly dispatched huge numbers of the men from the drug dealers' operation. There had been limbs everywhere – it was truly the stuff of nightmares. But Shirdal hadn't killed for years before that. Maybe if he'd let the urge out in a more controlled way – say once a year – most of those men could still be alive. Don't get me wrong; I didn't shed any tears for the drug dealers. They had sold a deadly drug to anyone, including minors, with the full knowledge that it was potentially lethal. No, no tears for them.

'This way,' I called to Gato and he trotted over. 'Put the empty ice-cream carton in the bin,' I chastened. He turned back, picking it up gently with his soft lips and carefully deposited it in the bin.

'Good boy.' I gave him a pat and a full body rub. 'Do you know the way to the café?' I asked Shirdal.

He grinned. 'Sweetheart, I know Portmeirion like the back of my hand.'

'Prove it.'

He offered me his right hand. 'There's a freckle at the base of my right thumb.'

I shoved his hand back at him, laughing. 'Prove you know the *area*, not prove you know the back of your hand.' I rolled my eyes.

'This way then, Jinx.' He looped an arm through mine and led me through the pretty village.

I spotted everything from ogres to dryads to elementals to perfect vampyrs as we walked; it was a melting pot of the Other. 'What's going on?' I murmured to Shirdal. 'Why is there a bit of everything here?'

'Portmeirion is special. It is a strict sanctuary for all of the Other, creature or human. There are wards painted on every house. If you're in the Other and you come here with violence in mind, the wards won't let you gain entry.'

'Derek and Arlo had violence in their minds.'

'For that reason, they didn't carry it out here,' Shirdal retorted grimly.

'That's so wrong.'

'At least Portmeirion is safe.'

'Wait, didn't Arlo get killed here?' I asked, suddenly confused.

Shirdal nodded solemnly. 'Yes, he did.'

I frowned. 'But how?'

'That's the million-dollar question.'

'Well, the obvious answer is that whoever did it was in the Common realm at the time,' I surmised. 'That doesn't mean that the killer wasn't Other, just that he bypassed the wards here by being in Common at the time of the murder. That's assuming that the wards were not tampered with.'

'The first thing the witches did was assess the wards,' Shirdal confirmed. 'They're in good working order. That's why everyone is so on edge – they should have been safe here but they weren't. Something – or someone –

bludgeoned Arlo to death. Someone slipped through the perfectly working wards and killed him.'

There was another explanation. 'Could he have been killed elsewhere and his body dumped in Portmeirion?'

'We considered that, but no. The site where the body was found was covered in blood splatter that is consistent with the injuries.' Shirdal spoke matter-of-factly. After a couple of centuries of practising assassination, I had no doubt that he knew a great deal about things like blood splatter.

'Where was the body found?' I asked.

'Just around the corner.'

We turned the corner and I paused as we entered the central piazza. It was beautiful, like nothing I'd been expecting. There were rolling green lawns, several beautiful fountains and a large pool of water. There was even a life-size chess set. A water elemental was playing in the pool, making the water swirl and dance. His expression was melancholy; the whole feeling in the village was subdued.

'Where exactly was Arlo killed?' I asked.

'Just here.' Shirdal led me to the chess set. 'His body was found here.' He pointed at the black-and-white board.

'On the game itself?'

'Yes.'

I frowned. The sign next to the game told people clearly that it was an ornamental installation and shouldn't be played with. Somebody had killed Arlo but also done a bit of a fuck-you to the authorities by placing the body where it shouldn't be.

'There was blood all over the board. Luckily the board was waterproofed so it could be kept outside, so it's cleaned up nicely.' He sounded relieved; Shirdal's priorities are a little strange at times. Screw the dead guy; it was the games board he was concerned about.

Ignoring the sign, I walked onto the board to see if I could find the place where Arlo's body was found. I couldn't; the whole place was spotless. I closed my eyes and let the ocean in my mind recede, then reached out with my empathy. I kept my search to the immediate area. I could feel curiosity from Shirdal, but nothing else.

I knelt down and touched the board.

Rage. Surprise. Fear. Satisfaction. The feelings were like echoes, and just as faint and impossible to grasp. They slipped away, leaving me none the wiser. Had I sensed the killer *and* the victim as well?

I hauled my mental shields back up and looked around. The murder had taken place in the middle of the piazza and bludgeoning someone to death couldn't be a quiet procedure. 'No witnesses?' I asked Shirdal.

'Not a single one.'

'What was the time of death?'

'Around 2am.' That was probably why there were no witnesses: everyone was in bed.

I took one last look around the area but sadly there were no flashing neon signs pointing to clues, so I gave it up as a bad job. Killers can be so unhelpful sometimes.

Chapter 8

We didn't have much by way of clues. We needed to speak to some willing people. Buying someone a coffee is almost as useful as buying them a pint to get a conversation going, and it was still too early for a pint.

'Let's go to the café,' I suggested. 'Which way is it?'

'The Town Hall café isn't far. Come on, it's this way,' Shirdal explained, pointing the way forward.

He led me up some steps onto a concrete path that curved left. It didn't take us long to reach the café. The building was painted a delightful shade of yellow and, like everything in the village, it had columns and stonework to give it that quintessential Italian feel.

That was where the Italian vibe ended. Inside the café were booths with green-leather seats, and it was set up more like a 1950s American diner. Still, the menu clung to the Italian theme with plenty of pasta and pizza options. I was hungry, so grabbing a pizza seemed like a good idea.

The place was bustling; despite the murders – and the village being shut to tourists – it was still doing a roaring trade. I wondered if the residents of Portmeirion had gathered for safety in numbers.

Like the piazza, there was a little bit of everything Other here. There was a table of what I guessed were air elementals. Their hair was long and constantly gusting and blowing like they were standing in front of a fan. They must have had to take a hairbrush everywhere with them. The knots must be a real pain in the ass; my hair knotted if you looked at it funny, so I couldn't imagine how all that gusting affected the air elementals' manes. If it were me, I'd have shaved it short but I guess it was a part of their identity and they didn't seem bothered by it.

Shirdal and I ordered some food, and I also ordered a few sausages for Gato so that he didn't feel left out. My tummy was growling and I hoped it wouldn't take too long. We ordered a hot drink each and settled down to do some people watching before we got to the serious stuff: interrogating the local yokels.

The café felt like a fast-food joint and, sure enough, it wasn't long before the food arrived. As we chowed down, we listened surreptitiously to the people around us. It wasn't long before the air elementals started to talk about the murders.

'He had it coming,' one of them commented, sounding grimly satisfied.

'Arlo wasn't *that* bad. He was a misogynist, but he didn't deserve to be pulverised into little pieces,' another disagreed.

The first one snorted. 'He absolutely did. I saw him at Alma de Cuba in Liverpool one time. He was getting thrown out by the bouncers because they'd seen him put something in a girl's drink. You don't spike people's drinks. What an asshole. He was more than a misogynist, he was a twat. A rapist.'

'You know none of that stuff was ever proved,' the third elemental said disapprovingly. 'You don't gossip about the dead. It's just not done, even if they *were* twats.'

'That stuff was never proved because the girls always upped and left. With all of his damned lottery winnings, Derek was able to threaten them. I know he did. It's so unfair that such an asshole won so big,' a male elemental complained.

'I wonder where his cash will go?'

One of the others leaned forward. 'I heard he made a new will.'

'Who? Derek?'

'Yup.' He nodded smugly.

'Leaving it to who?' his friend asked.

'No one knows.' He was almost whispering; this guy was full of drama. 'His lawyer is on holiday so the Will is still in the vault.'

'Who is his lawyer?'

'Ettinger.'

'So when is Ettinger back?'

'A few days, apparently. Then we'll know who Derek liked.'

'Imagine if it was me!' the first elemental said. 'What I wouldn't do with a million pounds.'

'Obviously it's not being left to you,' her companion sniggered.

'I can dream.'

'Yeah, me too. I can dream about a twenty-two-year-old buxom brunette, but that doesn't mean she's going to fall into my lap.'

I decided I'd better intercede before the conversation moved too far away from Derek and Arlo. I swivelled around in my seat. 'Sorry to interrupt. I'm Jinx. I'm visiting Portmeirion, and I heard all about Derek and Arlo. Did you know both of them well?'

One of the men's mouths dropped open. 'Holy fuck! It's a young buxom brunette falling into your lap!' He cleared his throat and said loudly, 'I can dream about a million pounds just falling into my lap.' Nothing happened. 'Damn.'

His mates started to laugh.

'I'm twenty-five and not especially buxom,' I interrupted their laughter. 'What can you tell me about Derek and Arlo?' I repeated my question.

'They were local celebrities. You'd often find them propped up at the bar. When Derek was feeling generous he'd buy rounds of drinks for everybody. He could be quite generous.'

Another elemental snorted. 'That was nothing more than buying people's forgiveness, making them look the other way when he did shit he shouldn't have. When he was hitting on the girls, everyone would just say, "Oh that's just Derek. He's a harmless sleaze." But he wasn't harmless, not if what I saw in Alma De Cuba was true.'

'Why didn't you tell people what you'd seen?' I tried to keep the censure out of my voice.

He grimaced. 'What if the bouncers were wrong? You can't go around accusing people of spiking drinks without evidence. I didn't have any security footage or anything like that. I'm not going to ruin someone's life on half a piece of information. But I kept my eye on them.'

'Well? Did your eye see anything else?' I asked.

'Other than them being general sleaze balls? No,' he admitted. 'I saw them hit on a lot of girls, but as far as I saw they listened when they were told no.'

Somehow I doubted it, but I tried to keep an open mind. I'd follow where the evidence led me.

Chapter 9

After we had eaten, Shirdal and I cleared the table and started to work the room. We spoke to a lot of the people in the café, moving around the tables, buying people hot drinks to get them chatting.

Interestingly, a lot of the men thought that Derek and Arlo were 'lads' lads', but the feeling was that they were largely harmless. The women that we spoke to painted a very different picture. They often felt creeped out by them, unsafe if they were alone with them, though nobody could pinpoint what exactly it was that made them feel that way.

After we'd covered most of the customers, I asked one of the waitresses, a dryad, if I could speak to the manager.

'Oh,' she said, flustered. 'Was something not to your liking?'

I smiled warmly. 'Not at all. The food and the service were absolutely wonderful. I wouldn't hesitate to recommend the café to anybody.'

Her shoulders slumped with relief. 'Oh, great. Okay.'

'But I really could do with speaking to the manager about another issue,' I reiterated.

'Sure. I'll see if he'll see you.' She looked doubtful. 'Although...' She slid a glance at Gato and visibly brightened. 'He's in the office doing rotas. One moment.' She disappeared for a moment before coming back. 'He'll see you now. This way.'

I was starting to follow her when, out of the corner of my eye, I caught sight of someone familiar and my breath caught. Impossible – of course it was impossible. From behind, the man to the side of me looked like Stone: the same broad shoulders, the same haircut... But no; where Stone's hair had been a rich brown, this guy's was littered with grey. Not the same guy. Of course not. Anyway, it was impossible to tell from behind.

Stone had been on my mind because of the office break-in a few weeks earlier, where his prints had been planted as some sort of cruel hoax. The subconscious likes to play cruel tricks sometimes. I craned my neck around, willing the guy to turn so I could see him properly.

'I'm going to tell Emory that you're panting after other men, Prima,' Shirdal teased me.

I gave him a flat look and turned back to the waitress but she'd disappeared. Crap, where had she gone?

'That way.' Shirdal pointed towards the corridor and I hastened down it. There was only one door at the end and the waitress was holding it open awkwardly.

'Sorry,' I apologised.

'No problem. Enjoy.' She winked and fanned herself a little as she walked away. Weird.

When I strode into the office, I understood her cryptic remark. Her manager was hot, if you liked the muscley, blond look. Which virtually everyone does. His eyes were twinkly and blue, like pools of water I could dive into.

Suddenly I was having a hard time stringing my thoughts together. My brain felt sluggish. Magic, some sort of magic. This wasn't *me*; I didn't drool over guys – except for Emory, of course. But this guy, he was just so—

'Pretty,' I murmured aloud.

'Sorry.' He sighed and rubbed a hand over his perfect features. 'I've just been to the portal so my magic is pretty strong right now. Give me a second. I wasn't expecting guests.'

I wasn't sure whether a second would be enough to change how absolutely awesome he was. He was splendiferous. Marvellous. Magnificent. A specimen of male perfection—

It was like your ears popping in an aeroplane. Suddenly the drop-dead-gorgeous male in front of me appeared normal; good looking and handsome but not quite haul-out-your-altar-and-start-worshipping-him gorgeous as he had been a second earlier. I'd been a heartbeat away from building a shrine.

I blinked. 'What?' I said in confusion.

'Sorry,' he repeated with a grimace. 'I'm a siren.'

'A strong one,' said Shirdal cheerfully. A very strong one. Yikes. The manager's magic had all but wiped out my brain power and my free will. Scary stuff. 'How are you doing, Stan?' Shirdal asked.

The man glared. 'It is Marco, as well you know, Shirdal.'

'I'm trying to help you be less sexy for Jinx here. Stan isn't a sexy name.' Shirdal winked roguishly, but Marco was not in the mood to be charmed and his glower deepened.

'You can call me Rossi if you prefer,' he said firmly. 'But not Stan.'

'Marco Rossi,' I interrupted. 'I'm Jinx. I'm—'

'I know who you are. You are Emory's.'

I glared. 'I am *mine*,' I corrected decisively, 'but yes. Emory and I are dating.' I don't know why I said that – we were getting *married*. My brain was thick like glue, and for some reason I didn't quite want this Adonis to know that I was unavailable. His siren magic was back, still playing with my emotions like a cat plays with a ball of string. I'd never been a cheater and I didn't intend to start now.

I willed my brain to clear, but sexiness rolled off Marco like waves crashing onto a beach, and it was so hard to concentrate. I knew it was wrong and I really wasn't interested, but he was just yummy. So super yummy.

'Yum,' I said aloud. I wondered if I was visibly drooling.

'Sorry.' Marco sighed, carding a hand through his hair in frustration. 'When I'm annoyed it flares up a bit. And Shirdal is annoying.' He concentrated visibly.

Pop. I was back to me again. Thank goodness. Nevertheless, I stepped back a little. Maybe a bit more distance would help. Marco winced as I moved away from him. 'That must be difficult for you,' I commiserated.

'It really is.' He sounded grumpy.

'The Connection forbids him from using his magic to get sexual partners,' Shirdal confirmed.

Marco glared at him. 'I don't need my powers to get partners, thank you.'

'You're welcome.' Shirdal winked at him.

Man, we were off track. 'Andrea,' I blurted out.

'Sorry?' Marco blinked.

'Andrea Lyons,' I tried again. 'She was a waitress here while she was on shore leave.'

'Yes, of course, the mermaid. I remember her well. She was hard working.'

'Did you hit that?' Shirdal waggled both eyebrows suggestively and I elbowed him sharply in the ribs. He was definitely a liability.

'No,' Marco snarled. 'I do not mix work and pleasure. Andrea was lovely, but very young and a bit naive.'

'Why did she leave your employ?' I probed.

'I don't know. She simply said it was time to move on.'

'And?'

'And what?' he asked.

'Did you believe her?'

He tilted his head, considering. 'She'd been ... jittery for a few weeks. A few customers had made complaints about her absent-minded behaviour. Things weren't right with her.'

'And you didn't ask her about it?' I asked.

'I was her boss, not her psychologist.' He looked a bit guilty. 'After she left I heard some rumours.'

'What kind of rumours?'

'The kind that suggest she was targeted.'

'By whom?'

'Derek the satyr.'

'The dead one?' I clarified just in case the name Derek was the 'Mr Smith' of the satyr world.

'Indeed.'

'Did you speak to Derek about it?'

Marco flexed his muscular arms, linked his fingers and put them behind his head. 'I did. I warned him that if I found out he'd touched another of my workers, I would use my call to make him walk into the sea and drown.' *True.* Marco didn't pull his punches.

'What did he say?' I demanded.

'He denied touching Andrea inappropriately, but I think he took my warning seriously. I'd see him around town but he skirted around me if he could. He knew I was serious.' Marco looked at me and then at Gato. 'I've been meaning to reach out to you,' he said finally, talking directly to Gato. 'I found something a week ago which is not mine, Lord of Time.' He stood up and opened an adjoining door. 'Come on,' he called. 'Don't be shy.'

A fast blue-grey blur ran in.

A puppy.

My eyes widened. It was a Great Dane puppy. Yipping gleefully, she ran to Gato. She bowed her back and pounced on him with her huge paws before leaping back in case he retaliated. But Gato didn't retaliate; instead he grinned a huge doggy grin, bowed back to her and swiped at her playfully.

My vision swam. The whole time I've known Gato, other dogs had run away from him; not once had I ever seen him play with another dog. They sensed his Otherness and they kept far away. But not this pup. She was delighted to see him, as he was to see her. I wiped my eyes; it was ridiculous to be tearful over such a small thing, but I knew it wasn't a small thing to Gato.

The next time she leapt, Gato was ready. He pressed his snout to her snout and suddenly she grew black spikes and red eyes. She grew taller too, though she was still relatively small, the size of an adult Great Dane rather than a horse. She went to yip but this time it came out as a deep reverberating bark.

Gato wagged his tail furiously. He touched his snout to hers again and she shrank, losing her red eyes and spikes. She darted forward and started to gambol around his feet. He looked down at her indulgently, real affection in his eyes. He was content to let her frolic about – until she went to gnaw on his paw. She chewed a little too hard and he gave a deep, warning growl that had her leaping back, staring at him wide eyed.

She was only shocked for a moment before she started to chase her own tail instead.

'My goodness, a hellhound pup,' I breathed. 'Where did you get her?'

'I found her half drowned on the beach.' Marco was looking at her fondly.

'You saved her.'

'Yes, but now she needs to be with her own kind.' He reached out and stroked her steel-grey fur, and his eyes softened with warmth. He liked her. 'She's too young to be alone. She needs to be taught to master time, and I can't teach her that.'

'But won't you miss her?' I couldn't imagine giving up Gato.

'With all my heart,' Marco confessed softly. 'Perhaps, if it is meant to be, she'll come back to me when she is older.'

'What's her name?'

'I've been calling her Indy – short for India, like the blaze on her chest.' He gestured to the splash of white on her torso. She was a blue Great Dane and the only patches of white were on her toes and her chest. He was right: that last one looked a lot like the shape of India.

I held my hand out to her. 'Hey, Indy, how are you doing, girl?'

She sniffed my hand before licking it enthusiastically then immediately starting to mouth it, nibbling at it lightly. I pulled my hand away. 'No. No biting,' I said firmly. She looked at me blankly and then tried to nibble my shoes instead. I sighed. Puppies are hard work.

I looked at Gato. 'Do we need to take her?'

He gave a firm bark and wagged his tail once. That was a yes. Damn. It looked like I'd got myself a new pup.

Chapter 10

Mike caught up with us as we arrived back at the piazza. 'I've got you a meeting with the head horn but there's a slight problem.'

Of course there was. 'What is it?'

'He wants to meet tonight in Liverpool.'

'Then it looks like we're going on a road trip.' I sighed. 'We'd better get a move on.' I frowned, considering Indy. 'I think we'd better drop off the puppy at the castle.'

Mike turned to me in surprise. 'How exactly did you acquire a puppy since I walked away?'

'I'm just lucky, I guess.' I patted Indy's head as she happily danced around my feet. She took the head pat as an invitation to start nibbling my hand again. 'No,' I said firmly. 'No biting, Indy.'

She looked up at me with bright blue eyes, wagging her tail enthusiastically and unrepentantly.

'It's a shame,' Shirdal muttered as we strode towards the car park.

'What is?'

'Portmeirion. It's normally a party town once the Common realmers have left. Lots of laughter and games and drinking. It's weird to see it so quiet. Apparently the circus last week was a real hit, but you'd never know it from all of the glum faces. You'll have to come back for one of the festivals.'

I wondered if the circus had been The Other Circus; I knew they'd been touring in Wales before returning to Liverpool. It seemed likely, and I was disappointed to have missed the chance to catch up with them. It would have been nice to check on Bella and Ike.

I turned my thoughts back to the village. 'It's a beautiful place – kinda weird, but beautiful.'

When we arrived at the car park we looked dubiously at the car. It was an Alfa Romeo Giulietta, a nice *small* car. It hadn't been a problem on the way with Gato in the back and me and Mike in the front. But with Shirdal and the puppy...

Shirdal huffed. 'Looks like I'm flying then. What a ridiculous puny car.'

'It's fast!' Mike said defensively.

'And beautiful,' I added. 'But not quite Great Dane size.' Let alone two Great Danes.

'We'll manage,' Mike asserted.

'You'll have to,' Shirdal muttered. Mike shot him an unfriendly look and the griffin's eyes narrowed when he caught it. He glared right back. 'No magic, no guns, silly car. What exactly do you bring to this operation? How are you supposed to protect the Prima?'

'Prima-to-be,' I corrected. 'And Mike has lots of skills and insider knowledge.'

Shirdal snorted. 'He's as helpful as a dryad in a desert.'

'At least I don't kill people for fun,' Mike sneered back.

'That's because you don't know how to have fun. I expect it's the rod up your ass that's the problem.'

'If I have a rod up my ass, it's only because you put it there!' Mike flushed. 'That came out wrong.'

Shirdal smirked. 'I didn't put anything up your ass but it's good to know where your thoughts are at.' He shifted onto four legs and, as always, I had a moment where my heart froze. In his griffin form, his golden-eyed stare was predatory and it was oh-so-apparent that he could destroy you in seconds. Some ancient instinct made my mouth dry.

'See you back at the castle,' I managed, with a wave.

'Where we are picking up a bigger car,' Shirdal stated with a further sharp look at Mike. It was odd to hear his voice come from the depths of a beak.

'We'll take my Mercedes,' I promised. Shirdal didn't acknowledge me; instead he spread his wings and leapt into the air.

A few months earlier, someone had set my Mercedes G-wagon on fire, which had upset and pissed me off in equal measure. Emory had given me that Mercedes. It had been a ridiculous gift at the time, but I'd grown attached to it. Then, after my Mercedes' untimely death, Emory had bought me an almost exact replica. I shuddered to think about the expense. Maybe he'd got them on finance? It wasn't likely, but it was preferable to thinking that he'd spent nearly £300,000 on my cars in a matter of months.

'Shotgun!' I called quickly and Gato gave me a flat, unfriendly look. 'More space for you in the back,' I tried to mollify him. He liked to ride shotgun and let his huge head hang out of the window, tongue lolling in the wind.

Gato and Indy climbed grudgingly into the small back seat. Indy looked to be around five or six months old, which meant that she was now the size of a pretty large Labrador, so it was a tight squeeze. Luckily it was only just over thirty minutes from Portmeirion to Caernarfon – a little less the way that Mike drove. I approved; he's a speed demon like me.

I sent Emory a text to let him know that I was on my way home but I'd be going to Liverpool later. I told him I had a surprise. He sent back a thumbs up and a winky face. I looked at Indy in the rear-view mirror. She probably wasn't quite the sort of surprise he was hoping for.

Chapter 11

As we pulled up to the castle, the tourists were leaving and it was being closed to the Common realmers. Emory was waiting for me in the courtyard just past the turnstiles. His eyes widened when he caught sight of Indy. 'Gato,' he said in surprise. 'What have you been up to?'

I laughed. 'Indy isn't Gato's. A nice siren found her at a beach and rescued her, but she needs to be with her own kind so I guess Gato's fostering her.'

'And by extension, we are fostering her?' Emory clarified.

'Yup! Our very own baby. Think of it as a test, a challenge,' I said cheerfully. 'Dragons like challenges.' Was I over having my friend kidnapped and shoved on an island in the name of a challenge? Not really. I liked to remind all the dragons of that fact where possible, including Emory.

'I do work well under pressure,' he said modestly, ignoring my jibe. He stepped closer to give me a smouldering look. 'As you well know.'

I felt myself blush. Mike was right next to us. Jeez. And he was grinning. Ugh.

'It's a test,' I repeated. 'A challenge. If we can't raise a puppy together, we definitely can't raise children. Not yet, at least.'

'You do know that dogs and children aren't the same?' Emory pointed out.

I rolled my eyes. 'Obviously. But think of it as a dry run. If we can raise a puppy, we can definitely cope with kids – one day. I'm not saying now. But I'm warming to the idea of kids ... one day.'

'I'll take one day.' Emory gave a soppy sort of smile and kissed my forehead.

Gato barked and did a happy turn. My dad was excited at the idea of grandchildren – or Isaac was. Working out who was thinking what was a bit hit or miss sometimes.

'Not you two as well.' I glared at Gato. Everyone was on board the Jinx-baby train except me, though I was warming to it; I was at the station now, even if I hadn't bought a ticket. That was something. Gato gave me a big doggy grin.

We had taken our eyes off Indy, and that was our first mistake. She was off, haring around the courtyard like an Olympian on speed. 'She's energetic,' Emory commented.

'She gets it from you.'

'I *am* energetic. I can go for days.' His voice dropped to innuendo territory again. He wasn't wrong; the man had stamina.

'Did you have oysters for breakfast or something?' I asked suspiciously.

'That would be an extravagant breakfast even for me. No, my ardour for you needs no aphrodisiacs. I just missed you.'

'Aw. That's nice – but I was only gone for a few hours.'

'I missed you like a plant misses the sun.'

I grinned.

'Too much?' he enquired.

'Just a smidge, but I'm rolling past it. I appreciate it. Although you'd think that after two hundred years, you'd have mastered chat-up lines.'

Emory snorted. 'I was raised in the Victorian era when complimenting a women's ankles was scandalous.'

I extended my foot. 'Go right ahead, my love. You have my permission to be scandalous.'

Mike had a fist in his mouth, trying to stop his laughter from spilling out. He stepped away so we could continue our bad flirting with a little more privacy, but he still kept eyes on us ready to do his bodyguard thing.

'Why Jessica Sharp, what fine ankles you have,' Emory purred at me. It instantly made me think of the big bad wolf.

'I see where this is going,' I whispered back. 'And what big teeth you have. Are you going to promise to eat me later?'

Emory grinned. 'See, this has improved my mood no end.'

'What was wrong with your mood?' I asked, concerned.

He cleared his throat and stepped closer, wrapping his arms around me. His tone became serious. 'I've received news,' he murmured for my ears only. 'The Elders are travelling here.'

'Uh-oh. That doesn't sound good.'

'It's not,' he said grimly. 'The Elders rarely travel.'

'Audrey travels,' I pointed out.

'She's not an Elder.'

'She's old, though.'

Emory shook his head. 'Not particularly. Not by dragon standards.'

I frowned. 'But she told me she was in her last years?'

'Her time will come sooner rather than later because she bonded with Cuthbert.' The words came out thick and heavy. He hated admitting to Audrey's shorter lifespan; it was a lifespan that he would have to accept too when he formally bonded with me. At our wedding he would kiss a new wife and kiss away several centuries.

Some days it felt like too much, but mostly I tried to respect Emory's right to make his own decisions. He was a big boy and it wasn't for me to dictate his life choices, any more than it was for him to dictate mine. We were partners, not dictators.

We both watched as Indy leapt over the huge boulder in the courtyard. It marked a secret entrance into the catacombs below the castle, but she was just using it as a hurdle. Sure, why not?

'What does it mean that the Elders are coming?' I asked softly.

He sighed. 'It means our time is up. I guess that they've learned about my – intercession with the gargoyles.'

'How?' I frowned.

'The Elders aren't just from Britain, but from all over the world. They are the oldest of us that still remain.'

'You're immortal. Surely you all remain,' I pointed out.

'You've learned by now how deadly the Other realm is. We're long-lived, not indestructible. A sword to the throat kills us just as easily as the next guy.'

'True, but it's a heck of a lot harder to cut through dragon scales than to slice a jugular.'

'You've thought that through. Should I sleep with one eye open?' he asked, amused.

'Your jugular is safe with me.' I kissed his neck lightly. He gave me pointed look; it was one of his rules that there were no Public Displays of Affection – PDAs – in the castle. 'How do you think the Elders have figured it out?' I asked.

'The gargoyles will have upped and disappeared all over Europe and someone will have noticed. One of them may have talked.'

'I doubt it,' I disagreed. 'Part of the issue with made-brethren is that they're fanatically loyal to you. They're not going to spread the word about you. Besides, will the gargoyles that weren't present when the curse was broken know what happened?'

Emory scrubbed at the back of his neck. 'I don't know, but I can feel them. Not like I can feel you, but there's something in the back of my mind... The gargoyles are coming closer.'

'All of them?'

'All of them,' he confirmed.

I blew out a breath. 'Okay, so who is going to get here first? The gargoyles or the Elders?'

'We'll see, I guess.'

Indy had stopped zooming around like a nutcase and was bowing and wagging to someone on the other side of the boulder. I'd bet good money it was Evan; he often lurked there.

Evan was Emory's ward on paper only, but I'd pointed out to Emory that the boy deserved more than that. I was pleased that Emory had started to step up; Evan had too, though in typical teen fashion he tried to hide it.

Since the completion of the challenge, I'd pushed Emory to meet with Evan more, and he'd agreed with the proviso that I went too. As he'd pointed out, we were a package deal these days. We'd had a few stilted dinners with Evan before I'd suggested a movie night instead. The movie gave us a focus other than just ourselves as well as something to talk about. It turned out that Evan was a movie buff and it didn't take long to find some common ground. We all liked *Die Hard*; we even promised tentatively to watch it together the following Christmas.

Evan had opened up across our evenings together. He had a younger sister, Harriet, who he missed terribly. His father had made it entirely clear that Evan wasn't to try and contact his younger sister. He'd obeyed because his father was "scary". Evan hadn't come out and said it exactly, but he'd explained that his mother had died soon after the revelation that she'd had an affair with a dragon. It didn't take a genius to work out that Evan's father had been the one to take Evan's mother away from him. Poor kid, he'd already been through so much. I would add finding a way he could speak to Harriet to my to-do list. He deserved that much.

I looked at the boulder and, sure enough, I spotted Evan's messy hair being tousled by the breeze. I gave him a big wave; he returned it with a grin before continuing to play with Indy right next to the catacombs. If Indy was anything like Gato, she'd be able to see right through the illusion that kept the entrance to the catacombs hidden.

The catacombs were a part of the castle's defences; in the event of attack, the young were supposed to shelter in them so it made sense that Evan was familiar with them. The brethren guards were supposed to be the only ones with keys, but I'd snaffled a set a few weeks earlier and hadn't given them back. I wondered how many other people had done the same.

'Do you need me to stay tonight? For the Elders, I mean?' I asked Emory. Maybe jetting off to meet with the head horn wasn't the best idea.

'No, it's fine,' he reassured me. 'Go to Liverpool and meet with Hardman. I'll be interested to hear what you think of him.'

'You didn't mention the other deaths,' I said accusingly.

There was a pause while Emory worked out how to not quite fib to me. 'It's not certain that they're linked. I wanted you to look at them with fresh eyes.'

'Why these deaths and not others?'

'They're closer to home, for one thing.'

'And?' I asked drily.

'The satyrs are under my purview. The elemental is not.'

'The dryad is,' I pointed out.

'Yes, the dryad is,' he agreed. 'But he was less local.' Emory frowned. 'Truthfully, I'm concerned. There's been a rise in Anti-Crea sentiment and attacks. Normally the Anti-Crea are content to spout vitriol about us, but lately things have turned violent.'

'You think the murders have been carried out by the Anti-Crea,' I surmised. 'But what about the elemental? She's on the human side.'

'An outlier, for sure. Maybe it's a red herring, maybe she pissed off the wrong Anti-Crea and they took action. Maybe it's nothing to do with the Anti-Crea. I can't be objective about this. I'm getting a lot of pressure to turn the tables on them. The creatures have turned to me as their Elite and they want protecting. I've sent teams of brethren out as a visible deterrent and I'm hoping that will prevent further ... incidents.'

'I didn't see any brethren at Portmeirion.'

'I had them pull out while you and the Connection were there.'

'Are they back in place now?'

'Yes, and patrolling visibly.' Emory paused. 'Before you dash off, there's something else you should know. Hardman asked for you specifically.'

'He did? You didn't say that before.'

'I didn't want to inflate your ego,' he teased.

'So am I hired by you or Hardman?'

'Me,' Emory said firmly.

'Good. I'll make sure to bill you some sexy new underwear.' I winked, trying to inject some levity into to the conversation.

'Please do.'

'Has Shirdal arrived?' I glanced around but I couldn't see the griffin. I frowned; he should have beaten us back. He could fly much faster than we could drive – according to him, anyway. It was possible he was shovelling me some shit when he told me that, which I'd swallowed whole.

'Did he not ride in the car with you?' Emory asked.

'Mike's car was a bit cramped with Gato and Indy. We'll take my Mercedes to Liverpool.' I paused. 'And we'll leave the hellhounds with you. I think you'll need allies more than me.'

Emory watched as Indy started barking at Evan. 'You're leaving me with the liability.'

'Don't call our baby that!' I grinned. 'Best of luck, Emory.'

I spotted Shirdal – or at least, a massive fuck-off griffin – in the skies above us, coming into land. He whumped down beside us with such force that the ground shook.

'You've got incoming,' Shirdal said urgently to Emory.

'I know, the Elders are en route.'

'Not the Elders. Something I've never seen before with black wings. Like freaking avenging angels.'

'The gargoyles,' Emory and I said in unison.

It looked like we knew who was going to arrive first.

Chapter 12

I was torn: on the one hand, I wanted to see all of the gargoyles again, especially Reynard. The French gargoyle had grown on me when we'd fought together, and besides he was Lucy's friend, which made him mine. On the other hand, I despised being late and I had a date with the head of the satyrs who was related to one of the murder victims I was investigating. Things were getting dicier at the castle; I wanted to wrap this investigation up fast so I could focus on helping Emory.

He saw my quandary. 'Go. I'll ring you if I need you. You can always head back tonight.' He frowned at Evan who was playing with Indy in the distance. 'I'd better get him tucked away. I have no idea what the gargoyles are going to bring.'

'Is there any chance that the gargoyles are hostile towards you?' I asked quietly. 'You know – for ending their gargoyle life and making them human-ish again?' Reynard had gone from being a short, squat gargoyle with grey skin, scaly wings and shark-like teeth to being a handsome human man with black-feathered wings. His skin glowed with orbs of light like constantly moving constellations. I had no idea if his dramatic transformation had applied to all the gargoyles, or just those present at Emory's little life-saving magic ritual.

'No,' Emory said firmly. 'They're grateful, so grateful that it's kind of awkward, really. I can feel it all of the time and I have to try to put it out of my mind. Pulling my bond with you closer helps.'

I knew what he meant. I used my bond with Emory to help block out my bond with Nate, the vampyr whose life I had accidentally saved. In doing so, I had inadvertently bound myself in a master-slave bond that I tried hard not to call upon. 'Okay, I'll go. But I'll come back tonight,' I said firmly. That seemed like a reasonable compromise.

Emory's eyes softened. 'I'll look forward to that.' He gave me a chaste kiss on the forehead. Flirting was all right, but there could be no tonsil hockey in front of the brethren. He had all these rules, and I guessed that with all the current Anti-Crea friction, he needed to keep himself even loftier than usual.

'Keep your eyes on Hardman,' he advised. 'He's harmless enough, and I suspect he's little more than a figurehead for the satyrs, but there's a reason why he's asked for you.'

My eyes narrowed. 'Because I'm a kick-ass PI?'

'Let's hope so. I question his motives.' He worried his bottom lip with his teeth. I wanted to kiss it better but that would probably distract us both – and besides, no PDAs. Emory was fine with a PDA outside the castle, and I missed the days when we could fool around and kiss wherever we wanted to.

I dragged my wanton brain back to Hardman. 'Emory, I always question people's motives. It's part of the job description. I've got to go or I'll be late. I'll see you on the flip side. Be safe and say hi to Reynard for me.'

'I will.'

'Take care of Indy and don't let her chew anything,' I added. 'I'll leave Gato here to look after her.' Emory looked slightly relieved. 'And don't do anything I wouldn't do.'

'That's not very limiting,' he teased, throwing my words back in my face.

Mike followed me to my car but, visibly torn, he kept looking back at Emory. As he went to get into it, I moved in front of him and put a hand on his chest. 'Stay,' I said firmly.

'What?'

'Stay,' I repeated. 'You want to protect Emory, and I'm only going to question a goat.'

'A very annoying goat,' he muttered.

'You want to protect Emory from the gargoyles and the Elders, and I want you to do that too. Go on. I've got Shirdal riding shotgun with me. I'll be fine.'

Mike glared at Shirdal. Shirdal smirked smugly. 'Go on, little brethren boy. I've got this.' Mike's nostrils flared. Men!

'*I've* got this,' I declared. 'Go keep Emory safe from the threats coming to our door.'

Mike wavered. 'Are you sure?'

'Positive. I'm going to a bar in Liverpool – how much trouble can I get into?' Even as I said it, I grimaced internally. A lot: I could get into a lot of trouble. I kept my face sunny. 'Protect your Prime. That's an order.'

He straightened. 'Yes, Prima,' he said and marched away.

'Glad you got rid of the asshat,' Shirdal said.

'Mike's not an asshat! He's a good man.'

'Exactly. He's so boring.'

I couldn't help but smile; Shirdal's definition of fun was different to everyone else's. I slid him a sideways glance. 'If I didn't know any better, I'd say you were trying to put his pigtails into the inkpots at school.'

'Is that your subtle way of asking which team I bat for?' He raised an eyebrow.

'Only if you want to tell me. I'm just saying. It sounded like there's some unresolved sexual tension there.'

Shirdal scoffed. 'There is zero sexual tension with Carter. Regardless of which team I bat for, Carter is straighter than a Roman road. Unless I'm very much mistaken, he's got his eyes on your fiancé's PA.'

I would be only too happy if Summer and Mike hooked up. I was very invested in securing Summer's happiness. Not that I didn't trust Emory one hundred per cent, but I'd still feel happier if Summer was happily in love with someone else. Anyone else.

We slid into my Mercedes with me behind the driver's wheel. 'Can you drive?' I asked Shirdal out of interest.

'Of course I can drive. What kind of an idiot doesn't drive in this day and age?'

'Emory doesn't drive.'

Shirdal snorted. 'I bet he could if he wanted to. He's much too cautious not to have learned the basics. He might not have a licence, but I bet he could slide behind the wheel in an emergency.'

'Maybe.'

'Definitely,' Shirdal said confidently.

'Have you seen him drive?'

'Well ... no.' The griffin started fiddling with the radio station before settling on a country station.

'Country, really?' I mocked. 'I thought you'd be a rock-and-roll type.'

'Sure, if I'm killing things. But when I'm cruising, I love me some country tunes. Eyes on the road, sweetheart.'

'You're going to be an annoying backseat driver, aren't you?'

'I'm in the front seat, so it's fine,' he quipped.

'Uh-huh,' I sighed.

Shirdal cleared his throat. 'Actually, I play for all teams. I'm an equal opportunities player. I like the person, their gender is irrelevant. Does that bother you?'

'Not in the slightest. You do you.'

'Mike wouldn't be interested in me,' he said dismissively. 'Nor I in him. He may be pretty but he's got no sense of fun.'

'Have you thought about projecting a less—' Drunken? Debauched? Murderous? '—messy vibe? A shower might help your chances.'

He folded his arms. 'I shower. And anyway, I don't care about my chances with anyone that judges me on my appearance.'

'Good point.' I conceded.

Shirdal cleared his throat and changed the subject to country songs, and I let him.

The hour-and-a-half drive to Liverpool flew by next to the loquacious griffin, who told me tales as we drove, each one taller than the last. My lie detector was working overtime, pinging me as he told me falsehoods, but he was enjoying himself so I let him continue. He made me laugh – and that was a rare commodity these days.

Chapter 13

Sean Hardman wanted to meet us at Smugglers Cove, a bar on the Albert Dock. He had reserved us a parking space right outside, proper VIP stuff, so we left the car and headed inside. Smugglers Cove was relatively new; it hadn't been there when Lucy was a student, or maybe we just hadn't been either cool or rich enough to frequent the affluent docks.

As suggested by its name, the whole bar was pirate themed. We gave our names to the maître d' and were shown to an area that had been cordoned off. There were tables made of huge barrels as well as long wooden ones with benches alongside them. Ropes and vast swathes of fabric, reminiscent of a ship's sails, hung from the walls.

The cordoned-off area was full of the Other. A wizard was stirring a drink using the IR. Two witches, one younger and the other older, were poring over a book of runes. The latter had some sort of yellow lizard on her shoulder – a bearded dragon, maybe. If I'd known pets were welcome, I could have brought Gato or Indy with me. Though honestly, Indy was a riot – it was probably for the best that they were relaxing at the castle. Still, the bar room was a hodgepodge of all things Other and a couple of hellhounds would have been fine. There were ogres and dryads and vampyrs and, sitting on the comfy-looking sofas, were three satyrs. Bingo.

I went over to them and touched my hand to my heart. 'I am Jinx. My honour to meet you.'

One of the satyrs gestured for the other two to leave, and they obediently sloped off to prop up the bar on the other side of the room. The satyr gestured to the sofa opposite and I sat down. Shirdal paced behind me, keeping an eye on the ogres at my back, guarding my six. I blocked him and everyone else and focused on the man in front of me. He still hadn't introduced himself. Rude.

'Sean Hardman, I presume.' I didn't try to keep the edge out of my voice. Emory had taught me a lot about the Other realm. I'd known it was dog eat dog from the beginning; it was full of little tests like this to see whether I'd roll over when the power games started. I needed to make it clear that I wouldn't.

Sean had shaved his head, so his black horns that jutted backwards were even more pronounced. He carried the look off by having beautiful cheekbones sharp enough to cut your hand on. He was dressed in a shirt and smart black trousers. His hands were twitching on his lap. He swept his gaze over me. 'I see why he picked you.' He gave an exaggerated leer.

Yuck. Even cheekbones like his didn't make such comments welcome.

I wasn't going to do small talk with this sleaze, so I went straight to the heart of the matter. Maybe Arlo and Derek weren't the outliers, maybe Shane was. 'Arlo Hardman and Derek Ives. Both were brutally murdered within days of each other. What can you tell me about them?'

'I think you'll find that *I* hired *you* to tell me about them,' he said snottily.

'No. In this instance, I am retained by the Prime Elite,' I responded levelly.

'As if he gives a fuck about their deaths.'

That made me want to glare. Emory did give a fuck – of course he did. If anything, he cared too much.

I studied Hardman. 'The deaths happened in the Prime's back yard. He doesn't want a murderer sloping around, killing off the Others. Arlo was your cousin and you'd been told he didn't care too much about consent.'

The satyr snorted. 'What a ridiculous woke society we live in. A girl has too much to drink, makes bad choices and the next morning cries rape.'

My eyes narrowed and my nostrils flared. What a twat. 'There have been suggestions that Arlo and Derek used date-rape drugs.'

He waved it away. 'Nah, nothing like that. Just a little persuasion to help people relax. Nothing more. I spoke to them about it.'

'And you believed them?' I was fighting to keep my tone non-judgemental but, despite my best efforts, I was failing.

'Yes.' His tone was equally pugnacious. Oops; we were rubbing each other up the wrong way. His hands were constantly fiddling but I saw a slight tremor. Drugs? I studied him carefully. His eyes looked a little watery and feverish and something about him seemed off. My gut was making me feel edgy.

I tried to bring the conversation back to a professional level. 'Do you know of any enemies that Arlo might have had?'

'No real ones,' he said finally. 'Just petty shit. I think his death was a random attack.'

'A random kill of two roommates ... on two separate occasions?' I couldn't hide my incredulity.

He grimaced. 'Well, maybe not totally random.' He thought about it. 'There were some complaints against Arlo and Derek. I've got records of them.'

'Can you send them to me?'

I could see he was debating whether or not to cooperate so I used my magic to lean on him a little. I didn't even feel bad about it. People's lives hung in the balance, and I didn't doubt that the baseball-bat killer would strike again.

'You want to get to the bottom of this, right?' I pointed out, coaxing him to the right course of action. 'If Derek and Arlo didn't do anything nefarious with these women then you've nothing to hide.'

Hardman rubbed his jaw thoughtfully; he seemed to be warring with himself. Eventually he pulled out his phone from his back pocket and tapped away at it before asking, 'Email address?'

I gave him my details and heard the whoosh as he mailed me. 'Thanks. What can you tell me about Arlo? What kind of things did he like?'

'In the bedroom?' he leered.

I didn't hide my distaste this time. 'No,' I snapped back. 'In general.'

'He liked football and women. He was a simple guy with simple pleasures. A bit like me.' He reached out a hand and squeezed my knee.

'Fuck off,' I told him forcefully and pushed his hand away. Total sleazeball.

'Oh, it's like that is it?' He glared. 'You're good enough for dragon cock, but all this fine goat energy is below you? Whore.'

'I think you'll find that's the very opposite of being a whore.'

His lips drew back in a snarl and then, without warning, his fist flew back and hit me solidly in the eye. The force of the blow sent me back into the sofa.

Before he could do anything more, I had a fireball in my hand. I suspended him in the air with the IR with an abrupt, 'Up!'.

Rage and instinct got me that far, but now logic clicked in and I didn't know what to do. I could let Shirdal handle it – he was already barrelling in – but no, *I* needed to deal with this. If I was going to be Prima of the dragons, the

Other realmers needed to know that I couldn't be messed with.

As if in answer to my quandary, Glimmer was already on my hip, heavy and familiar. Enticing. It was always there when I needed it, so it must have thought it was required. I let the fireball fizzle to nothing and drew Glimmer. Hardman was still floating in the air, suspended by my force of will.

'Do you know what this is?' I asked, holding the dagger up to his eyeline. I turned the blade so he could see its distinctive pommel.

He swallowed hard. 'It's Glimmer.'

'And do you know what Glimmer can do?' I watched as he began to squirm.

'Steal your magic.'

'That's right. With one stab of my blade, I can take your magic from you. I can leave you nothing more than a sad little misogynistic man.'

'Please, I don't know what came over me. That's not me. I swear it.' *True.* The truth of that sentence gave me pause.

A lady pushed forward from the crowd around me. I hadn't even noticed that the punch had attracted attention. She was one of the witches, the older one who'd been tutoring the younger one with the book of runes. 'Allow me,' she offered.

I had no idea what she was offering but now didn't seem like a good time to admit ignorance. I slid my eyes to Shirdal and he gave a minute nod. 'Sure.' I gestured her forward.

The witch had a huge backpack, like Amber had her ever-present tote bag. She swung it around to the front of her body, unzipped it carefully and hauled out a jar of gloop. She had a paintbrush ready and, before Sean could object, she sketched a quick rune onto his hand. It shone for a moment with a light glow before turning red. Red was never good.

'He's been influenced by a daemon,' she confirmed grimly. 'He's not the first we've seen lately. Someone is stirring up trouble.'

'A daemon?' Sean stared in horror at the rune on his hand. 'Get it out of me!'

'You're not possessed,' the witch said scathingly, 'just *influenced*.'

I grimaced. Too many things in this realm could fiddle with your thoughts: pipers, sirens, wizards, daemons ... the list went on.

'How?' Sean asked.

'Daemon magics are complicated,' the witch said archly. 'But I'll do what I can to remove its hold over you. Stay still, please.'

'Um, should I lower him down first?' I asked.

'No, keep him up there in case the daemon compulsion hasn't run its course.' She hastily painted some more runes on him. They all shone red once before rapidly shrinking and disappearing. 'There,' she said with satisfaction. 'All done.'

I lowered Sean down to the ground. 'Thanks. I don't know what we would have done without you,' I admitted.

She eyed Glimmer. 'Stabbed him, I expect.'

'Well, yes.' *Lie.* I wasn't going to stab him but he didn't need to know that. Let the Other realmers think I would steal their magic if they crossed me; maybe it would give me a bit of street cred. It had been years since my misspent teenage years, but I could still remember that a bad reputation helped a lot. You didn't actually need to *do* bad stuff. I hoped it worked the same way in the Other realm.

The helpful witch introduced herself as Kass Scholes, mother of the Liverpool coven of witches. Now she had painted the runes to remove the demon influence from

Sean, he was like a new man. 'I'm so sorry,' he stuttered again for the millionth time.

'It's really okay. It wasn't you.'

'No – I'm not like that. I *did* investigate Arlo and Derek and what I emailed you before was a full investigation that I was preparing to send to the Connection. The date-rape allegations were new, but as soon as I heard about them I knew they were above my pay grade. I'm head horn but the role doesn't really mean anything – it's a popularity contest among the satyrs and not much more. The Trip rules the satyrs – I'm just a frontman because none of them wanted to waste time being on the symposium.' I knew from Emory that The Trip was the ruling council of the Satyrs. 'Besides, I run every vote past them and they tell me what to do. I'm a puppet, nothing but a nice puppet. I would never hit a lady.'

'Punch and Judy are puppets,' I pointed out.

'But not nice ones. I'm a nice one.' He was desperate for me to understand.

'It's okay, Sean, really.' I looked at Shirdal. 'I think we're done here.'

Shirdal was still glaring at Sean; I'd forgiven Sean for the punch, but he had not. We stepped out of the bar and went back to the car. I was anxious to return to Emory and the gargoyles and the Elders. I felt like I was juggling too many balls and I didn't want to drop any of them, but the most important thing was being there for Emory. A host of elder dragons travelling to the castle didn't feel good. The going was about to get tough, and I wanted to get going – back to his side.

I beeped the car unlocked. Before I climbed in, I turned self-consciously to Shirdal. 'Does it look bad? The eye?'

'It's too dark for me to see. Step under the streetlight.' I stepped closer to the light so he could peer at my poor puffy face. 'It's red and swelling already. You're going to look a mess,' he promised gleefully.

I looked back into the bar. I should have asked Kass to paint a healing rune or two on my face whilst she was giving away freebies in the name of the common good.

Shirdal read my thoughts. 'We could go back in.'

'No, Let's just go.' I turned back to the car.

Just as it exploded.

Chapter 14

My ears were ringing and I couldn't see; I was wrapped up in a bundle of white feathers. Shirdal had shifted and protected me from the worst of the explosion with his wings, but the force had thrown me to the ground.

When I could think straight, I carefully pushed away his wings. He resisted for a moment before relenting and letting me go. I stood up slowly and dusted myself down. I'd probably ache later when the adrenaline left me; adrenaline really is a clever little drug.

I checked on Shirdal. Some of his feathers were scorched, others were missing and his body bore a few cuts from stray shrapnel. 'Are you all right?' I asked him.

He shifted back into a man. Thank goodness his clothes shifted with him. He grinned and rubbed his hands with pleasure. 'Now we're talking. This is fun.'

I rolled my eyes and immediately regretted my actions. That hurt. 'Someone bombing my car is *not* fun.'

My phone rang: Emory. 'Jess, are you okay? I just got an alert that the tracker on your car has gone offline.' Of course he had a tracker on my car. I didn't get wound up about it; it had already come in handy a time or two.

'I'm fine, though my car isn't.' I paused, not quite sure how to admit the next part. 'I'm sorry. Someone bombed it.'

'Someone bombed your car?'

'Yes. I'm really sorry.'

'It doesn't matter; it's just a car. It's replaceable. You aren't,' he growled.

'I don't want you to replace it again. That's two Mercedes I've destroyed. Maybe I have a curse. Is that a thing? Could I have a car curse?' Sirens were wailing in the distance. Uh-oh: the police were on the way.

'I don't know about car curses,' Emory said, 'but I'll get you another one anyway. Maybe a different brand.'

'That might break the curse,' I agreed sagely.

'Did you hit your head?' he asked with concern.

'Not in the explosion,' I said. Best not to mention the punch right now. 'The police are here so I'd better go. I love you.'

'I love you, Jessica Sharp. Stay safe.'

'Stay sharp,' I quipped, then I hung up.

The police car screamed to a stop, closely followed by a fire-fighter's truck. The firemen piled out and started battling the flames and my poor car was soon a smouldering wreck. If I'd thought about it, I could have used my water elemental powers to put out the flames, but this was a busy and popular area and there would be CCTV cameras. It would be hard to explain, and the Connection would have to wade in and start clearing people's memories. Nope, it was better that I'd done nothing.

The police rapidly cordoned off the area. One of the officers came over to me and I immediately spotted the triangle on his cufflinks which meant he was Other. He was a crossover cop, an inspector for the Connection and a detective for the local police force. There was something passingly familiar about him, but try as I might, I couldn't place him. 'Name?' he demanded brusquely as he pulled out a small notepad.

'Jessica Sharp.'

'And I'm Shirdal.' Still grinning like a loon, the griffin introduced himself.

The cop viewed him with visible distaste and his lip curled in a sneer. 'Which of you is the owner of the car?'

'That'd be me,' I said.

'Any gang affiliations?'

I blinked at the baldness of the question. 'Erm, no?' It came out as a question because I was so surprised at his abrupt manner.

The cop put his notepad away without making a single note in it. 'I think it's best if you come to the station.'

'What? Why? I'm the victim here,' I protested.

Another police car came in, hot and heavy, and Elvira stepped out with Bland. I gave her a relieved smile and a finger wave. I was grateful to see them, though it must have sucked for them. It looked like the inspectors pulled long shifts. 'Hey,' I greeted Elvira.

'Jinx, what have you done now?' she sighed.

I shrugged. 'Pissed off the wrong person apparently.'

'Any idea who?'

'No. None.'

'Any threats to your person?' Bland asked.

'Not recently.' I shrugged.

'Inspectors Garcia, Bland,' the newbie cop interjected. 'I was just taking Ms Sharp in for questioning.'

'Why?' Elvira asked, quirking an eyebrow.

'Why? Because she is withholding information,' he spat out.

'About what?' Bland demanded.

'About the perpetrators of the crime.'

'She is the victim here.' Elvira spelled it out slowly.

The cop snorted. 'No one who's innocent gets their car blown up.'

'What about innocent until proven guilty?' I muttered.

Elvira glared at me, a clear '*shut up*' in her gaze. Oops. 'I appreciate your zeal, Detective Randall, but that won't be necessary. I've got it from here. Please do some crowd control,' she ordered.

'Yes ma'am,' he said tightly, glaring at me as he stalked off.

'What did I do?' I asked.

'Shagged a dragon,' Elvira explained.

'He's Anti-Crea?'

Bland spelled it out for me. 'You bet. His father is Elliot Randall.'

At my blank expression, Elvira sighed. 'Elliot Randall – the current leader of the Anti-Crea movement here in the UK?'

'Right. I knew that.' *Lie.* I did not know that. 'How the hell did Detective Randall get a job on the force?'

'His dad is rich and money talks.' Bland sighed. 'It's a shame, but it is what it is. The world is a crooked place.'

'Money talks,' Shirdal agreed loudly. 'It says, "Here, I'm an asshole who needs my rich daddy to bribe people to give me a job because I'm so thick as shit I can't get a job all by myself".' His voice was loud enough to carry to the cop and his back stiffened. He paused mid-step, warring with himself, but he didn't return.

'There'll be a contract out with your name on it if you don't stop,' Elvira warned Shirdal.

'He can put as many hits out on me as he likes,' Shirdal laughed. 'I love it when people try to assassinate me. It really starts my day off right.'

'Griffins are so weird,' Elvira muttered. She turned to me. 'I'll email you a copy of your statement for you to e-sign. Did you see anything or anyone suspicious?'

'No.'

She peered more closely at me. 'What happened to your eye?' she asked.

Good point. I thought of Sean Hardman being influenced by the demon; maybe that influence had extended to planting a bomb. Why hadn't that occurred to me earlier? The explosion had clearly addled my brain.

'One second.' I turned and went back into Smuggler's Cove. Elvira was close behind me.

A lot of the patrons had hustled out with the explosion but the bouncers were trying to cajole them back in with promises of drinks on the house.

Sean was where I had left him in the back room of Smuggler's Cove with his two satyr companions. 'I thought you were acting weird,' one of them was saying. 'The shaved head thing was a surprise.'

'Why didn't you stop me before I cut it all off?' Sean whined. 'My head is cold all the time. Surely a daemon would appreciate a warm head.'

'Maybe it would have if you'd been possessed,' his other mate offered.

I interrupted their oh-so-essential hair conversation. 'When did Sean start acting weird?' I asked. I should have asked earlier; the punch had rattled me more than I'd admitted even to myself.

'About two days ago.'

'After he went to the races,' the other satyr agreed.

Sean glared. 'Next time I start acting not like myself, please can you do something about it rather than just waiting for me to shave my head and punch someone in the face?'

'To be fair, Sean, we didn't know you were gonna punch the PI,' the first satyr pointed out.

'Talking about punching me, did you by any chance also plant a bomb in my car?' I asked casually.

'No!' Sean looked aghast. *True.* I turned to the other satyrs. 'Did either of you plant a bomb in my car?' I asked hopefully. If it was either of the satyrs then the mystery would be solved, and I really wanted one less thing in my headspace.

'Not me,' the first one confirmed. *True.* Damn.

'I wouldn't know a bomb if it exploded in my face,' the second one said. *Lie.*

It was a lie and an evasion, so I pressed the point. 'You didn't plant the bomb?'

'No ma'am.' *True.*

Damn – but that would have been too easy. 'Okay, thanks,' I said. 'Sean, do you remember anything weird happening at the races?'

'I won!' He grinned. 'But no, I don't remember any daemons putting some hoodoo magic on me.' *True.*

'Daemons don't do hoodoo,' his mate sniggered.

'Whatever,' Sean rolled his eyes.

'Why did you want to hire me?' I asked.

He frowned. 'I don't know.' *True.* 'Do you think it was the daemon influence that made me do it?' If he didn't know why he'd hired me, then it certainly seemed that way.

Elvira had her notepad out and was busily scrawling notes. She was a better cop than Randall. 'What's this about a daemon?' she asked.

'They'll fill you in,' I told her. 'I'm going home. I'm beat.' Literally. 'You have my number if you need anything else from me.'

'Sure. I'll see you tomorrow. I was in two minds, but then I thought – why not?' Elvira beamed at me.

I had no idea what she was talking about but I gave her a vague smile. I guessed she'd have follow-up questions and she could find me at the castle if she needed me. I gave her an awkward wave and marched back outside to stare forlornly at the wreck of my car. The flames were out but it was still smoking. My poor baby.

A chill ran down my spine. Normally at a pub or club like this, I would have left Gato in the car. Imagine if I had brought him and Indy along? Thank goodness they were safe and sound back at the castle.

Shirdal was being considerate for once, staying silent and letting me process what had happened. 'We have two options,' I said finally, when I'd processed things enough. 'We can grab a taxi all the way to Caernarfon or I can ride on your back. Which would you prefer?' I had an uneasy feeling between my shoulder blades, and I was itching to get home to Emory.

Shirdal read me like a book. 'It'll be quicker to fly if you're game,' he offered.

'Always.' I gave him a goofy thumbs-up. I'm such a dork.

'Let's go back to the bar. I can shift on the roof away from prying eyes, and we can get high quickly so no one will see us.'

'Are you all right to fly me for an hour and a half?' I asked dubiously.

'It won't be that long. Probably an hour. And yes, I'll be fine.' Shirdal confidently waved away my objections.

I frowned at him. In his griffin form, he'd been injured by the shrapnel. 'What about your cuts and scrapes?'

'They're already gone, healed in the shift. That's why I changed to human right away.'

That made sense. We slunk back into the bar and made our way upstairs past the door marked 'staff only'. My heart was hammering, but no one stopped us. Normally I have nerves of steel – I skydive, for goodness' sake – but the punch and the bomb had left me feeling antsy.

We climbed out onto the flat roof and moments later Shirdal was back in griffin form. It had been about three weeks since the challenge, but I still had to battle to convince my legs to move forward and climb onto his back again.

Once I was in position, he swept back his mighty wings and ran towards the edge of the roof. Before I could say anything, he leapt. A scream wanted to rip from my throat as we started to fall, but a second later Shirdal's wings snapped out and then we were soaring.

Chapter 15

We were nearly at the castle when Shirdal shouted, 'Incoming!' He stopped flying forward and held us still in the air, moving his wings gently to keep us airborne. A moment later, someone with black wings shot towards us.

Shirdal extended his claws, ready to fight. Shit: I didn't want to be on the back of a battling griffin. Aerial combat is not my strong suit. 'Play nicely!' I shouted.

The black-winged former gargoyle came to a stop and hung effortlessly in the air. It was Reynard.

Without forward motion, it was possible for us to speak even though we were several thousand feet up in the air with the wind gusting around us. 'Shirdal, this is Reynard. Reynard, this is Shirdal,' I shouted to introduce them.

'My honour to meet you, Reynard,' Shirdal responded, eyeing the other man's black wings. 'Bastion's report outlined the great bravery you have shown in assisting Lucy Barrett.'

'Bravery or foolishness? I'm not sure which,' Reynard laughed. 'My honour to meet you, King of the Air, you feckless lionbird.'

Shirdal didn't blink at Reynard's insult. He knew of the gargoyle's propensity to blister the air with swear words; it wasn't personal, it was just his thing. 'Ah, we have dispensed with the title "King of the Air" these days.' Shirdal explained. 'It made the air elementals grumpy. And we must move with the times – kings are so last century.'

'Are all of you here?' I asked Reynard pointedly.

'Every last dew-beating one of us.'

I blinked. 'What on earth does dew-beating mean?'

'It means getting up early, my fine wench.'

'Does that mean you don't have to be nocturnal anymore?'

'Got it in one, sassenach. We have seen the sun for the first time in centuries – well, without being turned into stone immediately afterwards.'

'Um, congratulations,' I said. 'That must have been amazing.'

'It truly was.' Reynard's tone was wonderous.

'What about your immortality?' I pried.

'Funnily enough, my little trollop, there wasn't a spate of volunteers willing to fall on their swords and test whether or not we've still got a good dose of fucking survival going on.'

'Still got the cursing thing though, huh?'

'It's a bloody hard thing to turn off, and frankly I haven't fucking tried. I like my expletives. They may not be a necessary part of my vernacular now that the curse is lifted, but I'll be fucked if I'll change the way I speak.' He grinned. 'Plus, it's fun to shock the genteel courts.'

No doubt. I turned back to business. 'And the Elder dragons, have they arrived?'

'Not yet, but apparently they are due any minute. That's why I'm here, beating the air, keeping an eye out for the Prime Elite.' Warm affection suffused his tone when he spoke of Emory.

'And how do you *feel* about Emory?' I asked Reynard cautiously.

'Like he is a god among men. He saved us all. He didn't have to but he did, and now we are free. Truly free – pain free and not cursed to the night. It's a bloody miracle. We owe him our lives and our fealty,' he declared passionately.

'And has he accepted your fealty?'

'He has. We had a ceremony in his big old hall with two hundred of us flapping our wings like crows on the pull. We're brethren now, through and through. And nothing those cantankerous Elders say will change it, the cumberworlds,' he declared grimly.

'You think they're going to take issue with it?' I asked.

'*Oui*. We stayed away as long as we could, but the pull to serve the Prime Elite was too strong. We have created *un petit problème* for him.' He looked sad.

'It can't be helped,' I said encouragingly. 'We'll get through it.'

'Yes, all things are to be enjoyed or endured. Let us see what the Elders bring.' Reynard shrugged then abruptly dropped a few hundred feet. 'Ah, one mustn't shrug and fly,' he muttered. 'Good to know.'

Shirdal was sympathetic. 'You'll get used to it. We'll see you down there.' Then he folded his wings and dived us down towards the castle – and certain trouble.

I let out a shriek as we plummeted, though I wasn't sure if it was because of joy or fear – perhaps a bit of both. At the last minute Shirdal's wings snapped out again and we banked to the left, closer to the castle's tower. The brethren manning the walls had spotted us coming in and weapons were being pointed our way. Shirdal landed us expertly on the top of the tower.

'Prima.' Jackie greeted me. She was one of the brethren that Emory trusted; she frequently stood guard outside our rooms. 'What happened to your face?'

I grimaced. 'Is it bad?'

'No, not really.' *Lie.* Thanks, Jackie.

'I got punched by a satyr.'

'What did you do?' Jackie's partner Dave asked incredulously. 'Satyrs are the most fun-loving beings in the Other realm.'

'He was being influenced by a daemon,' I explained.

'That's not good,' Dave said.

'No shit.' Jackie rolled her eyes.

The door to the roof opened and in strolled Mike. 'Carter,' Jackie greeted him. 'The Prima was just explaining how she got punched in the face by a satyr.'

I figured it was best to divulge information the way you take off a plaster: nice and quick. 'Yeah. And my car exploded.'

'What?' Mike exclaimed.

'Yup. Kaboom.' I mimed an explosion with my hands.

Mike squeezed the bridge of his nose, then assumed a falsetto voice. 'You look after the Prime. I'll be absolutely fine, I'm just meeting a goat,' he scoffed. 'That's the last time I leave you alone. You'd better give me the full story because the abridged one is giving me an ulcer. What happened?'

I gave him a rundown of our trip to Liverpool, complete with the snot-nosed officer and the rescue by Elvira. 'Does the Prime Elite know about all of this?' Mike frowned darkly.

'Most of it. I'll give him the full details now.'

'Do it fast, the Elders are inbound.'

'Roger that.' I gave a quick salute.

'Smartass,' Mike muttered. He turned to Shirdal. 'And what were you doing, Mr High and Mighty, while our Prima was getting punched and exploded?'

'To be fair, *I* didn't get exploded – just my car – and that's due in part to Shirdal's protection,' I objected.

'He didn't defend you from the punch though, did he?' Mike sniffed.

'It was a sucker punch,' Shirdal snarled. 'He wouldn't have got a second hit in. Besides,' he raised his voice so it carried to all of the brethren on the ramparts, 'our Prima didn't need help. She had him suspended in the air, and she had a fireball in one hand and Glimmer in the other. He was sweating bricks when she told him she was going to take his magic for daring to accost her. Of course, that's when we realised he was being influenced by a daemon, so the Prima let him crawl away with his magic and his life.'

Who needed a PR agent when Shirdal could do the job? 'Thank you for that blow-by-blow account,' I said drily. 'I'm okay from here, so you go do whatever you need to do.' He must have been knackered; he'd flown me miles on top of an already busy day. I wanted to pat his back but I wasn't sure if that would be welcome or if he'd rip my hand off. Discretion said not to bother, just in case.

'I'll go have some more fun,' he said. More fun? Christ. I wondered briefly what he did for pleasure and hoped it didn't involve maiming.

Shirdal bowed his eagle head to me in a mini-bow then leapt up and took to the skies once more.

I made my way to Emory's suite of rooms, nodding at the various brethren that I recognised along the way. Mike followed me at a discreet distance on Jinx-bodyguard duty again. Sarah and Jacob were on guard duty outside Emory's door.

'Indy – no! Drop!' I heard him shout from inside. Sarah and Jacob were both suppressing sniggers.

'The dog training's going well then?' I asked drily.

'It's going something,' Sarah agreed.

I knocked once and let myself in to the rooms. Emory appeared to be playing tug of war with Indy. She had his suit jacket in her mouth and he was trying to unhook her teeth without damaging anything. 'Bad dog,' he muttered. 'Drop it.'

'We haven't trained her on "drop it" yet,' I pointed out.

'She's a hellhound – she's bright enough to understand, she just chooses not to. She's a stubborn bitch.'

Technically, he was right; since Indy was a female dog, she was indeed a bitch. Even so, I frowned at him. 'Don't be mean. She's just a baby – and she can hear you.'

Emory gave up on the suit jacket, turned to me – and then he froze. In a second he was by my side. His vampyric speed took me off guard; generally, he works hard to hide the extra skills he got from his tangle with Glimmer. His fingers reached out to touch my jaw and gently turned my face towards him. 'Who did this to you?' he growled, his voice full of fury.

It took me a beat to remember what he was talking about. With the explosion at the forefront of my mind, I'd momentarily forgotten about the punch to the face. Though now that he mentioned it, my left eye *was* throbbing. 'Sean,' I admitted.

'Hardman?' he snarled, his voice low and gravelly.

'Yes.'

'I'll kill him.' *True.* Oops. Nope, no letting Emory kill people on my behalf.

'Not necessary,' I said hastily. 'It wasn't his fault. It turns out he was being influenced by a daemon, and he was very apologetic once the witch runed the influence out of him. It really wasn't his fault.'

Emory's eyes narrowed. Through our bond I could feel his fury that someone had hurt me and his self-flagellation that he'd let me go without adequate protection. The latter pissed me off. 'I can protect myself,' I bit out.

'Clearly.' He spoke through gritted teeth, gesturing to my face.

I glared back. 'He took me off guard. It was a sucker punch, and he wouldn't have got a second one in,' I said, parroting Shirdal's words. 'After the first punch he was suspended in the air with a fireball ready to roast him. I was all prepared to do something nasty when the witch stepped in and said it wasn't his fault.'

Emory's jaw worked. 'Fine. But I'm still punching him next time I see him.'

I'm a strong independent woman, but some prehistoric part of me preened at the thought of him punching Sean for me. At the root of it all, humans are still such basic creatures.

Emory picked up the soggy suit jacket that Indy had now dropped. Gato was stretched out in front of the fire, and he gave me a tap-tap of his tail to say hello. He'd been too busy toasting himself to listen to our conversation, but he stood up as soon as he spied my eye and leapt towards me. I braced myself for his weight and caught his forepaws on my shoulders. He pushed his cold snout towards me, touching it to my cheek with a sad whine.

'I'm okay.' I gave him a quick rundown of the events while we had a cuddle. Eventually he stood down, but he didn't move from my side. More guards.

Emory laid the jacket over a chair and came closer to me, budging Gato over. 'Let me make that better,' he offered, touching my cheek lightly. Rage had gone now and something else was swirling inside of him. He closed the remaining distance between us and gently kissed my eye. He swiped his tongue over it and I felt a tingle as his healing saliva did its work.

'Does anyone in your court know about your vampyr skills?' I asked curiously.

'Not a single one.'

'Why not?'

'Information is power. You know vampyrs and dragons are sworn enemies, so even my allies might have difficulty swallowing the news that I've got a vampyr's powers,' Emory explained evenly.

That was a fair point. Without centuries of prejudice clouding my judgement, I'd only thought of the upside – the fact that he could heal, move super-fast and phase to travel huge distances in a blink. But he was right; I couldn't imagine stalwart Elizabeth taking it well. 'Got it. No telling the Elders about your magic spit,' I affirmed.

'Gato. Indy. Out you go,' Emory ordered. Gato obediently herded Indy to the next room, shutting the door behind him. He was a smart pup.

'What do you need privacy for?' I asked.

'So you can come here and let me heal any other damaged parts.' Emory lifted me up and carried me to his bed. He unhooked the top snap of my jeans and started to pull them down.

'I'm not hurt there.' I assured him.

He flashed me a wolfish grin.

Oh.

Chapter 16

Much later, there was a discreet knock on the door. 'Sorry to disturb you, sir. The first Elder dragon has landed,' Mike called.

We were embroiled in a tangle of heavy, sweaty limbs. Emory pressed a kiss to my lips before replying, 'I'll be there in a moment. Who is it?'

'Darius,' Mike replied.

'Okay. See that he's offered food and drink right away – you know what he's like.'

'Does Darius like his food?' I asked.

'Loves it. Total foodie,' Emory told me.

'Is he huge?'

'No, dragons don't get fat. Awesome metabolism.'

I poked a roll on my stomach. 'Wish I were a dragon,' I muttered.

'I'd love you if you were as fat as Mr Blobby.' I loved that it was true.

I smiled. 'You say the nicest things.'

Emory flashed me a grin then climbed out of the bed, leaving me lonely. He pulled the duvet up to cover me and tucked me in before he padded to the bathroom for a quick wash before dressing in his customary sharp suit.

I checked the time: it was nearly midnight. Weariness was trickling down my spine. I was relaxed and happy, and sleep was chanting my name, but I pushed myself up reluctantly. Was I expected to greet the Elders with Emory? I didn't want him to get into trouble because I didn't know the protocol.

'Should I come with you?' I asked with as much enthusiasm as I could muster. No doubt the bond gave away the reluctance I was trying to hide.

Emory gently pushed me back down into the sumptuous pillows and gave me a long kiss. 'Go to sleep, love. I have to greet all of the Elders and get them settled into appropriate accommodation, but there's no obligation for you to do the same. You get some rest. The next few days will be busy.'

'And that will be different to normal how?'

He laughed. 'Situation normal—'

'—all fucked up. I wouldn't have it any other way,' I admitted.

'Oh, and Jess?'

I felt a very unusual shard of anxiety from him. 'Yeah?'

'Are you any further along with finding the Eye of Ebrel? Leonard is getting an ulcer over it.'

Leonard wasn't the only one; Emory was really worried about it too. He hadn't been before, despite its supposed doom-and-gloom portent. If he had been, it would have topped my to-do list. But now ... yeah, he was worried.

I grimaced guiltily. 'I'll get to it tomorrow. I'm sorry. You didn't seem too worried before.'

'Honestly? I thought it was a prank. There hasn't been a whisper of it on the black market, and there would have been if someone had tried to sell it.'

'And now you don't think it's a prank?'

'If it is, it's gone on long enough.' Emory frowned. 'I was hoping the pranksters' morals would have made them come forward, or at least put the jewel back. But no, I guess I'm giving them too much credit.' He ran a frustrated hand through his hair. It still looked perfect. 'Not everyone is taught right from wrong by their parents. I know I wasn't.'

'You were taught it by Audrey and Cuthbert.'

'But not my father.'

Emory rarely spoke of his father. His mother had died in childbirth and his father had been a waste of space. He hadn't taught Emory about the Other and he'd died – or abandoned – his son when he was six or seven. I'd done some digging, but they didn't keep good records back in those days and there wasn't anything about Emory's birth, let alone his father's death. Without the birth certificate, I had nothing to go on. To complicate matters further, the name Emory was unusual now, but it was a standard Victorian name back in the day.

'No. Not your father.' If I *could* find Emory's father, it would only be to slap his child-abandoning face. I hoped for Emory's sake that he was truly dead and gone. I deliberately turned the conversation back to the Eye. 'Pranksters or not, I'll focus on the Eye now. I'm sorry it's taken me so long.'

'No problem, but if you could find it... The Elders will want to use it in a ceremony. They can be traditional and crotchety, not to mention paranoid. So we need it.' He was being as casual as possible but through our bond I could feel pervasive worry. He was downplaying the paranoid-Elders thing, too.

He'd told me once that the immortality was no cakewalk; the centuries weighed on you and eventually warped your mind. It could make the Elders erratic; there was a delicate tipping point between wisdom and madness.

Emory had told me a horrific tale about a very elderly dragon losing his mind completely. He'd killed his entire brethren, a visiting dragon and two dragon younglings. Audrey had killed him, a necessary evil because a dragon-hunt was the last thing anyone wanted. There was no saying what could set an Elder off, so I'd best find the damned Eye.

I felt another surge of guilt. 'I'll sort it, I promise. Don't worry about the Eye.' It looked like justice for Derek and Arlo would have to wait a little while longer.

'Thanks. Be careful out and about today.' He hesitated. 'That thing with Hardman...'

'He got the drop on me,' I said firmly. 'It won't happen again.'

'I hope not, but it's got me thinking. There's a daemon out there influencing people.'

'Yeah?'

'I'm wondering if that's really why the Anti-Crea have stepped things up lately.' Elizabeth had been meeting with

Emory on a daily basis, and most days she passed on reports of more violence against the Other creatures.

'You think that their Anti-Crea sentiment is being stirred up by a daemon?' I felt like Emory was being optimistic again, hoping that the rash of violent clashes were something other than the die-hard prejudice that it was.

'Stirred up or amplified,' Emory said. 'I don't know. There have always been Anti-Crea in the Other and I'm not naïve enough to believe that has changed, but they used to just chant shitty slogans and do some horrible graffiti. Lately the physical attacks have increased in number. Elizabeth was telling me about another attack yesterday. She thinks that's why the Elders are coming.' He grimaced.

'Maybe it is,' I offered. Now who was being optimistic?

'It's not,' he said firmly. 'They're coming for me and for the gargoyles. But I feel like something else is going on. That daemon is definitely doing something.'

'Then we need to find him.' I mentally added that to my to-do list, under find the Eye and find Derek and Arlo's killer.

'Derek and Arlo...' I said slowly. 'You don't think the Anti-Crea had something to do with their deaths?'

'I considered it,' Emory admitted. 'But the other two deaths include an elemental.' Elementals are on the human side of the divide; the Anti-Crea wouldn't have hurt them.

'You said that the four deaths weren't definitely linked,' I pointed out, playing devil's advocate.

'Maybe they're not, but I don't think that's likely.'

No, it wasn't likely, but it wasn't out of the realms of possibility. Maybe our killer wasn't Anti-Crea, but I couldn't rule that out just because of the presence of an elemental on the deceased's roster.

Emory gave me a long, slow kiss farewell. 'Stay safe, Jess.'

'Stay sharp, Emory.'

He left. I snuggled into the covers and tried to sleep but lassitude had long since fled my limbs. I felt awkward alone, and my mind wouldn't stop turning over my conversation with Emory.

In the end I fetched Gato and Indy from the adjoining room. They piled on the bed with me and Gato nudged Indy to watch. He carefully touched his snout to my forehead to send me to the Common realm, then he turned three times and settled down next to me with his heavy head on my abdomen.

It was familiar and reassuring, and the routine settled me. I cleared my mind to meditate. I pictured the ocean

and its powerful waves and restless sleep claimed me soon
afterwards.

Chapter 17

I awoke after a scant six hours but, try as I might, I couldn't get back to sleep. After tossing and turning fruitlessly for ten minutes, I gave sleep up as a bad job.

Gato sent me back to the Other realm and I dressed quickly for a run. I set off with the two hounds in tow. It was still depressingly dark as we headed out to run along the river but I set a fast pace and the dogs followed effortlessly. Then there was a noise to my right and I automatically reached for the fire within me.

It was a squirrel. I blew out a breath and let the fire go. I was jittery; I'd had dreams all night long, not about the car explosion and my brush with death, but about the relatively minor punch to my face. The nightmares had been mixed up with a faceless man calling me a 'dragon whore' as he hit me. He had set my arms on fire and I had screamed while my skin had cracked and burned.

It was the most horrific dream I'd had in some time, and I was struggling to shake it off. I knew it was just my subconscious being a bitch, stringing together the punch along with the graffiti some shithead had spray-painted on my office wall when they'd broken in. Even so, I couldn't quite get the feel of burning skin out of my mind.

I've been exposed to a fair amount of violence in recent times but most of it had been once removed; somehow throwing fireballs and using sentient daggers seemed a little less personal than being punched in the face. What pissed me off most of all was that, for a split second when my eye was hurting, I had wished with all my heart for my mum to kiss it better.

Ludicrous, I know – I'm in my mid-twenties and not a child – but emotions have no rhyme or reason. I'd woken this morning after the nightmares with a hollow, aching heart, wanting my mum to cuddle me and kiss it all away. For a moment I had forgotten that she was dead, but then reality had cut in, sharp and raw. My mum was dead and gone, and today I wanted to stamp my feet like a toddler and scream that it wasn't fair.

I focused on clearing my mind, acknowledging my feelings and letting them go. Mum was dead, no matter how much I raged. All the anger did was wear me out, and I would need all my energy in the coming days. Emory had broken dragon law and the Elders had come to be the judges and the jury. I prayed they weren't planning to be the executioners because, if they were, I would be fighting a bunch of ancient dragons.

Whatever they decided, there was no appeal process. I had no idea what the repercussions might be: Emory losing his title of Prime, certainly. That was the one sanction we had discussed, and it was the one he feared most. He'd spent the last decade doing everything he could to modernise his court, but he was all too aware that it hadn't been a popular move. Dragons *liked* pomp and ceremony; they rolled in their traditions like pigs in mud.

To pass muster, I'd need to polish up my best social graces that Mum had instilled in me. Not that I *cared* about passing muster – not for my own sake – but I did care about Emory. I didn't want to be an embarrassment to him. I'd been a lone wolf for a handful of years and social soirées were more Lucy's thing than mine... I brightened. I'd give her a call after I'd had a shower; she always helped sort out my headspace.

The run didn't clear my mind like it usually did but my body was still grateful for the exercise. I nodded hello to Dave and Jackie, the brethren on duty at the turnstile. Jackie had three kids and she was joking with Dave about how much easier it was coming to work than staying at home with the tribe. Dave was twenty-two and pre-kids, so he thought that work was harder. I left them with Jackie wiping tears of laughter from her eyes.

I jogged back to our rooms and hopped in the shower, then dressed for the day. I'd decided to forego my usual jeans and boots and instead I selected some smart black trousers. I added a cute but professional blouse and slung on my leather jacket; hopefully the ensemble said professional but tough. I've never quite learned the knack of choosing clothes, but hopefully this would do the trick.

Even though I felt better for having exercised, washed and dressed, I still called Lucy for a quick chat.

'Hey, love,' she answered cheerily. She's an early riser too.

'Hey. How are you?' I asked

'I'm okay. I snuck into the kitchens to do some baking. The kitchen feels weird without Mrs Dawes.' She sighed.

I grimaced. 'Sorry about that. What are you baking?'

'Cookies and bread.'

'That's a weird combination.'

'Not together,' she laughed. 'How are you, Jess?'

'I'm okay. The Elders have started arriving.' I didn't need to say more than that.

'I'm on standby to kick dragon butt,' she promised.

I grinned. 'Thanks. I just needed to hear your voice this morning.'

'Back at you. Let's pencil in a hug real soon.' I could hear the longing in her voice; I wasn't the only one in need of a hug.

'Yes, please,' I agreed fervently.

'Phone hug.'

'Phone hug.'

'I'll speak to you soon,' Lucy promised. 'Keep me updated on the Elders.'

'Will do. Enjoy your cookies.'

'They're not for me, they're for a friend.'

I felt an absurd flash of jealousy and wished I was close enough to be the recipient. 'Lucky duck,' I managed to say lightly.

I heard Lucy's oven start to beep. 'I've got to go; the cookies need to come out. Love you, Jess.'

'Love you, Luce.' We hung up. I felt better for touching base with her and I loved that she'd volunteered to kick

Elder ass. If I needed to, I wouldn't have to fight an army of dragons by myself. We would still lose, but at least I wouldn't die alone. Silver linings and all that.

Indy was flopped on the bed, resting after her run. Gato was waiting patiently by the door. He looked at me pointedly; he wanted food. 'Come on pups,' I called to them. 'Let's get breakfast.' My stomach growled audibly, agreeing that was a brilliant idea, and we headed to the kitchen.

As always, the indomitable Mrs Jones was at the helm. She beamed as soon as she saw me. 'Prima Jinx! Come on in! I've got pancakes with your name on them.'

Yum. 'Yes, please!' I said eagerly.

I sat next to her as she ladled out some of the mixture. She used lard to grease the pan and the smell instantly transported me back to pancake night with my parents. I looked sorrowfully at Gato but he was busy wolfing down some biscuits and raw food so I stomped on my grief. Not today.

Indy was getting the same breakfast as Gato. They were both wagging and happy.

Mrs Jones flipped my pancake expertly. 'Banana or strawberries?'

'Strawberries, please.'

'Chocolate sauce and cream?'

'Oh yes, please!' This was the way to start the day!

She served up the overloaded pancake and a cup of tea, then started making me another one. I wasn't going to say no. After I was stuffed full, I pushed back my plate. 'Adopt me?' I asked, only half-joking.

She laughed. 'I'm glad you enjoyed them.'

'So much. What will you be serving the Elders for breakfast?'

'They won't get up for hours yet. The last of them came around 3am, and they all stayed up until everyone had arrived. But I've got vats full of porridge with their names on. They're not like our Prime, they like a good solid start to the day.'

'No Danish pastries for them,' I surmised.

'No, indeed. Good stout porridge.'

'You'll still make it delicious,' I said confidently. Mrs Jones could make anything taste nice, even a salad. Of course, she'd added so much cheese to one of my salads that I doubted it was still healthy. Tasty, though.

'Oh yes, they'll have the options of berries and honey and syrups and all sorts. It won't be gruel.' She sounded horrified at the idea.

I took a sip of my tea while I tried to think of a graceful way to segue the conversation back to the topic I wanted to discuss, but I drew a blank. Blunt force it had to be, then. 'So, Emory was telling me about the Eye of Ebrel. He made it sound like a big deal.'

'The Eye of Ebrel has been one of the dragons' treasures for centuries.'

'Is it an actual eye?' I knew it was a jewel, but was it shaped like an eye or something?

Mrs Jones laughed. 'No. It's a huge yellow diamond set in a bunch of white diamonds. It's worth millions, I should think.'

Eek.

She continued, 'Of course, its true value isn't its monetary worth but its use in our ceremonies. A prophecy once dictated that if the Eye of Ebrel is lost, the fate of the dragons is similarly doomed.'

Emory had mentioned the Revival Prophecies before; Elizabeth was apparently obsessed by them and kept copies of the scrolls in her rooms.

'And where is the Eye kept?' I sipped my tea. I couldn't have appeared more casual if I'd started whistling.

'In the hoard under the castle.' Mrs Jones started washing up the pancake-mix bowl.

'In the catacombs?'

'Exactly, dear. Safe and sound, under lock and key.'

Mmm-hmm. Totally safe.

It looked like it was time to head to the catacombs again.

Chapter 18

Indy was tired, and frankly she was a liability, so I dropped her off at Emory's rooms. Hopefully she would have a snooze; the run had taken it out of her and she was still growing.

I fired up my laptop and started searches on the other two people who'd been killed: the dryad and the elemental. When they were in progress, Gato and I headed outside. My catacombs' key was burning a hole in my pocket.

I had my lock picks and a flashlight in my bumbag; they ruined the look of the outfit but practicality stumps fashion every day of the week. I still looked tough. On a last-minute impulse, I hooked Glimmer onto my hip using the holster Emory had got me. Now I *definitely* looked tough, even with a bumbag.

As much as I would have liked to wander around the catacombs by myself, I needed a guide. It didn't take me long to hunt down Mike Carter. He was finishing a coffee and chatting in the brethren mess hall. He looked up as I walked in. 'You're looking better,' he commented, then he reddened. 'Without the shiner I mean,' he added hastily.

'Good save,' his friend Dave smirked.

I ignored their remarks. 'Mike, are you free this morning? I could do with a guide.'

He hesitated. 'I'll keep an eye on the gargoyles,' Dave promised.

Mike nodded and pushed away from the table. 'Sure. Where do you need a guide for?'

I waited until we were out of earshot. 'The catacombs.'

'What? Why?'

I pitched my voice low. 'The Eye of Ebrel is missing.'

Mike paled and then he stumbled. '*What*?'

'It's not lost,' I said firmly, 'just temporarily misplaced. Emory has asked me to find it.'

'Shit. We'll need it tonight at the opening ceremony.' He was visibly distressed.

Fuck. Emory hadn't said it would be needed so soon. 'So we'd better get a move on, hadn't we?' I said calmly. I was going to have to take extreme steps to find it in such a short time. Luckily, I was a woman on a mission; there was nothing I couldn't achieve with hard work, dedication and a time-travelling hellhound.

'We'll need to go to Leonard first to get permission to visit the hoard,' Mike explained.

Leonard is a stick in the mud who wears fussy spectacles he doesn't need perched on the end of his sharp nose. He hadn't warmed to me, and I'd taken to calling him 'NotLeo'. 'I'm not his favourite person,' I said.

'It doesn't matter; this is business. No one accesses the hoard without Leonard's knowledge and say so. For starters, we have to sign in the book.'

'So in theory, our thieves' details should be in Leonard's book?'

'In theory,' Mike agreed, but his tone was doubtful.

'You think it was an outside job?' I asked.

He frowned. 'No, that's even less likely. We have both brethren and dragon patrols, as well as security cameras. Emory insists on top-of-the-line security. The chances of someone infiltrating the castle and the hoard, then escaping without notice, are almost nil.'

'There are security cameras around the hoard?' I was impressed.

He grimaced. 'No, the Elders were against such "modern innovation". They were worried someone would hack the camera footage and use it to find a way in.'

Ah. Less impressed. 'I'm surprised they know the word "hack".' I thought about our next steps. 'Okay, so we've got – what? The book, and the cameras outside the catacombs?'

'Yes,' Mike confirmed.

'Well, let's get permission to sniff about and then we'll go to the hoard and then to the security room,' I suggested.

'Okay. We'll get the staff out of the security room – the fewer people who know about the Eye being missing the better. We don't want to cause mass panic.'

Sheesh. The Eye thing was a big deal.

I had been to Leonard's stuffy office once before, but I let Mike lead me through the tight castle walls and up to the turret. On the way we passed Veronica's office, and through the closed door I heard her giving a lecture to some naughty younglings who had dared to cross her. She seemed pretty strict, but her bright pink hair suggested she might have a fun side – though I hadn't seen much of it.

I looked forward to getting to know her better; so far, she was the only dragon who'd thrown me a bone.

During the challenges she'd helped douse the wicker dragon in something highly flammable and she'd told me that she hoped I'd survive, which was nice. Yeah, it was slim pickings but I'd take what I could get. I felt sympathy for the unknown kid being told off; *I* wouldn't want to be chewed out by her.

Leonard gave a gruff, 'Come in,' when Mike knocked. His welcoming smile vanished when he caught sight of me. Charming.

'Hi.' I greeted him, foregoing the 'NotLeo' greeting in the name of securing his cooperation. 'We need to get into the hoard,' I said without preamble.

'What for?' His eyes narrowed suspiciously.

'To hunt around for the Eye,' I explained.

'Finally.' Leo huffed and folded his arms. 'I told the Prime Elite about the theft weeks ago.' *True.*

'Supposed theft. It's possible it has simply been misplaced,' I offered optimistically.

'It has not been *misplaced*. You should have found it weeks ago.' All *true* – as far as he believed. But dragons can only speak the truth and, though it was hard to imagine NotLeo as a dragon, he definitely was one. I struggled to imagine him with razor-sharp teeth and a spiked tail that could rip you to shreds.

'It only went missing a few weeks ago,' I pointed out.

Leonard took his glasses off his nose and gave them a clean with a cloth from his desk. He popped them back onto his face and studied me for a moment, his mouth tight. I tried to keep my impatience off my face.

He tapped his fingers rhythmically on the desk for a moment before he blew out a sharp breath and opened his desk drawer. He withdrew a strip of something, selected a pair of scissors and carefully cut around it, then peeled back the cellophane from the strip. 'Hand,' he demanded.

I gave him my hand. He placed a piece of paper on my skin and looked around for something. He picked up a sponge and frowned at it. 'Too dry,' he muttered.

I summoned some water and aimed it at the sponge. The water I summoned was a little ... excessive. I'd meant to send a trickle, but instead I sent a mini-river. It was like turning on a hose, and it sprayed Leonard liberally before I hastily shut it off. 'It's not too dry now,' I offered lamely.

Mike gave some very loud coughs that seemed like they might be designed to hide guffaws. Leonard's mouth dropped open. His desk was soaked, his clothes were soaked, his glasses needed windscreen wipers. Oops.

I held my hand out again. Leonard pressed his lips in a tight line, took my hand with a little more force than necessary and dabbed the paper with the now-thoroughly-wet sponge. When he lifted away the paper, there was a rune on my hand. 'This rune will enable you to access the hoard. After you leave, you will wash your hands and the rune will be removed. I am giving you this for one-time access, and one time only.' He turned to Mike. 'Hand.'

After Mike had accepted his temporary rune tattoo, Leonard pulled out a leather-covered book and neatly wrote in our names, the date and the time. 'Can I see that?' I enquired.

He passed it over reluctantly. I took a quick photo of each page during the period when the Eye had gone missing, then handed it back. 'Thanks, NotLeo.' I couldn't resist tweaking his tail now I'd got what I wanted. My gut just didn't like him one bit. His nostrils flared but he didn't respond; he had apparently decided that ignoring me was the best policy.

'Let's go.' Mike grabbed my arm and all-but heaved me out of Leo's office. As we started down the turret, so did his lecture. 'Is there a reason why you're antagonising one of Emory's inner circle?'

'He didn't exactly greet me with open arms,' I muttered. I admit I sounded a tad petulant.

'And is calling him names the best way to get him to see you as an ally?'

'I'm not calling him names!' I protested. 'He said his name was not Leo, so that's what I've been calling him. He should be more careful about how he introduces himself.'

Okay, so once in a while flashes of immaturity still creep into my behaviour. Mike was probably right, I shouldn't call Leonard NotLeo, but he had looked down his spikey nose at me like I was below him and I'd wanted to rile him. Objective achieved.

Mike was also right that I needed a new objective. I'd passed their sodding challenge with flying colours and now it was time to focus on something else. I could have a get-along-with-Leo objective; maybe I should start by calling him Leonard.

'Leonard isn't so bad. He likes fine dining and days at the races. He even visited the circus when it came. What I'm saying is, he's human, like the rest of us.'

I resisted the urge to point out that he was a dragon, but that was a rather Anti-Crea sentiment so I kept it to myself, even in jest.

Mike was giving me a disapproving look but he didn't say anything else – he didn't need to. He'd made his point. Dammit, I hated feeling like a schoolchild being lectured by a teacher.

We left the castle walls and strode across the courtyard to the huge boulder. Just behind it was the super-secret entrance to the catacombs – so naturally, everyone knew where it was.

Chapter 19

'Gato, you didn't get a tattoo because of all your fur, so you'd best stay here and keep watch,' Mike instructed.

Gato gave two affirmative tail taps and sat in guard mode with his back to the illusion, head swinging this way and that. I gave him a pat. 'Thanks, pup,' I said, then walked through the illusion leaving Mike swearing behind me.

'How did you find the entrance?' he spluttered when he joined me on the other side.

'Long story.' I produced the key to the catacombs and his eyes bulged. 'Another long story,' I quipped, though it wasn't; it was a very short story but I didn't want Joe, the brethren who'd given me the key, to get into trouble. After all, I'd tricked him a bit, so it really wasn't his fault.

I used the key to open the iron gate and we stepped inside. I locked the gate behind us and we delved into the darkness of the ancient catacombs. I turned to Mike. 'You'd better lead the way.'

'You seem to know the way already,' he said drily.

'Not to the hoard – luckily I didn't stumble across that. I assume it's guarded by huge rolling boulders and spikes coming up from the floor and arrows being shot out of the walls.'

Mike sent me an amused look. 'You've been watching too much *Indiana Jones*.'

'Is there such thing as "too much"?'

'Yes.'

I sighed. 'So no spikes and arrows?'

'No, but there are plenty of witches' runes and curses.'

I brightened. 'See? That's okay.' I rubbed my hands together in anticipation. Spells and curses, here we come. No matter how long I'd been in the Other, I still hadn't quite got over the excitement that magic is real. Curses? Cool!

I followed Mike down the long corridors. There were plenty of forks in the path, and I tried to keep track of his route; not that I was planning on coming back to the hoard alone, but if we got separated I had to be able to make my way out. The catacombs' tunnels were huge and far more extensive than I'd imagined, maybe stretching beyond the castle's walls and underneath the town.

Eventually we came to a dead end – where Mike strode through a wall. Another illusion. I closed my eyes and followed him. I couldn't keep my eyes open and convince my legs to march through what looked like solid stone.

Beyond the illusory wall was another gate. Mike withdrew a huge, heavy key that looked like a theatrical prop, slid it into the lock and turned it with visible effort. The gate swung open with a creak. 'We need to get some oil on that,' I suggested.

He grinned. 'The creak is so loud that it's picked up on the camera feed.'

'It's deliberate?' I asked incredulously.

'Well, we didn't put it there but it's proved useful. This is where the security feed ends. Come on.'

'Why don't the cameras extend into the hoard itself?' I huffed. 'It's ridiculous.'

'The cameras are monitored by some of the brethren,' Mike replied. 'We're dragon offspring, but we're only men. Even the best of us could be tempted by what lies in the hoard. Better not to have it on camera constantly tantalising us.' He had a point.

I entered the last corridor. As we walked down the pathway, flames leapt up on the torches on the wall. Dramatic. 'Motion-detector torches?' I surmised.

'The Prime Elite likes the drama of it,' Mike confirmed. Hard to disagree with that – they looked effortlessly cool.

We rounded the corner. I had been prepared to see a significant pile of gold, but the sheer magnificence of the hoard took my breath away. It was like stepping into Aladdin's cave. There weren't just piles of gold everywhere, there were other expensive items like paintings and fine furniture. The gargantuan cavern was the gaudiest warehouse I'd ever seen.

There was a roar and a jet of flames as a sleek, sapphire-blue dragon with silver wings flew over. He landed neatly on a pile of gold near us. 'Hello Tobias,' Mike greeted him familiarly.

'Carter.' The dragon inclined his head. 'You bring our Prima-to-be to inspect the hoard?'

'Nothing so prosaic, I'm afraid. She's here to see if she can locate the Eye.' Mike grimaced as he said the words aloud.

The blue dragon regarded me hopefully. 'I'd be glad if you could find it. If you don't, I'll have to fall on my sword for my abject failure. Emory won't let me redeem myself until you've at least had a chance to find it.' Geesh. Death seemed like an overreaction, but the dragons are all about their oaths. If Tobias had sworn an oath to keep the Eye safe...

'I'll find it,' I said with a certainty I didn't feel. I was happy when my radar buzzed *true*. Deep down, I knew I'd find it, though I hoped my confidence in myself wasn't misplaced. 'Tell me what happened when it was taken.'

'I'd popped up to the castle for my morning coffee with Mrs Jones,' Tobias admitted shamefacedly.

'Is that part of your routine every day?' I probed.

He bowed his head his head further. 'Yes, every day – though I have stopped going since the Eye was taken.'

'It's not necessarily your absence that is the issue but the predictability of it. Just change up the times that you go – 6am one day, 7am the next, 8am the day after, 6.30am the next. Never do the same thing twice and *never* in a pattern,' I explained. 'So you were gone for how long?'

'Half an hour at most.'

Whoever had taken the Eye knew the catacombs well, then. I thought of Mike's earlier comment about brethren members being tempted by the hoard. He might be more on the nose than he realised.

Tobias cleared his throat. 'On my way up to the kitchen, I thought I heard a noise. I stopped and listened but I didn't hear anything else, so I dismissed it as nothing.'

'It may well have been nothing,' I reassured him. *Lie.* I turned to Mike. 'And what about the security footage for that half-hour period?'

'The footage appears to have been looped,' he said grimly. The situation was looking even worse now for the brethren.

'Has anyone who works in the castle unexpectedly stopped turning up to work or been off sick?'

Mike's mouth tightened; he knew where I was going with this. 'No,' he said firmly.

Tobias interrupted. 'There's been no murmur of the Eye on the black market. Not a hint. Something like that ... there'd be noise.'

'Maybe there would be, but not the type of noise that they'd let a dragon hear,' I pointed out.

'I have sources among other species. I'd have heard *something*,' Tobias said firmly.

'From down here?' I asked dubiously.

'Tobias is a ... collector,' Mike explained. Aren't all dragons?

'I'm not a collector; I'm a purveyor of rare artefacts. There is nothing I can't source.' Tobias lifted his head and puffed out his chest proudly. 'I would have heard something. Besides, I only guard the hoard in the morning. Leonard guards it in the afternoon, and Samara guards it through the night.'

I searched my brain for any knowledge of Samara but drew a blank. 'I haven't met Samara yet.'

'You wouldn't. She sleeps through the day so she's alert at night,' Mike said.

'It seems like a bum deal,' I said wryly.

'We rotate the dragon guards on a three-monthly cycle. I'll be off hoard guard duty in two weeks.' Tobias sounded happy about that.

'But the theft definitely happened during your stint as security?'

He bowed his huge head unhappily again. 'Yes. It was there when I left and not there when I returned.'

'What did you do next?' I enquired.

'I alerted Leonard, who alerted the Prime and Tom. We reviewed the footage together and ascertained that it had been looped. We knew then that it was no accident that the Eye had gone missing.' Tom is Tom Smith, Emory's right-hand man and head honcho of the brethren. He is head of all things security.

'Why was there no man hunt?' I queried.

'How can we hunt when we don't know who took it? We had no leads, no footage, nothing.'

'What about scent?' I pushed.

'What?' The dragon blinked at me.

'Did you have a werewolf or hound come here to see if they could find a scent?'

Mike and Tobias both looked blank. 'No, we didn't,' Mike said finally. 'We waited to see if there was evidence of one of the curses being invoked.'

'What would the curses do?' I asked.

'Cripple or kill the thief, depending on which curse they invoked.' Mike shrugged.

'And how do they work?'

'The place is covered in runes. Ill-intent triggers them.'

'Ill-intent? What if the thief had good intentions? Like they were desperately poor and they needed money to get potions to heal their mother, something like that? Say the theft is for a good reason – will that bypass the ill-intent curses?' I had to get to the bottom of this.

Mike grimaced; the possibility hadn't occurred to him. 'I don't know,' he admitted reluctantly.

We both looked at Tobias. 'I don't know. I'm not a witch,' he grumped. 'This whole thing has been an absolute nightmare.'

'I'll find it,' I promised again, this time with more certainty in my voice. After all, this time I had a plan.

Chapter 20

After we had spoken to Tobias, Mike and I walked back to the brethren security hubs. There were two: one dealt with the whole of the castle security, and one that dealt solely with the catacombs. We went to the latter. It was located in the centre of the catacombs so that brethren security could get to an emergency quickly.

When we walked into the room, Mike asked the men to leave and surround the catacombs. They did so instantly and without comment. Then Mike showed me the damning camera footage, such as it was. I noted the time that the footage changed: 7am. At that point, the time stamp flicked back to 6.30am. We fast-forwarded through the loop; at what should have been 7.30am, the screen flickered once and the time stamp returned to the correct time. The footage had been looped for half an hour, then the real live footage had come on again with a snap, like a switch had been flicked.

We checked the feeds for the surrounding areas, but no one approached the cameras or the security hub. There was no one visible in the corridors before the 7am cut off; whoever had done this had timed it to perfection. I had done object retrieval a time or two, so I couldn't help but admire the slickness of it all.

'Come on,' Mike sighed. 'We'd better wash the rune off and report our lack of success back to Leonard.'

Hmph. Speak for yourself, Mike. 'Just a minute,' I said. 'Let's check with Gato and see if there was anyone fishy lurking around the entrance.' Mike shrugged – he obviously didn't think it was likely – but he followed my lead like a good soldier.

We let the security team back into their office and left the catacombs. I had an excellent mental map, and I was busy putting every route that I knew in the catacombs onto it.

Gato was still guarding the main entrance. I turned to Mike. 'There's another entrance, isn't there? By the kitchen? Why don't you go and examine that for any evidence of a forced entry?'

'Don't you want to come?' he asked, a little suspicious of my motives. His question was enough to warm the cockles of my heart – he was getting to know me already.

'I'll check over this gate,' I promised. 'You do the other entrance.'

He raised his eyebrows but in the end he left. With Mike gone, I was free to decide my next steps without worrying about a witness. Sometimes I play hard and fast with the rules, and this was going to be one of those times.

'Hey, pup, are you ready to hop to the Third?' The Third realm is accessible only by portal or by hellhound, and it controls time itself. It's not something to play idly with. If the situation had been less dire, I'd have been less inclined to hop through to it, but I couldn't let Tobias kill himself and I couldn't let the curse of the Eye come into effect. I was Prima – well, near as dammit – and I wasn't going to let the dragons' fate become as lost as the Eye, as it would be if the Revival Prophecies could be believed.

Gato gave a wag; he was ready for a spot of time travel. I'd been tempted to do exactly this to solve Derek and Arlo's murders, but ultimately the Third isn't something to use as a shortcut. I only use it when I think that it's absolutely essential, like for saving a life. Derek and Arlo were already dead on a mortician's slab, where they'd been sliced and diced in a post-mortem; I couldn't go back in time and save them because I'd already *seen* them dead. The past is fixed, but sometimes I can amble around in it. However, using the Third realm takes its toll on your mind. I only had to speak to the rambling elf Leo Harfen to be sharply reminded of the dangers of using it willy-nilly. I didn't want to lose my mind to time.

I cleared my throat. 'We need to go back three weeks, exactly at 6.55am,' I instructed Gato. 'Give me a minute to prepare us.' I reached out a hand, put it on his shoulder and closed my eyes. Summoning the IR, I gathered the intention within me and willed Gato and I to become invisible. 'Invisible.' I released the magic with my utterance.

Gato vanished, but luckily I could still feel him under my hand. 'Shit. I didn't think this through,' I muttered to him. 'You can't see me to touch your nose to my forehead.'

He let out a huffing laugh. Suddenly I felt his muscles ripple under my hand and then his familiar weight on my shoulders. Muscle memory: he didn't need to see me. Nice. Something cold touched my forehead and the world tilted sideways.

I opened my eyes to darkness; 6.55am was still dark in April and three weeks earlier we'd still been in March. I could just about see my hands, which was a relief, but I couldn't see Gato. 'Am I invisible too?' I asked him.

He tapped his tail twice in the affirmative – I couldn't see his tail but I heard the thumps.

'Phew. Okay, you stay here and keep guard in case I miss the thief. Keep an eye on anyone slipping out.' He tapped his tail twice again.

I checked my watch. The minute the hands hit 7am, I opened the gate and hustled into the catacombs. Invisible or not, the cameras were now in a loop so I wouldn't be seen, nor would pesky doors be seen opening and closing by themselves.

I broke into a run. I didn't want to miss anything because I wasn't in the place that I needed to be. I ran hard, praying that I'd remember the route to the hoard, then I turned the corner and nearly ran smack-dab into Tobias in his dragon form. At the last second, as I swerved around him, I prayed his footsteps had hidden my own.

I froze, pressed against the wall and held my breath so he wouldn't hear my heavy breathing. Tobias stopped too and swung his huge head back and forth, then shrugged and carried on walking past me. Shit, that had been entirely too close. I guessed *I* was the noise Tobias had said he'd heard. Oops.

I waited until he'd turned a corner then started moving again, more slowly this time. When I felt sure that Tobias was too far away to hear my footsteps even with his excellent dragon hearing, I broke into a run and jogged all the way to the final gate. I didn't have the heavy key for that so I had to wait flush against the wall until the thief came.

I hoped that the thief wasn't one of the brethren that I had come to know during the last few weeks; I'd be crushed if it was Mike, Dave or Jackie, who were my favourites. But I'd be upset too if it was Sarah, Jacob or Joe. They were the ones who guarded me most.

I sat down on my heels and waited for betrayal.

The thief and his companion didn't keep me waiting long. There were two of them: a girl I didn't know, and a boy I did. Evan.

What had he been thinking? Of course, I reminded myself, this was all taking place before Evan had started movie nights with me and Emory, but still... I felt sick. Emory was going to be so upset. And they were *giggling*. What did they think they were doing?

The girl took the heavy key from her pocket and opened the gate. They both winced as the gate squealed then froze, waiting for an alarm to be raised. Nothing happened. 'I told you Luke would sort the cameras!' the girl crowed.

'Come on, let's get to the Eye quickly,' Evan said. 'Let's hustle.'

I hoped to hell I wasn't about to witness some sort of death or maiming. Idiot children. They left the gate open and I crept in behind them, shadowing their steps. We rounded the corner past a huge pile of gold. There, on a pedestal in the centre of the room, was the Eye of Ebrel.

It was every bit as stunning as Emory had said. It was beautiful and awe-inspiring, and my invisible jaw dropped. The golden-yellow jewel nestled unsecured on a velvet pillow. When all of this was over, I was going to have a long chat with Emory about appropriate security. He was normally so on the ball with that sort of thing. There was no need to rely on witches' curses when good old technology could play a part, too. Screw the Elders and their sensibilities.

I watched as Evan picked up the Eye. To my surprise, he didn't pocket it but slid it into a pile of gold. The girl giggled. 'Shush, Louisa!' he hissed. He piled more gold on top of the Eye, then said, 'Let's go!'

They went towards the exit. Shit. I put a sprint on and got out of the gate before them. 'Did you hear that?' Louisa asked, frowning. Oh crap. Had she heard me?

'What?' Evan looked around nervously.

'I thought I heard something.'

'Let's get the hell out of the hoard before Tobias returns,' Evan urged.

'I can't wait to see his face,' Louisa giggled. *Bitch*, I thought, perhaps a shade uncharitably. They were kids and they hadn't appreciated the repercussions of their actions. Well, I'd make sure to spell it out for them in short words that even they could grasp.

'We can watch from the room back there.' Evan pointed to an antechamber.

A prank: this whole thing was a childish prank. Emory's guts had been tied in knots and Tobias had been thinking about falling on his sword all because of a couple of thoughtless teenagers. Man, I was going to kick their asses.

But first, I needed to return the Eye to its rightful place.

Chapter 21

I ran to the exit ahead of the kids. They had ducked into one of the side rooms to watch Tobias's face drop when he realised the Eye had been stolen. Little reprobates – and poor Tobias.

I ran through the huge catacombs back to the entrance where I hoped Gato would still be waiting patiently for me. I locked the gate behind me and crept forward to the boulder, still holding onto the IR. 'Gato?' I whispered. 'Are you there?'

Gato gave a low gruff and I moved closer to where it sounded like he was. I let out a low whistle and heard him snuffling towards me. Suddenly he walked into me, nearly knocking me on my ass. 'You found me,' I whispered drily, suppressing a slightly hysterical giggle. I pulled myself up and brushed off the dirt. 'Let's go back to our proper time,' I pleaded.

He tapped his tail twice. That sound was all the warning I had before I felt the heavy weight of him on my shoulders. How he could manage to jump up at me accurately when he couldn't see me was beyond me. I felt a touch of a cold nose and then we were back in bright sunlight. I released the IR.

'Thanks, pup, you're the best.' I gave him a cuddle as he winked into existence and he gave me a big lick in return, happy to see my face again. 'I need to go and find the Eye,' I told him. 'Why don't you head to the kitchens and see if Mrs Jones will get you something nice? And then maybe you should go and check on Indy.'

After rewarding me with a big, lolling, doggy grin, he trotted off towards the kitchens. I descended into the catacombs again; I would soon know this place like the back of my hand. I gave a light knock when I arrived at the gate that secured the hoard.

Tobias came forward, shimmered and shifted into human form. He had light-brown hair and blue eyes; he looked to be about my age but, despite his excellent complexion, his eyes gave away his age. Eyes that had already seen too much. 'Back so soon?' he asked, surprised, as he unlocked the gate for me. 'Did you forget something?'

'I've found the Eye for you,' I announced triumphantly. 'At least, I think I have.'

He froze for a second. 'Don't tease me! It would be amazing if you have.'

'I'm not teasing, I think I know where it is.' If it hadn't been moved again somehow.

I walked around Tobias to the hoard and plunged into the golden depths where the Eye had rested before it was stolen. Next to its pedestal was the golden pile of coins and trinkets into which Evan had thrust the Eye. I had seen roughly where he had placed it so I started digging, carelessly thrusting pieces of gold to one side.

'You're making a mess,' Tobias complained.

'You'll forgive me when I find the Eye,' I pointed out.

'I absolutely will. *If* you find it.'

'Ye of little faith.' My fingertips brushed against something which felt likely. I closed my hand around it and pulled it out. Bingo.

I grinned triumphantly at Tobias as I turned and held out the Eye on the palm of my hand. So that was why none of the witches' sinister curses had clicked into effect: the kids hadn't stolen the Eye at all, they'd entered the room with the intention only of moving it. That had caused no end of heartache, but thankfully it hadn't maimed the children.

Tobias gasped in shock then threw his arms around me, laughing with giddy relief. 'You found it! You really found it! Thank all that is holy.' He picked me up and spun me around.

'Okay, okay, set me down,' I laughed. He put my feet back to the floor but the grin didn't leave his face. I handed him the Eye. 'Don't lose it this time,' I teased lightly.

He groaned.

'Too soon for jokes?' I asked.

'Much. Emory has already made me swear not to leave when it's my turn to guard – not even for coffee. I am not letting this thing out of my sight – I'm going to take it with me when I prowl around the rest of the hoard.'

'That's probably a good idea for now, but the Eye could really do with some additional security.'

'Emory is already looking into it.'

'Great. I'll go and tell him the good news.' I patted Tobias's shoulder and left him still grinning. I was looking forward to seeing Emory with a similar smile on his face. I knew he was a bit worried about the presence of the Elders, but at least the missing Eye was one less thing to worry about.

I went to find Emory. Summer was in his antechamber office looking fierce. 'Is he in?' I asked, tilting my head towards his door.

'Yes, but he made it clear he is not to be disturbed, not even by you.' She frowned at me. 'This gargoyle pickle has caused quite the furore.'

'What are the Elders doing about it?' I asked. Knots started to form in my tummy.

'For now, they're just settling in – they move slowly. Emory has arranged a lunch out with some helicopter rides. He's convinced they'll love the experience since they like flying, and he's hoping it will make them more enthusiastic about technology.' Her tone said she thought that was highly unlikely. 'They'll leave shortly. After the niceties have been observed, the Elders will start questioning everyone.'

'About what?'

She gave me a flat look. 'About the gargoyles and how that whole mess came about.' Summer looked at me pointedly; it was clear she laid a lot of the blame at my door.

I couldn't object because I was at least partly to blame. I had taken Emory with me when I rode like a white knight to Lucy's rescue; I'd even travelled on his back, and God forbid the Elders found out about *that*. That was another rule that we'd smashed that day.

My faults didn't end there because it was me who pointed out that the gargoyles had bent the knee to Emory; after that, they were under his protection and he should do everything in his power to protect them. And he had. So yeah ... I was at least partly to blame, maybe even mostly.

My stomach was roiling at the thought of what could happen to Emory, but if I could go back in time – which I could – I would have done it all again. It wasn't the easy thing to do, but it was the *right* thing to do. Hundreds of gargoyles were alive thanks to Emory. Hundreds of lives. That wasn't nothing.

'Where are the gargoyles?' I hadn't seen them in the courtyard while I was romping around the castle.

'The great hall has been transformed into a gathering area for them, and they've been given some temporary accommodation in the village while we work out what is to be done.' Summer's tone seemed overly grim.

'Why so dour?'

She hesitated. 'I've been doing some research for Emory to help with our case. When this form of making brethren was outlawed, all of the made-brethren were put to death. Every last one.' Her lips pressed together.

Fuck. That wasn't good. Emory wouldn't save hundreds of gargoyles only to allow them to be killed later; his morality wouldn't let that happen, and neither would mine. If the Elders tried to order the made-brethren's' deaths, things were going to get really messy.

'Can you let Emory know that I swung by? I've got some good news for him.' Rather pettily, I didn't want to tell Summer about the Eye, partly because I wasn't sure whether she'd known it was missing but mostly because *I* wanted to tell Emory the good news first.

'Sure, I'll let him know.' I was relieved when that buzzed *true*. Summer and I were working on a friendship, but it was heavy going and I still didn't totally trust her.

I wanted to go and see the gargoyles, but I thought I'd better check on Indy first because she was still at puppy-destructive stage. I went up to Emory's rooms – which I had gradually started to think of as "our" rooms – to check on her and to look at my computer whilst I was there. I hoped that the searches on the other two victims would have finished running; now that I'd found the Eye, I could turn my attention back to Derek and Arlo's deaths.

I knocked once on the door because Indy was in there and that seemed polite, and there was no one around to judge me for being polite to a dog. Predictably there was no response so I strode in – and then stopped abruptly. 'Indy!' I chastened. 'What the hell?'

Indy had taken the bedsheets off of the bed and dragged them around the room. Two of Emory's leather shoes had been chewed to pieces. From different pairs. 'Oh you little shit,' I muttered. 'No! No eating shoes. Bad Indy.'

She wagged happily then leapt at me, trying to mouth my hand. 'No. No biting,' I said firmly, folding my hands and glaring at her. She didn't look chastened in the slightest and started chasing her tail.

With a huff, I tidied up the tip she'd made of our room. I straightened the bed and put the remains of Emory's shoes in the bin. Rest in peace, shoes.

I opened my laptop, relieved she hadn't seen fit to chew on that or its cable, fired it up and looked at my emails. There was an incredibly helpful one with attachments from Elvira's personal email address setting out information about all four deaths. She was certainly treating them as connected, and my gut didn't think she was wrong.

The fire elemental's death had occurred about one week before Derek's, and the dryad's a few days before that. As far as I could tell, the dryad was the first victim. There didn't seem to be any similar crimes, at least none that were flagged on the Connection's system that Elvira was willing to admit to.

I looked at the crime scene photographs. They were all pretty grim; I had tell myself that they were all just meat and bone because it made me feel ill to think of them as people who had lived and loved and were now forever lost.

I tried to look at the pictures analytically. I wasn't a crime scene expert but they looked *similar* though not identical by any stretch of the imagination. A footnote from Elvira confirmed that the Connection's pathologist thought the same weapon had been used. She'd attached a photo of a page of the report and I saw with interest that Noah, the guy who had showed me Derek and Arlo's bodies, was the pathologist in question. It looked like he had a foot in both Emory's court and the Connection.

A blunt object had been used in each case, a baseball bat or something similar. There was certainly nothing Other-worldly about that. None of the blood had been drained, so that tended to remove the vampyrs from the equation though I didn't discount them entirely. I knew from Nate that it was possible for a vampyr to feel blood-hunger and still walk away unless they were very newly turned.

The fire elemental was Clarissa Sands, fifty-six, no surviving spouse or children. A note on Elvira's email said that she was 'not well liked', even within the fire elemental community. I read through the search results that my computer had spat out. Clarissa was listed as a financial adviser who, interestingly, was currently under investigation by the Financial Standards Authority. That hadn't been included in the information Elvira had sent to me; either she didn't know about it or she hadn't given me everything. My computer's slightly less legal searches told me that Clarissa was being investigated for negligence and embezzlement; a lot of her investors had lost a *lot* of money.

I sent Elvira an email flagging up the FSA's investigation and asking if she could dig into who had suffered financially as a result of Clarissa's purported negligence. Elvira and Bland had a whole team under them at the Connection, although one of them was that dick, Randall. I hoped he'd be chosen to sift through the mountain of information this would involve. I couldn't see why one of

Clarissa's victims would attack Derek and Arlo, but it had to be investigated; I needed to dot the Is and cross the Ts.

My final computer search had been to try and find ties between any of the four victims. It hadn't picked up any links, save for the one that I already knew about between Derek and Arlo. Damn.

I picked up my phone and dialled Roscoe, head honcho of the fire elementals.

'Hey Jinx,' he greeted me cheerfully. 'How are things going at Casa Dragon?'

'It's ... complicated.' I thought of the Elders and gargoyle situation, then cleared my throat and tried to focus on the matter at hand. 'I'm working on a couple of murder cases. They seem to have a common element, namely that the victims were bludgeoned to death. Not very nice stuff. It threw up Clarissa Sands' name.'

Roscoe sighed. 'Yeah, her. Listen; between you and me, Clarissa was a bitch. No one liked her. I did some digging – of course I did! I can't let someone kill one of my fires without me doing something about it. But honestly? I've not met a single soul that's upset by her death.'

What a horrible thing for Miss Sands to be so universally disliked that people would actually speak ill of the dead. 'The people that she advised, were they Other?' I asked.

'Most of them were. Some of them weren't.'

'Did you know that she was being investigated for embezzlement?' I asked.

'I only found out after she died,' Roscoe admitted. 'She wasn't very sociable. She wasn't an active member of the fire elemental community and she never came to me for help or anything like that.'

'Do you think she's guilty?' I probed.

'Yes, I do. She always seemed to have too much money for a job like hers, though I just thought that the finance industry must pay well and maybe she knew what she was doing with her money. But with hindsight? No, it doesn't surprise me in the slightest.'

'It's still a horrible way to go,' I said.

'No doubt. She was a bitch but she didn't deserve that.'

'No, she deserved to be locked up by the Connection.'

'Absolutely.'

I had exhausted my enquiries with Roscoe; if he hadn't talked with her, there was very little he could add. I changed the topic. 'In other news, my car got firebombed.'

'Oh shit!' he exclaimed. 'In Wales?'

'No, in Liverpool.'

'What did you do?' Roscoe sounded amused. 'Who did you piss off?'

'Me?' I protested. 'I didn't do anything. The only thing I've done recently is investigate these deaths. I think someone doesn't want me to get to the bottom of them.'

'What are the names of the other victims?'

'Two satyrs, Derek Ives and Arlo Hardman. And a dryad, Hugo Arnold.'

'Well, I've heard of Hugo,' Roscoe told me, 'but the others aren't known to me.'

'What have you heard about Hugo?' I asked.

'There was a scandal some years ago. Someone accused Hugo of selling drugs.'

'What happened?'

'The person who accused him disappeared,' Roscoe said grimly.

'So naturally everyone assumes Hugo was guilty,' I stated drily.

'Definitely – though no one accuses him loudly anymore.'

'What sort of drugs was he into?'

'He sold to Common folk, which was why the dryad Elders looked the other way. That, and the fact that Hugo is the eldest son of one of them.'

Huh. I hadn't got to that piece of information. Someone was hushing things up. 'Was he still selling drugs when he died?' I wondered.

'I've no idea,' Roscoe said. 'The accusations stopped after his accuser disappeared, although the whispers persisted.'

'Can you remember the name of the person who disappeared?' I queried.

'It was a bloke. Sorry, that's all I can remember.' Roscoe paused, then added, 'Hold on. His wife disappeared too.'

'At the same time?' My eyebrows rose.

'Yeah, they both vanished. They appeared to have packed their bags and left.'

'Appeared?' I said suspiciously.

'Yeah. Everyone assumed that Hugo had them offed and packed their bags to make it look convincing when he said that they'd gone wandering. There was a kid, too. That caused some waves, as I remember. That's right, the whole family disappeared – or was wiped out.'

'Thanks, Roscoe. This has been helpful.'

'The car bomb... Any evidence it was done by a fire elemental?' he asked cautiously.

'Nope. Elvira said it's a regular Common bomb. Why? Are you having problems with rogues?'

'No, but I don't want to start now.' He laughed. 'Just keep your eyes peeled, hey?' He hung up.

The interesting thing was that he was lying when he said he didn't have any rogues.

Chapter 22

I re-jigged all the information I'd got from Elvira and Roscoe in my head. On my computer system, there didn't seem to be anything to link each victim, but in reality they all had two things in common: they weren't well liked, and they had supposedly done bad things. I'd even go so far as to say some of them were actively hated. We had two alleged rapists, an embezzler and a drug dealer; none of them were going to win philanthropy awards any time soon.

What we had on our hands was a vigilante – but why would a vigilante kill them all by bludgeoning? The weapon used was a baseball bat or something similar, so it wasn't like an ogre's mace. The victims were all Other but the deaths were all ... ordinary. Non-magical.

Something was itching in the back of my mind. I emailed Elvira and asked her to send me any details she had on Hugo and the family that had accused him and subsequently disappeared. She seemed to be embracing the spirit of co-operation, bar that little omission about the investigation into Clarissa; maybe she hadn't dug it up or hadn't thought it was relevant. I'd give her the benefit of the doubt. I also asked if she could dig into who benefitted from Derek Ives' death. He had apparently won millions so who would inherit them? According to his file, he had no next of kin. Unless he'd had a Will, the Crown was going to cash in.

There was a knock on the door: Mike. I closed the laptop and called for him to come in. 'Here, this came for you.' He handed me an envelope. 'And Emory is free to see you now, just for a minute before he takes the Elders to lunch.'

How kind of Emory to fit me in, I thought somewhat ungenerously.

I took the envelope from Mike. It was an A4 brown envelope with no postmark, which meant that somebody had handed it in at the castle. Something told me to be careful, so I grabbed Glimmer and used it to slice open the envelope.

I slid out the letter. Uh-oh – red flag. It was made up of various letters cut out from magazines and newspapers. Amateur criminal hour: anyone could type and print a letter these days, so going to such ridiculous lengths was telling. This wasn't a professional. The letter said: *Jinx, stop investigating the dead or you're next.*

When I showed it to Mike, he swore loudly and vociferously. 'The envelope was hand delivered,' I pointed out. 'No stamp.'

'I'll see what I can find out. Maybe there'll be some CCTV footage of the person handing it in.'

'Maybe,' I agreed, though it didn't seem likely. So far the killer had avoided CCTV cameras. It didn't seem likely that he – or she – would slip up on a postal run, but I could hope. The letter was certainly amateurish. 'Let's not mention this to Emory,' I suggested. 'He worries, and he has enough on his plate right now.'

Mike made a face. 'You're suggesting I lie to my Prime?'

'Not lie – omit. It's different.' Trust me, I know. 'Let's do some more digging before we worry him,' I compromised. 'Maybe you'll be able to tell him someone was spotted on CCTV.'

'Okay,' he agreed reluctantly. 'Just this once, and only for a little while because he has the Elders to sort out.'

'Do you think he will?' I asked abruptly.

'Will what?'

'Sort out the Elders?'

'I have every faith in Emory.' *True.* Mike might have had faith in Emory but that answer was an omission, too. He had swerved the question.

'You go and question the brethren at the turnstiles and I'll go and see Emory,' I instructed.

'And not mention the threatening letter,' Mike muttered disapprovingly.

'Exactly.' I nodded.

I turned to Indy. 'Come on, trouble, you'd best come with me.' I frowned suddenly. What was keeping Gato? He was supposed to be checking on Indy, too.

I took a slight diversion on my way to Emory. A buzz of worry was starting to churn in my gut and I hoped I'd find Gato in the kitchen, still snaffling down Mrs Jones's food.

The kitchens were incredibly busy but I spotted him straight away. He was lying down in front of a fire, getting his belly rubbed. 'Hey!' I said. 'I was worried! You were supposed to be looking after Indy!'

Gato stood and gave me a huge lick. 'Being cute doesn't help,' I warned. 'I'm mad at you.' I stood legs akimbo and folded my arms. Gato gave me another lick and leaned his body against mine. I huffed and gave in. 'Indy ate two of Emory's shoes,' I whispered as I gave him a full body cuddle. 'From different pairs.'

Gato gave a little growl at Indy, who promptly ignored him and started to play. 'Not in the kitchen!' Mrs Jones shouted loudly. 'Out! Outside if you're going to play.' Indy stopped playing. Huh. All I needed was Mrs Jones to look after the pup.

'You're cooking up a storm,' I noted, admiring the organised chaos.

'I've got to feed the gargoyles a hearty lunch,' she said with a sad look.

'Why?'

'Well ... in case it's their last,' she stage-whispered.

I grimaced. Did no one have faith that Emory would sort his out? Was I being overly optimistic? Surely the Elders would appreciate that he'd done the right thing?

Gato gave a sad whine. 'I know. Go on, take Indy out and have a play. I'm going to see Emory and give him some much-deserved good news.'

The two hellhounds trotted off and I went to Emory's office. Summer was looking stressed. 'Is he free?' I asked.

'Yes, you can go right in, but his helicopter is due to leave in fifteen minutes. He's taking the Elders to the Panoramic Restaurant in Liverpool.'

'Oh, fancy. He's pulling out all the stops.' That told me he was more worried than he was letting on. I gave Summer a tight smile and went in.

Emory was at his desk, looking even more stressed than Summer. He smiled when he saw me but it didn't reach his eyes. He stood up and came round to me. 'Hi, Jessica Sharp,' he said as he kissed me. 'It's good to see you.'

I relaxed as the scent of him surrounded me. Come what may, we had each other. 'It's good to see you too. It's going to be okay,' I reassured him. I hated when it buzzed *lie*.

Chapter 23

'I have good news.' I pushed away so I could see his face. 'I found the Eye!' He grimaced. That wasn't the response I was going for. 'That's not good news?' I asked in confusion.

'No, it is. It definitely is. If it was missing ... well, negligent is the nicest thing the Elders would say about me.'

'So why the frown?'

'The Elders will use the Eye to judge me,' Emory admitted.

'Judge you?' I didn't understand how a jewel could judge anything. Surely it was something that just looked pretty? And was worth millions?

'Judge me about the gargoyle incident,' he elaborated.

I was none the wiser. 'How does the Eye work?' I asked.

'I have no idea,' Emory confessed. 'Knowledge of its use is entrusted only to the Elders.'

'Oh well, you'll know one day.' I had faith that he would be the wisest of them all; he was smart, and he wasn't allergic to change the way most of the Elders seemed to be.

Emory smiled and his frown lines eased. 'Not if we mate, I won't.' He kissed me lightly.

I shifted uncomfortably. It was the worst thing about our wedding: when we were formally joined, Emory would give up part of his immortal life span and gift those years to me. Yay for me, boo for him. He would never be an Elder because of me. 'Sorry.' It was my turn to grimace.

'Don't be. I don't want to live in a world without you in it. We'll eventually grow old together. It's better than the alternative.'

'The madness?'

'Yeah.' He frowned. 'Darius is acting strange. He won't come to the lunch and he'd normally jump at the chance to eat out. He's all about fine dining.'

'Are you worried about him going mad?' I asked baldly.

'No. There are usually clear signs of impending madness. I spoke to his staff and they say he hadn't exhibited any of them. Leonard was chatting to Darius earlier, and he said he seemed fine.' Emory shook himself. 'I'm borrowing trouble,' he muttered.

'How old is Darius?' I enquired.

'I have no idea, but he's served as an Elder for as long as I can remember.'

'He's older than Audrey?'

'Far older. Like me, she won't ever reach the age of Elderhood,' Emory explained.

'So all of the Elders never mated?'

'Exactly.'

'As the final deciding voices in dragon culture, having a bunch of old unmarried people doesn't seem representative. It seems like a bad idea to give the final say on anything to a bunch of ancient people who may or may not be mad.'

'It's worse than that,' Emory sighed. 'If they do descend into the immortal darkness, I'm the one responsible for taking them out.'

'Taking them out?' I was guessing that Emory wasn't talking about going for an afternoon stroll.

'Permanently,' he confirmed grimly. Eek.

'You and your dragons will take them out, right?'

'No, just me. It's part of the role of Prime – that's why we tend to be young whipper-snappers.'

'Ready to battle ancient evil?' I raised an eyebrow.

'Exactly. Only they're not evil, they're just old and lost. You remember I told you that Audrey had to kill an Elder once? She used to have nightmares about it.'

'It sounds awful,' I admitted.

'It is. I hope I never have to do it. Hopefully, Darius just isn't feeling sociable, but I'll post an extra brethren or two around him, just in case.'

'Even the best-trained brethren won't be much help against a crazy dragon,' I pointed out.

'You'd be surprised. A shot in the eye from a gun is lethal to us too – but preventing that isn't the real purpose in posting them.'

'What is it, then?'

'To get one of them to ring the ancient bell to alert everyone and give them time to run away and hide.'

I resisted the urge to hum 'Brave, Sir Robin' by Monty Python.

There was a knock at the door and we stepped a nice professional distance back from each other. The person knocking didn't wait for us to call 'come in'; she just strolled right in. And man, was she a knocker. She was the most drop-dead gorgeous woman I had ever seen – and I'm best friends with Lucy.

'Geneve.' Emory smiled warmly at her.

'Em, darling.' She beamed at him.

Em? Who the hell called Emory Em? No one, that's who. Fuck off, Geneve.

Geneve sashayed over, hips swaying hypnotically, to kiss Emory on the cheek. My eyes were narrowed and my nostrils flared. Jealousy blazed, loud and proud.

Emory looked at me, visibly surprised. He could feel my jealousy monster roaring, and that was something unusual for me, but Geneve was Jessica Rabbit come to life. She had gorgeous ginger-red hair, a teeny-weeny waist, and boobs and a bum to write sonnets about. She even had full lips that were just a shade under a trout pout. She wore a full face of makeup, which was subtle and tastefully done.

I hated her on sight. Maybe I was jealous of her stunning looks, but more likely it was the fact that she was pawing at my fiancé with one manicured hand. She looked at me with green eyes so like Emory's and shot me a smirk. Oh, hell no. You're going down bitch, I thought. I don't know who you think you are but I'm kicking your ass – one way or another.

'I'm ready to go,' she purred at Emory. 'You'll hold my hand on the helicopter, won't you?'

'A dragon afraid of heights?' I snarled. 'Now I've heard of everything.' I shot Emory a pointed glare. 'Allow me to introduce myself. I'm Jinx, Emory's mate.'

'Not quite,' Geneve responded with a sickly-sweet smile. 'I don't believe you've had a ceremony yet, have you?'

'Ceremony or not, I am his mate and he is mine. Touch him like that again and I'll happily test your immortality.'

She smiled condescendingly. 'She's a feisty little thing, isn't she?' she said to Emory as if I weren't there. She made me sound like a cute little kitten. I ground my teeth.

'She's the love of my life,' Emory replied smoothly. He moved away from Geneve and pulled me into his arms, sending a wave of love down our bond that was so strong it almost consumed me.

I took a deep breath and called up the ocean, letting the waves calm me. Geneve could go and have lunch with Emory but he'd be coming home to me. Always.

'How sweet,' Geneve said, but this time there was an edge to her voice. 'Shall we go, Em?'

'You know I hate it when you call me Em, Geneve. Please stop.' Emory gave me a slow kiss. Apparently he wasn't against pointed PDAs when they were necessary to prove a point to what I could only assume was a pining ex. He turned to me. 'I'll see you later, my love.'

'Have a lovely time,' I managed, my knees weak.

I watched them go with clenched teeth. I trusted Emory completely, and I had no doubt he wouldn't do a thing with that strumpet who was thrusting herself at him, but that didn't mean I had to like the thrusting.

As I walked out of Emory's office, I was mollified to see that Summer was glaring after Geneve as hard as I was. 'She just swanned in and started pawing at him,' I growled.

'Ugh, yes. She's a total bitch,' she snarled. 'She's always over him like white on rice.'

'Did they ever...?' I didn't want to ask, but I needed to know.

Summer grimaced; that was all the answer that I needed. 'They have a long history,' she said finally.

'Like what? They dated?'

'Worse than that. She told me – and I don't know if it is true – that she took his virginity. She was his first.'

Ugh. Most people have a soft spot for their first. But maybe it had been awful; I could hope it had been awful. I knew that Emory had a past, and his skills in the bedroom meant he had to have learned somewhere. He hadn't come to our bed a blushing virgin so he'd obviously had partners – hell, I'd met Lisette – but it was something else to have the past come and smush its boobs in his face while it called him 'Em'.

'She can be his first but I'll be his last,' I vowed.

Summer grinned. 'You can totally take her.'

I found myself smiling back. 'I totally can.'

Chapter 24

I'm usually pretty focused, but at that point my mind was sliding away from me. I had a vigilante killer to catch, Emory's career to save and some teenagers to yell at. The first two on the list seemed pretty tricky, and I was feeling all this righteous rage after Geneve's flouncing, so it was time to let Evan and Louisa get it in the neck. I was channelling my anger in productive ways. Go me.

I went to see Veronica, the dragon in charge of all things youngling, because I didn't want to step on her toes. I knocked on her door. 'Come in,' she called.

I had a warm spot for Veronica; when everyone else was baying for my blood, she had murmured a couple of words of encouragement so now she was in my 'cautiously like' column. Today she had vibrant pink hair, which absolutely worked with her dark eyes and alabaster skin.

'How can I help you, Jinx?' Virtually everyone around here called me Prima after I had smashed the consort challenge, but not the circle; to them I was still Jinx. Normally that was the kind of thing I liked, but now it served as a reminder that my position here wasn't secure. Not like Geneve's, the sexy Elder.

I was driving myself mad.

'Do you have a youngling called Luke?' I asked. Luke had been the one to fix the security cameras for Evan and Louisa to hide the Eye, so I was holding out a vague hope it was another kid in on the prank.

'No. No Luke.'

I grimaced. 'Is there a brethren called Luke?'

'Luke Caruso,' Veronica said finally. 'He works in the catacombs security, I believe.'

Damn. 'Could you have him brought here?'

She raised an elegant eyebrow. 'Why?'

'I believe he was the one who screwed with the camera footage on the day that the Eye was taken.'

Her mouth dropped open. 'The Eye was taken?'

Oops. 'It was – but it's been found,' I reassured her.

She picked up her desk phone and dialled six for an internal number. 'Lintle, bring Caruso here. You'd best escort him yourself. He may need taking into custody afterwards.' She hung up and we waited in awkward silence.

'I'll need to see Evan and Louisa afterwards as well,' I said finally.

Her lips pursed. 'They took the Eye?' She was a sharp cookie.

'Not exactly. They didn't steal it, they hid it,' I clarified.

'No wonder Tobias has been acting oddly.' She paused. 'More oddly than usual.'

'He was preparing to fall on his sword,' I admitted. 'It's been a difficult time for him. Is he still on shift?'

She checked the time. 'Yes. He's on until 1pm today.'

'I'll take the children down to apologise to him after I've spoken with them. It's the very least they can do.'

'Very well. I will be speaking with the younglings afterwards,' she said firmly. Her lips were tightly pursed and I felt a flash of sympathy for the kids. They were in *trouble.*

'Sure.' Silence descended again. Luckily, there was a brisk knock at the door and two men entered, dressed all in black. One was skinny and young, the other was bulky and older with a touch of grey at his temples, and they both had guns on their hips. The older one gestured to the younger lad. 'Caruso, step forward.'

Lintle stepped back behind Caruso, his hand lingering near his weapon. The room was small, so Veronica couldn't shift into dragon form without causing some serious structural damage. If Caruso caused problems, Lintle would sort it. Or I would.

I smiled in a friendly way at Luke Caruso. 'Hi, Luke. I'm Jinx, my honour to meet you.'

His eyes were wary and unfriendly, but he touched his hand to his heart, gave a little bow and a muttered 'honour to meet you' in response. Generally, the brethren liked me; I was human-ish like them, and I was marrying their Prime. It was a modern fairy tale. Caruso had nothing but hostility in his eyes. Maybe he hadn't liked *Cinderella* as a kid, although how you couldn't like talking mice was beyond me.

'The Prime Elite asked me to look into the theft of the Eye,' I started.

Luke shifted, though he didn't make any exclamation of surprise. The theft of the Eye had been kept quiet but he displayed no shock that it had been taken. Lintle, meanwhile, sucked in a sharp, shocked breath.

I smiled at him. 'We've got it back already,' I reassured him. 'We've found the perpetrators.' I paused. 'Haven't we, Caruso?'

Luke licked his lips as he met my eyes for the first time. 'They weren't supposed to take it. Stupid kids, they were just supposed to hide it. It was a *prank,* that's all.'

'Tobias was preparing to fall on his sword for his failure. Does that sound like a prank to you?' Veronica snapped, her voice sharp.

His shoulders slumped. 'No, ma'am.'

She glared at him. 'You will be remanded into custody and I will discuss what your fate is to be with the Prime Elite. Do you understand?'

'Yes, ma'am.' Caruso shrank in on himself. 'I also wish to say, ma'am, how sorry I am. It was an error of judgement on my part.'

'It was indeed, Caruso. A supreme error of judgement,' Veronica said heavily. 'Lintle, arrange for transport to the Liverpool detention house.'

'I will see to it personally,' Lintle ground out as he glared at Caruso. Caruso was a guard of the catacombs, of the hoard itself, and he had let his whole team down as well as himself. The way Lintle was looking at him...

'Lintle,' I said firmly. 'The Prime will mete out justice. Not your fists. Are we clear?'

A muscle in his jaw worked. 'Yes, Prima.' He removed Caruso's gun, grabbed him roughly by the arm and hauled him out.

As the door shut, Veronica voiced a very unladylike swear word. 'Fuck. What a mess. The 'Comb's guards are not going to be happy with a traitor among their ranks.'

'It *was* just a prank,' I pointed out.

'As far as Caruso knew or was told. But someone could have lied to him and done something far worse. He turned off the cameras and that can't be forgiven, no matter how little impact his actions actually had. This is going to be a headache.'

'I'll speak to Evan and Louisa before it gets out,' I suggested.

'Feel free – and then send them up to me.' She steepled her fingers. Poor bastards. 'They'll be in the courtyard now for lunch break.'

It didn't take me long to trot down the stairs and find Evan, though I couldn't see Louisa. 'Hey,' I greeted him.

He smiled at me. 'Hey Jinx!'

I hated this. I *liked* Evan, which made this next bit all the harder. 'Hey, Evan,' I replied but I didn't smile back. His smile faltered. I leaned against the boulder. 'Come and sit next to me.' He came and sat and I met his eyes. 'I think you know what I'm going to say, don't you?'

He licked his lips. 'Why don't you tell me?' Smart lad: he wasn't incriminating himself.

'Too many crimes to know which one I'm going to sass you over?' I quipped.

He blew out a breath. 'No. Only the one.' He shifted uncomfortably; he could no longer look at me.

'The Eye,' I confirmed. For a beat, he almost looked relieved. 'What were you thinking?' I demanded. 'Do you know how runed-up the hoard is? You could have been killed or maimed.'

'We didn't take it! We just moved it.'

'You deliberately deprived Emory of it and caused him weeks of worry. Tobias was preparing to fall on his sword.'

'What?' Evan was genuinely shocked.

'Tobias failed to protect the hoard. You used both him and Luke – what you did is tantamount to treason.' I was laying it on thick, but I wanted him to understand the consequences of his actions. I shuddered to think of the guilt he'd have felt if Tobias *had* taken his own life.

'No! I – it was just a joke. A prank!'

'Then why didn't you tell anyone? Why didn't you put it back?'

'Luke wouldn't fix the cameras again,' he said sulkily. 'So we couldn't put it back.'

'Why didn't you tell anyone?'

He swallowed hard. 'I didn't want to get into trouble.'

'And what do you think Luke is in?' I said softly. 'He turned off the cameras. His job is to protect the hoard and instead he turned off the cameras and left it vulnerable. He let a multi-million-pound jewel be taken.'

Evan's face was ashen. 'I wanted Emory to notice me, to know I existed. It was before … you know. Before movie nights and stuff. I just wanted Emory's attention,' he muttered.

'Well, now you'll have it,' I said sadly. 'And not for the right reason. And you've probably cost Luke his job.'

Evan's bottom lip trembled.

'Find Louisa then go and see Veronica,' I ordered. They might as well get the tongue-lashing over with first. 'Then we'll go and see Tobias to give him your apologies in person.'

Evan stood to attention. 'Yes, Prima,' he said firmly before marching away to fetch Louisa and face his fate.

I'd probably crashed and burned any chance of a good relationship with him. I rubbed at my chest where my heart had an odd ache. Dammit. Life had been so much simpler when I was a lone wolf.

Chapter 25

I watched to make sure Evan didn't duck out and go somewhere else. He marched up to Louisa braced for an uncomfortable conversation, his shoulders squared. I saw Louisa pale as he explained what was happening. She stood up shakily – obviously she was regretting her actions, too. Good: the kids needed a dose of reality. Life isn't always kind and the consequences of your actions always catch up with you, one way or another.

A bell suddenly tolled, deep and ominous. The sound bounced around the bare stone walls with a sinister clang. I looked around in confusion – I couldn't even see a bell tower – then fear gripped me as I suddenly understood.

Emory had said there was an ancient warning bell... I hoped to hell I was wrong.

Evan grabbed Louisa and whipped around, his eyes wide with panic. The younger kids in the courtyard started to scream. 'To the catacombs!' Evan shouted to the youngest ones. 'Just like we practised! Go!'

I ran to him. 'What's happening?' I demanded.

'That's the ancient bell. It's rung when a dragon goes wild.' His voice was unnaturally high and a bead of sweat had gathered on his lip. He wiped clammy hands on his trousers.

There was a deafening roar: Darius. Dammit, Emory had said he was acting strangely. I pulled out my phone and did a quick voice message to Emory. 'It looks like Darius has gone wild. I'm getting the younglings into the catacombs. You'd better get your ass back here.'

I ran to the catacomb entrance where the children were gathered. Where were the brethren? There was no one here to let them into the catacombs. This was an epic balls-up.

Darius was in dragon form, sitting on the castle walls. Any other time and I'd have taken the opportunity to marvel at his golden body and wings. He really was beautiful – but today he was beautiful and deadly. He'd lost his grip on sanity, and he was coming for the younglings.

I had to keep them safe. If I could at least get them into the catacombs, then maybe they'd stand a chance. If Darius followed us into the catacombs, he'd be fighting in close quarters. It would restrict the damage he could do with his claws and his tail. And I had fire, too.

'I have a key. Move out of the way,' I called to the children. Fear was written on their little faces and I felt awful for what they were going through. I moved some of them none too gently, but I needed to get to the gate *now*. I got out the key, opened the gates to the catacombs and the children poured in.

I locked the gate behind us. It might buy us a minute or two. The children were already running. 'Like we practised,' Evan was shouting. 'Split up into pairs. Stay silent. If he finds you, play dead.'

A part of my mind was horrified, but logic was gripping me and I had to focus on that. Splitting up and waiting for Darius to find them was a recipe for disaster. 'No,' I instructed. 'Stay together and get to the hoard. At least there, you've got Tobias to protect you.'

'We can't make it to the hoard, it's too far,' Evan protested.

'You can. You must! Go! I'll hold off Darius,' I promised with a confidence I didn't feel. 'Go!'

'I could shift and help,' Evan offered. For half a second I was tempted, but he was a child too and he also deserved protection. If anything happened to him, I'd never forgive myself.

'No,' I said. 'Protect the kids. Go, Evan. No more arguing. You're wasting time.'

He nodded sharply, all signs of fear gone now he had a purpose. 'Okay.' He turned to the little kids who were still gathered around him and looking up at him with trusting eyes. I did a quick headcount. There were seven in total – and I was determined to keep it that way.

'Let's go!' Evan shouted and they ran after him. Louisa brought up the rear.

Emory was in Liverpool having lunch with all the other ancient dragons and his circle. Veronica was somewhere in her tower, so she must have heard the bell. Surely she was on her way? I just had to hold the tunnels until then.

How do you fight a dragon other than 'carefully'? I needed to stop panicking and stay calm. I needed a weapon. I felt a weight on my hip: Glimmer. I drew it from its scabbard. 'As happy as I am to see you,' I said, 'it's a bit like attacking a lion with a spoon. You're too small.'

Somehow I could feel it was insulted. Before I could apologise, it started to grow. 'You've been holding out on me,' I accused my dagger. It sang smugly in my mind and continued to grow, yet it didn't get correspondingly heavy. 'Okay, I can work with this.' I had practised fencing for a time; Glimmer was a broadsword, of course, and this was nothing like fencing, but it was better than having a minuscule dagger with no reach.

Where were Gato and Indy? I hoped they were holed up somewhere safe. Like I had summoned them with my thoughts, I heard a bark and then a thump. There was a whine and my heart stopped. Oh God – please, no. Let the dogs be okay.

There was a monstrous crunch and then a roar reverberated down the tunnels. Metal clanged and my stomach dropped. That was the gate destroyed, so Darius was already into the catacombs. Time for me to shine. I wracked my brains. What did I know about dragons? They were immortal and they had a great sense of hearing? No point trying to sneak around, then, because he'd hear me.

I ran boldly forward to the entrance. I needed to buy the kids time to get to the hoard, to get safely behind the witches' runes that would surely strike Darius down if he tried to breach them. And at least Tobias would be there

– if he hadn't popped out for another coffee. I grimaced; I couldn't rely on Tobias saving the younglings. I had to do it myself.

I rounded the corner and there Darius was. My breath caught in my throat. He was huge, bigger even than Emory, at least twenty feet long.

'Hi Darius,' I called. Maybe we could talk this out? Or at least I could stall for help until Veronica came.

'Little girl, I'm going to smash you to pieces. Then I'm going to crunch on the younglings to restore my youth,' Darius snarled. Nice.

'It doesn't work like that,' I pointed out. 'You know it doesn't work like that. You've lost it. You've gone feral. You're a threat to dragons everywhere and you're going to get yourself killed.'

He laughed. 'It's not me that's going to die. I'm invincible. Didn't you know?' His laughter echoed around the walls and fear prickled the skin at my neck. I had a sword that I didn't know how to use and it was almost the size of his trembling claws. Think, Jinx, think!

I scanned his body, looking for any sign of weakness that I could exploit. He had a few scars but nothing that screamed out fragility. I looked at his eyes; they had the same feverish light that Sean Hardman had. And Darius's claws were definitely shaking a little. Was it possible that he hadn't gone feral but was being influenced by a daemon? That could be fixed by a good witch, but going feral was a death sentence. But the truth was that it didn't matter what the cause was. I had no witch closeted close by. *I* had to stop him. Permanently.

Darius let out a roar of fire that funnelled down the tunnel towards me. I had two elements under my control; which would be more effective at stopping his fire? Could I absorb it with more fire or douse it with water? Fire or water? I didn't know what to do but, at the last moment, I threw up a wall of water.

His flames hit the suspended H2O and I kept it flowing until they were doused. Great – now the tunnel was filled with a dense fog, just in case I wanted to make this situation more sinister than it already was. Now I couldn't see properly.

Darius laughed again. 'Are we playing hide and seek, little girl? I do like to play hide and seek. Tell you what, I'll count to five and then I'll come after you – ready or not.' His giggle was sinister and I took him at his word. I turned and ran as hard as I could for five seconds. Now at least I was out of the fog bank so I could see if he was coming for me.

'Here I come!' he said in a creepy sing-song voice that was going to haunt my dreams – if I survived.

My heart was hammering. Where was help? Where were the brethren in the catacombs? Where was Veronica?

Darius leapt forward out of the fog bank and barrelled towards me. I summoned air with the IR and did my best to blow him back. Cackling, he simply took to his wings and used my air to hover gracefully above me. I knew that when I let it go, he'd plummet towards me. His claws were already extended, ready to lacerate me.

My heart was racing. I was going to have to stop the IR soon because I didn't want to use up all of my magic. My magic gave me a fighting chance; if I got drop-kicked into the Common realm, Darius could kill me with no effort at all. Thank goodness Gato had sent me to the Common last night. I should have a good amount of power left in me, but who knew how long it would be until help arrived?

Daemon influence or no, I was fighting for my life and I couldn't pull my punches. I stopped the IR and, as Darius plummeted towards me, I thrust Glimmer upwards with as much force as I could muster.

I felt the weight of him on my sword – on Glimmer – and I cried out as his claws raked down my back. My leather jacket was shredded like wheat. God damn it, that was my new favourite leather jacket. I was losing possessions like nobody's business: first my car, then my jacket – next my life?

I felt Emory's worry down the bond – he could feel my pain. He was getting closer, but not close enough. This was all on me. Fuck.

Even though Darius had landed on Glimmer, I'd barely pierced his skin. He'd managed to rake mine, though, and I was bleeding like a butchered pig. I needed to finish this fight fast if I was going to survive. And I really wanted to survive.

I was all in; it was do or die. I ran at Darius and struck him with Glimmer with all of my might. It bounced off his scales ineffectually but I kept going; it was the only thing I could think of to do. Maybe one of my strikes would get lucky. Over and over, I swung my sword until my arms started to tire.

Then I felt another presence coming closer and Nate phased out of the shadows right next to me. 'I felt your pain and panic,' he explained breathlessly. 'I phased directly to you.'

'Crazy dragon,' I panted back, pointing at Darius.

'So I see. Go for the eyes, it's their only point of vulnerability,' he advised. Vampyrs and dragons had been enemies for so long that it made sense he'd know where to go in for the kill.

'What about the throat or the neck?' I asked.

'Nope. Neither of those. Eyes. I'll distract him, you kill him.'

'You say it like it's easy!' I complained. It wasn't easy; I'd been whaling on Darius with my sword with no visible effect other than to piss him off. I had a new wound on my left arm and I felt like there was more blood on the floor than inside me.

'Dagger size now,' I murmured to Glimmer. 'I'm going to need to sheath you for a minute.' The blade shrank obligingly and I slid it into the holster on my right hip so that I would have my hands free.

True to his word, Nate phased out of the shadows right in front of Darius's face. '*Vampyr*!' Darius roared in fury. When he saw one of his lifelong enemies, reason fled even further into the recesses of his mind.

Okay: Nate was doing well on the distraction front, but how was I going to get at Darius's eyes? I needed to get closer. I waited until Nate phased into the shadows before he popped out at another point in the tunnel, making Darius whirl around. With his back to me, I jumped over Darius's tail and ran as fast as I could up his back.

I used his spiky spines to haul myself up and clung to them desperately when Darius whirled around to try and dislodge me.

If he had been focused on me alone, the crazy dragon would no doubt have simply flown upwards and crushed me against the catacomb ceiling, but he was focused on his mortal enemy, the vampyr at his feet. Nate was taunting him as he effortlessly ran circles around the ancient, lumbering dragon.

It was hard to move up the dragon's body as he whirled about, but I gritted my teeth and did my best. My progress was achingly slow, but at least the kids would have reached the safety of the hoard by now. They'd have Tobias to protect them, and all those witches' curses ready to strike down anyone who entered with ill-intent. Killing the younglings would definitely qualify as that.

I balanced, then moved up two more steps until I was nearly at Darius's neck, but then he moved quickly and I lost my footing. I reached out for a spike and screamed as I impaled my hand on it instead of grabbing it. Tears of pain streamed out of my eyes, my nose was running and I was a complete mess. I used my left arm to scrub my face clean and tried to focus. With herculean effort, I wrenched up my right hand and lifted it off the spike. Blood poured out, so much blood. Just looking at it made me feel faint.

I stumbled forward another step and grabbed another spike, carefully this time. I was at the apex of his neck. I pulled Glimmer from its sheath, but my ruined right hand could barely hold the pommel so I swapped it to my left. I hoped I could deal a killing blow with my weaker hand. I *had* to – it was kill or be killed. It didn't matter if a daemon had started this; I needed to finish it.

Nate looked at me over Darius's head, then jerked his eyes left to indicate which way he was going to move. I gave him a quick nod and braced for Darius to follow him. Nate phased into the shadows and out to the left. Darius turned in that direction but I was ready for it.

I took a breath, let go of the spike I was holding and climbed over the ridge of his head. Adrenaline surged through me, making my heart hammer but helping me ignore the pain from my hand. As I stepped onto the flat of his head, I shoved Glimmer into his left eye with all my might.

Darius screamed, but the dagger thrust wasn't enough to kill him. 'You're not big enough!' I shouted desperately to Glimmer. 'Grow!'

Glimmer's pommel shimmered and I watched it lengthen into a sword and pierce Darius's brain. Thank goodness for sentient weapons. Darius screamed again; his dying sound would follow me in my nightmares. But although he was dead, his body hadn't quite got the message and it thrashed and thrashed as death gripped him. I tumbled from his head towards the hard flagstone floor.

I heard Nate scream my name, and then I heard no more.

Chapter 26

I expected pain, so when I cautiously peeled my eyes open I was pleasantly surprised that nothing hurt. I pushed myself up. Still no pain. Huh.

'Hey,' Nate greeted me with a smile. 'How are you feeling? Are you okay?'

I lifted my hand, which should have been ruined. Not a mark. 'Did you lick all of my wounds?'

'Like a popsicle.' He paused. 'Well, not really. I spat into them because of the whole "wizard blood makes us crazy" thing.' Nate did air quotes.

'Right.' I grinned. 'And you're not crazy.'

'Nope. I was busy healing you, and then Emory arrived. He called in a wizard who put you into a healing coma.

You were out for the rest of the day and the night. It's tomorrow now.'

I looked at my bedside clock. It was 8am.

'After the wizard dealt with you,' Nate continued, 'he sorted out Gato's ribs.'

'Gato's ribs?' I said, alarmed. 'What happened to Gato?'

'He's okay. Indy was trying to stop the dragon all by herself. The dragon came in for a killing blow and Gato threw himself in the way. He got busted up pretty good but the wizard has done his thing, so Gato should be fine after some rest. He expended a lot of his magical energy keeping himself alive, so he needs to restore his energy levels. No hopping around realms for a few days,' he cautioned.

'Okay.' I blew out a breath. Gato was going to be all right. I don't know what I'd do if I lost Gato – and also my dad and Isaac. It doesn't bear thinking about. 'Okay,' I repeated. 'Can I see him?'

'Emory's just checking on him next door. He'll be back in a moment and he can let you know the latest,' Nate promised.

I settled back down. Emory knew how important Gato was to me; he knew that I needed my dad at our wedding. I couldn't lose Gato, I just couldn't. It would break me.

The bedroom door opened and Emory walked in carrying a platter of food. 'Jess!' He ran to me in a vampyric instant, set down the platter on the bedside table and kissed me. It was soft and gentle, and I could feel his relief pouring down our bond.

Nate was staring at Emory, his mouth open. He closed it with a clack. 'Woah. What was that? That was...' He knew about Hes having vampyr speed because she'd been stabbed by Glimmer, and I saw the cogs turning in his brain. 'Vampyric speed?' he asked, eyes wide.

'It's a secret,' I whispered.

'I bet,' Nate muttered, still looking shocked.

'Thanks for spitting on me Nate,' I graciously thanked my vampyric hero.

He grinned. 'Any time.'

'I'd rather not need it again, to be honest,' I said drily. 'But thanks for rushing to my aid. How did you phase here? You've never been in the catacombs?'

'No,' Emory said in a tone that brooked no argument. 'No vampyr ever has.'

Nate shrugged. 'I just closed my eyes and phased to you.'

I was surprised. 'I didn't know it worked like that. I thought you needed to know the destination.'

'Usually I do. I have no idea how I did it. There've not been too many instances of a bond like ours.'

I cleared my throat. 'So is Hes okay with you coming here?' The last time I'd been in danger and needed Nate, Hes had deleted the message so he couldn't come to my aid. That had ended their fledgling relationship, yet here he was riding to my rescue. It had to have been contentious.

'I didn't ask her permission,' Nate said firmly. He shrugged. 'She knows the deal. I'm sworn to protect you and I'll come running if you need me. Any time. Every time.'

I felt teary. 'Thank you.' There was a time not too long ago when Nate had given off young, ebullient vibes. That was partly due to living the college lifestyle over and over again. Now he felt ... older. My vampyr had gone and grown up.

He leaned down and kissed my cheek. 'If you're all good here, I'll give you guys some space.'

'I'm fine. You're good to go,' I assured him. 'Thank you again, I really appreciate you coming. I would have been mincemeat without you.' *True.*

He snorted. 'You're a cat. You've got a lot more lives yet to live.'

'I did *not* land on my feet,' I pointed out drily.

'No,' Nate agreed. 'You landed on your head. Luckily, you have a thick skull.' He rapped my forehead gently with his knuckles and smirked before giving me another quick kiss. He shook Emory's hand in a farewell and I saw Emory murmur his thanks as he pulled Nate into a man hug. I felt all emotional. My menfolk were getting along.

Nate closed the curtain in one corner of the room to create a shadow then phased out, leaving me alone with an anxious mate-to-be.

Chapter 27

When we were alone, Emory checked me over, running his hands over where my wounds had been. 'Eat something, love,' he urged. The platter he'd brought in had a bit of everything on it: sliced melon, Danish pastries, porridge, toast and a bacon roll. I went with the bacon option. Mrs Jones had put tomato ketchup in it. Yum.

Emory watched me eat with relief. When I'd finished the entire roll, he sat next to me and took my hand. 'Don't scare me like that again.'

'Don't have an elder dragon going gah-gah on me, then I won't have to,' I sassed back, picking at the melon.

Emory shook his head. 'It's so weird. I know Darius wasn't being himself, but he wasn't exhibiting *any* of the warning signs. I would never have left him behind if I'd thought there was any risk that he'd go feral.'

'What are they?' I asked. 'The warning signs?' I clarified.

'Forgetfulness first, little things like forgetting where you've put your keys. Then it progresses to not remembering names, and general confusion. We normally have a lot of warning when the madness is coming. I spoke to Darius's staff before I left, and I've spoken to his brethren again this afternoon, but they all swear that he was still as sharp as a tack. They're in complete shock, plus they're grieving and feeling guilty that they didn't see the warning signs.'

'Maybe they weren't there,' I suggested.

'What do you mean?' Emory tilted his head in question.

I chewed on my lip. 'It's tenuous, but his eyes ... they looked like Sean's before he punched me. And his claws were shaking like Sean's hands were. I don't know enough about daemons, but...' I trailed off.

'You think he was influenced by a daemon?' Emory sounded surprised.

'It would explain a lot.'

His jaw was working. 'Dammit. This daemon is trying to fuck us up. First the increase in Anti-Crea attacks, and now this?'

'Maybe. We don't know for sure.'

'This is the last thing we need right now.' He ran a hand through his short hair.

I decided it was a good thing I'd kept the threatening note to myself; I'd keep it that way for now.

'How are you feeling?' Emory asked.

'I'm fine. The vampyr spit and the healing wizard have done the trick.' I yawned. 'I feel good as new.' I lifted my right hand and looked at my palm; there were no signs of the huge rip that had crippled it. Fascinated, I flexed my fingers and watched them move. I put my hand down. 'Hey,' I said to Emory. 'Come cuddle.'

Fully clothed, he climbed onto the bed next to me. 'I'm so sorry,' he apologised. Through our bond, I felt guilt swamping him.

'For what?' I asked, honestly baffled.

'For leaving you with Darius. For being too slow reaching you. For not having my brethren security there to help you. Pick one – all of them are true.' I could feel his frustration.

'The first two aren't your fault because you couldn't have known. But where was everyone – Veronica? The brethren?'

'Darius took Veronica by surprise and knocked her out before the bell was rung. A less hard-headed dragon would have died. Luckily she'll pull through.'

'What happened to the extra brethren you posted on Darius's door?'

'They both died,' Emory admitted with a sigh. 'Darius killed them after they rang the bell. They knew that he would, but they did it anyway.'

'What were their names?' I asked. It was important to remember them; they had rung the ancient bell and warned us all.

'Scott Dean and Jane Lindon.'

I didn't recognise either name and I felt guilty for the flash of relief I felt about that. Just because I hadn't known them personally didn't change the fact that they had died for us all.

'They rang the bell to alert everyone, But there was no "everyone",' Emory said grimly. 'The brethren had taken Caruso's little stunt with the cameras personally. They took him off site and beat the shit out of him.'

I winced. 'I told Lintle...'

'He didn't lay a hand on Caruso, he was very clear about that. The others did.'

'Damn this bloody realm and its stupid wordsmithing,' I grumbled. 'Poor Caruso.'

'Caruso bought it on himself. He betrayed us.' Emory's tone was harsh.

'It was just a prank,' I protested a shade weakly – even I didn't really believe that. Caruso had displayed some terrible decision-making skills.

'This time. And how could he be sure that's all it was? Veronica has already had words with Evan and Louisa, and I'll be speaking to them as well. Their actions were foolish, at best.'

Another thought occurred to me. 'Where were the gargoyles?'

Emory sighed. 'Creating a nice little mess for me. I'm in the helicopter, flying to lunch in Liverpool, trying to argue that the gargoyles won't be an issue, that they aren't *that* fanatically loyal to me … and then they burst through the clouds. Two hundred gargoyles flying alongside the helicopters to keep me safe.'

I winced. 'Shit.'

'Yeah.' He rubbed his jaw. 'I don't know what to do about this. The Elders are questioning the gargoyles today and tomorrow, then we'll have a formal trial to decide my status.'

'Is there anything I can do?' I asked, feeling helpless.

He shook his head. 'Just carry on being here. That's all that I need. No matter what happens with the trial, you're still all that I need.' I loved that it was true; he may not *need* to be Prime, but he *wanted* to be. But he *needed* me.

I bit my lip. 'Geneve seems ... friendly. Surely she'll vote in your favour?'

Emory grimaced. 'I'm not so sure. She suggested we renew our old friendship. Obviously, I said no.'

'She hit on you? After meeting me? What a fucking bitch,' I snarled.

He shrugged. 'She didn't take no kindly. I may have burned that bridge.'

'We don't need bridges. You can fly,' I said stubbornly.

'As long as I think happy thoughts.'

I flashed him a grin. 'Okay, lost boy, we need a plan. A good one.' I tapped my lip with my forefinger. 'What's our plan?'

'I've called Audrey,' he said decisively.

I smirked. 'Your plan was to ring your mum?'

Emory ignored the jibe and I resisted the urge to make a 'your mum' joke. Now wasn't the time. 'She has a longer relationship with the Elders. Maybe she can talk them into letting us at least have some time with the gargoyles to see how the made-brethren and their bond with me develops. The Elders don't need to see it as a threat.'

'Why would it be a threat?' I was honestly confused about why it would be an issue. How could loyalty be a bad thing?

'That's why made-brethren were outlawed – they got too fanatical. They were so convinced that their dragon was the best dragon that they started fighting the other brethren for their dragon's supremacy.'

'You are the Prime, you're king of the dragons as long as they don't take that away from you, so surely the gargoyles won't take issue?'

'I don't know.' Emory rubbed his jaw again. 'Listen, Reynard is their leader so I could do with having him elsewhere. He's already spoken with the Elders and I don't want him stirring things up. Can you take him with you to do something? Focus on the vigilante killer angle?'

'I can do that,' I agreed. The killer and the car bomb seemed like a lifetime ago and it was hard to switch gears in my brain. I was still thinking about Darius and the younglings he had wanted to murder. 'The kids – they're alright?'

'They're fine. They got to the hoard and Tobias was there, ready to fight Darius.' He paused. 'He was very upset he couldn't help you but I'd made him promise to stay with the hoard, no matter what. I've released the strong wording of that vow – I only meant he wasn't to pop out for coffee.' He sighed. 'But the vow stopped him coming to help you. I could have got you killed just because of some careless phrasing.'

'Don't be ridiculous. If I had died, it would have been on Darius, not on you or Tobias. It's not either of your faults.'

Emory grimaced again but didn't argue. He looked me over one more time. 'You're sure you're okay?'

'I'm fine. Stop fussing.' I gave him a long kiss. 'Go and convince those Elders that you're the best thing since sliced bread.'

'They probably think slicing bread is barbaric – it should be ripped into chunks like the Vikings used to do it,' he muttered grumpily.

I laughed. 'You were made Prime for a reason. Go. You've got this.'

He gave me another lingering kiss. 'Have I told you lately that I love you?'

'You've mentioned it a time or two. I love you, too.'

He stood up. 'Gato's next door. He's okay, but he needs rest.'

'Thanks. I'll go say hi and then let him sleep. Say hello to Audrey for me.'

'I will do. You keep out of trouble.'

'Sure,' I said airily. 'I'm just going to find a vigilante-killing car bomber. It'll be a walk in the park.'

'Take back-up,' Emory ordered firmly.

'I'm already taking Reynard,' I pointed out.

'Take Shirdal too. And maybe Mike.'

I could see he wanted to add to the list so I said hastily, 'we'll see. Off you go.' I didn't want to take a posse with me because it put people off answering my questions truthfully.

After Emory left, I popped next door to see Indy and Gato. Indy leapt up to say hello, her tail wagging enthusiastically as she jumped up and gave me a very wet lick across the face. 'Hey, little girl, are you okay?' I asked, checking her over.

She hopped down and wagged her tail again before apparently catching sight of it and deciding it was time to chase it round in a circle. Gato watched her with narrowed eyes and gave an audible huff. He was lying in front of the fire and his black fur was scorching hot as I stroked it.

'You were young once,' I teased him. 'You still chase your tail occasionally.'

He gave me a look as if to say, 'what, me?'

'Yes, you!' I stroked his great head. 'You gave me a scare. Are you okay?'

He tap-tapped twice for yes but lowered his head back down. He was tired. 'Poor pup. You'd better take it easy. Do you need anything?' He shook his head slightly. 'I'll leave Indy with you to keep you company.'

He shot me a slightly pained look. 'Sorry,' I mouthed to him. But I really didn't want to take the puppy on a hunt for a murderer. So far she hadn't learnt to listen too well, and I didn't want her skidding into more danger – because that was what I was heading for.

Chapter 28

I persuaded Mike to stay with Emory by pointing out how much help he would be at the castle. I also convinced him that he needed to bash the rest of the brethren into shape. It was inexcusable that no one had come to the younglings' aid when Darius had gone wild. I'd taken the Elder down, sure, but really it was only because Nate had provided a distraction. Without Nate, I would have been a goner.

My phone rang. It was Elvira. 'Remember your office break-in?' she began without preamble.

'Hi Elvira, how are you? I'm fine, thanks for asking. I just survived a brutal attack on my person,' I sassed.

'You're always getting your person attacked. Have you thought about being more amenable?' she suggested sarcastically.

'Hey! I'm super-amenable. Everyone likes me,' I protested.

'Not whoever broke into your office.'

'Okay. The office break-in. Tell me what you've got.' A few weeks earlier, my office had been broken into and one of the stolen files posted to Bentley Bronx. He'd come hunting for his ex-wife and got himself killed instead. The theft had consequences. Bad ones.

'I've got a hit on the fingerprints,' Elvira confirmed.

'Great!'

'Not really.' She sighed.

I dialled my enthusiasm down. 'Why not?'

'The reason I have his prints is because he's in the morgue. It was Hugo Arnold.'

'The bludgeoned-to-death-dryad?'

'That's the one,' she agreed.

'Dammit.' I wondered if Hugo's death was somehow on me. Was someone cleaning up shop after themselves? 'What's the deal with Hugo? I heard he was a drug dealer.'

'Never trust someone with two first names,' Elvira muttered.

'What?'

'Hugo and Arnold. Two first names.'

'You know that's not a real thing, right?'

'It was in his case.'

'So he *was* a drug dealer?'

'That is unsubstantiated at this time,' Elvira said firmly. Her voice lowered to a whisper. 'But between you and I, a butt-tonne of drugs was found at his residence.'

'Why is that a secret?' I asked.

'Because it was reported to the Connection.' She sighed again. 'And nothing was done about it. So now I'm not allowed to put the drugs in my report because it makes us look bad.'

'That sucks.'

'Yeah.' Elvira let out a harsh breath. 'I only got into this job because of Stone. I thought he'd be impressed that I could hack it. But now... I love it. I love the job, but I hate the politics. There's so much politics. It shouldn't be this way,' she said unhappily. 'It's not right.'

'It's not,' I agreed. 'It must be frustrating for you.' I felt like a shrink helping her identify and talk through her feelings, but maybe I wasn't acting like a psychologist but as a friend. Maybe we were just on the path to friendship. That thought made me happy.

'It's awful,' she groused. 'You either get used to it or you just make jokes like Bland. Either that or you leave.'

'Stone thought a lot of the Connection.'

'It does good stuff, but it's made up of people, and people are flawed. It could do better, *be* better.'

I admired how passionate she was about it. 'Maybe you should try to be the next wizard symposium member. You know, bring about change from within?'

She laughed bitterly. 'I hate politics, remember?'

'Right. That *would* be an issue.'

'Just a little one.'

I thought again about Hugo. The information I had him on so far was pretty sparse. 'Who was Hugo's next of kin? Wife? Husband? Mum?'

'No spouse – he never married. He dated a few women occasionally, but no one special. His mum died a couple of years ago. Only one surviving sibling.'

'Name?' I asked.

'Rebecca Arnold. She was a lot younger than Hugo. My money is on her being a surprise baby,' Elvira said.

'Did you do the death notification?' I queried.

'No, another officer did it. I've been up the wall.' Between the murders and my little car bomb … yup – she'd been busy.

'Where does the sister live?'

'One second.' Elvira tapped on her computer. 'Well now … she lives in Portmeirion.'

'And no one thought Hugo's death was connected to Derek's and Arlo's?' I huffed.

'Not initially. We do *now*. Hugo was killed in Liverpool,' she said defensively.

'And Clarissa Sands?'

'She was killed on the Wirral. Still a fair bit of distance between them.'

'Not all that much,' I disagreed. 'Has Clarissa got next of kin?'

'She didn't have anyone. She was an orphan, raised in children's homes. She got bounced around. A few years ago she had a best friend – question-mark lover – a seer apparently, but by all accounts their relationship ended abruptly and badly.'

I felt a surge of sympathy for poor unlikeable Clarissa. It was a tough beginning for anyone. It didn't excuse her later actions but it gave me some context. 'What happened to the friend?' I probed.

'We don't know.'

'Do you think she found out about Clarissa's embezzlement?'

'Possibly. It was a long-running scam. Clarissa was an independent financial advisor, but she also worked for a number of financial institutions. She was taking money from clients – skimming – and passing a little less on to the institutions. Not much, a few hundred here or there, but she did it for years. Recently she started taking more and that's when the red flag went up and the FSA started investigating. I spoke to the FSA and they recently passed her file to a crossover for prosecution. The future wasn't bright for Clarissa Sands.'

'Regardless of that, now she has no future at all.' I blew out a breath. 'Thanks for all this information, Elvira.' I guessed I'd better have a trip to Portmeirion. Maybe the sister could give me some insight into the break-in and Hugo's death.

'One more thing. You remember asking about Derek Ives' riches?' Elvira asked.

'Yeah?'

'His solicitor said he filed a new Will with them recently. He'll retrieve it from archiving and let me know the beneficiaries.'

I frowned. 'Derek *filed* a new Will? He didn't make it with them?' I clarified.

'No, apparently he did it himself. I'll text you when I hear from his solicitor. It should be soon – he said he'd go to the office shortly and retrieve it.'

Hmm. There was one more thing that I needed to mention. 'One last thing,' I said. 'I got a threatening note, hand delivered to the castle.'

Elvira sighed. 'Shoot me a picture of it. Do you want me to get forensics on it?'

'No. The person who delivered it hasn't been caught on camera. There's not going to be any prints.'

'You don't know that.'

'No, but when you're up the wall, you have to prioritise. Let's focus on the dead.'

'I'll send someone to pick up the letter,' she said, blithely ignoring me.

I laughed. 'Okay, fine. You win. I'll leave it at the castle entrance with some of the brethren. You're a good woman.'

'I try.' She cleared her throat. 'I'll see you later. And thanks for the invite. It means a lot.' Then she hung up. What invite? What the hell was she talking about?

I put it out of my mind. I had a crime to solve and I was determined to get to it. First, though, I needed to locate my new partner, Reynard. I wondered if Emory had given him the good news that he was being seconded to help me.

Reynard was in the great hall, surrounded by people also adorned by black-feathered wings. He was big news now, and I took a moment to study him. When Emory and I had met him, he'd been a squat, grey-skinned gargoyle; now he looked like some sort of avenging angel. I could still see hints of the creature that he'd been, but now he was all man. He wore trousers but no shirt, so I guessed the wings were an issue. It must have been chilly when he was flying high.

I gently manoeuvred my way through the crowd to his side. 'Hey Reynard,' I greeted him.

'Jinx, my saviouress. How's your sodding day going?'

'Not so bad, but I'd like to improve it. There's been a spate of deaths lately. Do you want to come with me to speak to one of the victim's sisters? I could use some backup.'

He brightened visibly. 'Of course, my Prima. I would be honoured to serve you. Emory will be so pleased with me.'

I winced a little at the adoration in his voice. 'He will.'

'I'll get some more of us to come... ' Reynard suggested.

'NO! No.' I held up my hand. 'Thanks for the offer but really, one gargoyle is enough.'

'We prefer to call ourselves the black-winged now,' he said pointedly.

'That's a bit of a mouthful.'

'That's what she said.' He winked lecherously and grinned at me.

I rolled my eyes. 'Come on. Let's go.'

'Shall I fly us?'

'Er, no. We'll take my car. It's not too far away.'

'Sure, Prima. Let me just give instructions to Tamsin, my second in command.' He joined a group of the black-winged and gestured back to me. Everyone nodded and smiled at me. Oh boy.

Before long we were making our way to a car. Since mine had exploded, we were taking one of the brethren fleet cars. Shirdal was leaning casually against one of them. 'So,' he started belligerently. 'Now this bozo has wings, you don't need mine anymore?' Uh-oh.

'Of course I need you.' I smiled. 'The more the merrier. I'd love you to join us.'

Kill me now. It was going to be a circus.

Chapter 29

Reynard and Shirdal were bickering over who should ride shotgun. Before they could decide, shouting broke out from behind us. I hesitated, but in the end nosiness won out. 'Let's go and see what the commotion is about,' I told them, locking the black Land Rover once more.

We jogged back to the turnstiles. Dave and Jackie had been on shift when we'd passed through on our way to the car, and a small trickle of anxiety wormed its way into my stomach. It turned out my anxiety was justified. Even from a few feet away, I could see both of them were on the ground surrounded by blood. Oh God, no.

Tom Smith was shouting orders into a walkie-talkie and the castle was being locked down. It had already been closed to visitors in preparation for the Elders' visit; a huge placard outside proclaimed emergency repair work was being undertaken and some scaffolding had been thrown up against one of the walls for good measure.

'What's going on?' I asked Tom, already fearing the answer.

'There's been an attack,' he said tightly.

No shit, Sherlock. No one was working on Dave and Jackie. 'Why isn't someone helping them?' It was a stupid question, but I didn't want to admit the obvious answer even to myself. I was in a river in Africa – De-Nile.

'It's too late. They're already dead,' Tom said grimly.

My mind went blank. Jackie had three children at home. Dave was only twenty-two and he'd barely had time for his life to start. I went over to them, clinging to a hope that Tom was wrong.

He wasn't wrong; both of them had had their throats slit. Their deaths had been quick and we must have only just missed strolling past their killer. I stared at their bodies, waiting and hoping to see a telltale flicker of life that would tell me it was an illusion but there was none. They were truly dead.

The only way to save them would be to go back in time, but Gato was down and Indy didn't know her paw from her nose. Despair and grief crawled into my heart. There wasn't going to be a miracle here; Jackie and Dave were gone and there was nothing I could do about it.

I *can* go back in time but the past is fixed by our present, so I couldn't go back and save their lives because they were already very dead in my present. It wasn't like Bella, when I'd known that her death was illusory because she hadn't been dead in the first place. Not so with Jackie and Dave; they were lifeless and the fixity of the past condemned them to stay that way. Even if Gato had been fighting fit, there would have been nothing I could do.

Jackie's eyes were wide with horror and it was too much to look into them. Somebody had written 'die dragon scum' on her body and scrawled the Anti-Crea symbol next to it. I pulled myself off the ground to touch the grim red graffiti. Spray paint not blood, despite its appearance.

'Go, Prima, please,' Tom pleaded with me.

'There is no way I'm leaving with a killer strolling around,' I hissed.

'If you're the target then I need you far away,' he said firmly.

'I'm not the target. If I was, they could have grabbed me,' I said impatiently. 'We must have walked right past the killer. Have you got camera footage?'

'Verifying that now.' His walkie-talkie blared to life. 'Footage being sent to your phone now,' a disembodied voice said: Fritz. Damn, the young electronic whizz kid shouldn't have been seeing stuff like this.

Tom pulled out his phone and impatiently refreshed its data. I sidled closer so I could watch the footage too. The selected clips had been trimmed; the first showed two people parking their black car, a Ford Focus. The numberplate had been covered with mud so it was wholly obscured. Two men piled out, with hoods up, covering their faces. They made their way towards the entrance, turning their backs to the cameras as they pulled on gloves and masks. The footage stopped and the next clip began from a different angle – inside the entranceway. It started as two masked and gloved assailants burst into the entrance. Dave and Jackie had their backs to it and were looking at something on their security screens. Their assassins closed the distance between them and sliced their throats from behind before either of the brethren even knew that they were there. I tried to console myself that at least they hadn't been afraid. Their deaths had been quick.

The murderers both took out cans and one sprayed the vitriol, the other the symbol. Then they left again. In and out in a minute or less. This had been carefully planned.

'Can we check the footage that Dave and Jackie were looking at?' I asked. 'Something drew their attention. This was too smooth, too slick. The killers planned it, including making sure Dave and Jackie's backs were turned – or at least one of their backs was turned.'

Tom nodded grimly. 'I'll get that sent to me now. This is a total shit show. The Elders are not going to be impressed.'

The Elders were the least of our worries. Jackie and Dave were dead; Jackie's three children were all aged under ten and they would never see their mum's sunny smile again. That hurt.

'At least the killers left the way they came in. The castle wasn't breached.'

Tom snorted. 'Small mercy. With all the shit that's gone on, I wouldn't be surprised if Emory fires the lot of us.'

I looked at him in surprise. 'He trusts you. You're his right-hand man.'

'If I'm his right-hand man, then he should amputate me,' he snarled. 'I'm failing him miserably. First the Eye, then Darius, now this? Go, Prima. Please. Go to where you were heading and let me deal with this. At least you'll be safe.'

I didn't want to leave, not for one second, but staying would undermine the last shred of self-worth Tom had right now. If I stayed, it said I didn't trust him to deal with this shit. 'All right. We'll be in Portmeirion if you need us.' I paused. 'Please get Jackie and Dave taken care of.'

His eyes softened. 'Of course, Prima.'

Delegation isn't in my skillset and it took everything I had to walk away. Shirdal and Reynard were hovering too close, eyes darting and hands tense. This was going to be a fun drive.

We piled into the car with Reynard carefully sitting on his folded black wings. I slid behind the driving wheel. In my rear-view mirror I noted four brethren men, all dressed in black, making a hasty dive for another black Land Rover.

I started the engine and peeled away and the other vehicle followed. Great – Tom had sent an extra protection detail. I saw Shirdal make them too, but he made no complaint about Tom not trusting him. Things were hotting up and I was worried we were all going to get burned.

The roads were clear so it didn't take us long to reach Portmeirion. I was struggling to get my mind focused back on Derek and Arlo. All I could see were Jackie's unseeing eyes.

The dryad's address wasn't far away from Derek and Arlo's, but of course nothing in Portmeirion was too far from anywhere else. The village was tiny. We parked in the car park with the other vehicle behind us. I noted that the village was still closed to visitors, though the blue-and-white police tape had been removed.

Reynard was whistling as we walked along and Shirdal was glaring at him. The dark seraph was trying to be light-hearted. I felt anything but.

'Where's the pooch?' Shirdal asked me.

'He got hurt when the elder dragon went nuts,' I explained.

'That's a bad business.' He frowned. 'If I'd known all the gargoyles would be flapping along after Emory, I would have stayed with you. Leaving the Prima unguarded...' He shook his head in disgust. 'The whole thing was a bloody shambles. An embarrassment.'

'It doesn't matter. I'm fine.'

'Only thanks to some healing.' Shirdal stopped walking and turned to me. 'I won't let you get hurt again.'

'Not today, anyway,' I joked.

'I let that asshole hit you, too. It turns out that it's a lot harder to protect someone than kill them.' Gone was his jovial smile; he was all seriousness.

'Go figure,' I said drily.

'You must feel worried with the attack on the brethren but I swear I've got your back,' he promised.

'So have I,' Reynard asserted. 'I won't let a fucking thing happen to you.'

'Pfffft.' Shirdal made a dismissive noise. 'What good are you? Are you going to flap your wings at an enemy?' He sneered. 'I need your help like a fish needs a bicycle.'

'I don't know why you're throwing stones. You let her get punched! You're as much help as a glass hammer.'

Shirdal's eyes narrowed. 'Me? You're as useful as a newspaper umbrella.'

Reynard's mouth twisted and he let out a very wolf-like growl. 'Fuck you.' His hands shimmered and in their places were sharp claws. Huh. 'I'll rip the bloody throats out of anyone that dares harm our Prima,' he snarled.

Shirdal made a slightly impressed face. 'Okay, maybe you're not a waterproof teabag. Have you been practising with those things so that you're not Edward Scissorhands?'

'I've been practising,' Reynard confirmed. 'I could slice you into pieces.' *Lie.* Ha! Even he didn't believe it.

Shirdal laughed, good humour restored. 'Not a chance, my aerial asshole.'

'Aerial asshole?' Reynard humphed.

'If you dish out the swears, you've got to be able to take them.'

Reynard glowered. 'I can take anything you throw at me!'

'Really?' Shirdal smirked, giving him a lascivious wink. 'We'll see. Let's just focus on keeping the Prima alive for now.'

'Agreed,' Reynard said tightly.

I knew they were both trying to help me, but it was rubbing me up the wrong way. 'I appreciate your protection, but I'm not a damsel in distress,' I bit out. 'Nor am I a precious little wallflower. We'll get to the bottom of all of this, we'll find out who killed Jackie and Dave, and then we'll mete out some justice.'

Shirdal grinned. 'I love justice.' He paused. 'By justice – we mean death and destruction, right?'

'Right,' I agreed grimly. I wasn't feeling charitable right now; death and destruction was exactly what the doctor ordered.

Chapter 30

We weren't far from Hugo's sister's house, so I took the extra few steps to her doorstep to calm myself back down. I called up the ocean in my mind and let the sounds relax me. 'Hands,' I said to Reynard as I caught sight of his claws out of the corner of my eye.

He blinked in surprise and then obligingly turned his claws back into hands. When he looked more or less human – bar the wings – I knocked loudly.

I tried to get my head screwed on straight. We were here about Hugo Arnold, the dryad bludgeoned to death who had also broken into my office. For now, I laid Jackie and Dave to rest; I had to focus on the task at hand.

The door opened, and the dryad waitress from the café stared back at us. 'Rebecca Arnold?' I asked in surprise.

She folded her arms defensively. 'I don't go by Arnold anymore.'

'What do you go by now?'

'Smith. Becky Smith.'

'Original,' Reynard snorted.

I shot him a warning look. 'Can we come in, Becky? We need to discuss some stuff of a sensitive nature.'

She sighed. 'You're here about Hugo then?'

'Can we come in?' I repeated.

She stepped back and let us into her home. On the outside, it was painted bright pink. There were flower baskets full of bright petals hanging underneath the windows, and she had baskets hanging from brackets next to the front door. Inside, the house was no less green. Plants covered virtually every surface. 'That's a lot of fecking plants,' Reynard commented.

'Dryad,' she confirmed drily.

'Right, sure – but still.'

'I don't have a tree yet, so I need more plants around me.' She might as well have been talking double-Dutch, but she was comfortable discussing her plants so I let her ramble on before I brought up Hugo again. She told us about the largest flower in the world, the *titan arums*: apparently they produce flowers ten feet high and three feet wide. They smell of decaying flesh and are known as corpse flowers. Gross.

After I had learnt more than I ever wanted to about corpse flowers, I hauled the conversation back to topic. I wanted to be back in the castle; I wanted to see Emory with my own eyes even though I could feel him across the distance between us. I could feel he was upset but he was trying to keep a lid on his emotions. I wanted to go home.

I tried to focus on the here and now. 'Can you tell me a little about Hugo?'

'What do you want to know?' Becky asked pugnaciously. 'He was a twat. Okay? He didn't have a single redeeming feature.' She met my eyes challengingly. 'I'm not even sorry he's dead. Mum would have been devastated, but luckily she's not here to see this day. It came far too late for my liking.' *True.*

'You didn't get on with your brother?' I asked, knowing it was a massive understatement.

'He was a bully ever since I was a child. He was always tricking me, getting me to say rude things or do bad things. By the time I was six, I'd caught on to the fact that Hugo was bad news. For all Mum loved him, she wasn't ignorant of his flaws. She often tried to keep him away from me. We didn't have what you'd call a normal sibling relationship, and by the time I was a teenager the rumours about him had started.'

'Did your mum know about the rumours?'

'Yeah, they just about killed her. Our father was a dryad elder, and having Hugo act like that sullied his good name and reputation. Dad's name and legacy was all Mum had left of him – he died soon after I was born.' She looked emotional about that for a moment, then she cleared her throat.

'It was my best friend's parents who told her about Hugo, so she knew the source was genuine. I honestly think it contributed to her heart attack. She was horrified at the thought of her son becoming a drug dealer, but she still loved him. I think she hoped to rehabilitate him – she was the only one who stood a chance. After she died, he went even further off the rails. That's when I changed my surname to Smith and moved out.'

'Your best friend's parents? What were their names? Can I speak to them?'

'Not likely. They went missing soon after they made their accusations. They told mum, but they also told the Connection. I argued with Hugo about their disappearance and that was the last time I spoke to him properly. He denied offing them – it's probably the only thing he said that I actually believed. He was an awful person but I don't believe he'd have hurt Emilia.'

'Emilia?'

'My bestie. We were still young and he wouldn't hurt a kid like that. No matter how scummy he got, I don't think he'd sink that low.'

'What were Emilia's parents called?' I asked.

'Mr and Mrs Ramirez. Erm … Maria and Juan, I think. Dryads. They'd moved here from Mexico.'

'You work as a waitress?'

'Yes, the hours are good, the pay is okay and the tips are decent. I love living in the countryside. My boss pays for my flat here – he does that for all of us.'

I thought of Marco the siren. 'He seems like a pretty decent boss.'

'He is. He'd help anyone. When the circus came and they broke one of their poles for the pole vault, he arranged for another to be delivered the next day. That's the kind of guy he is.' She smiled dreamily. Someone had a crush, and I couldn't blame her. Marco was handsome and he'd seemed kind when he'd dealt with Indy.

I brought the conversation back to Hugo. 'There is some evidence that Hugo broke into my office in Liverpool. Do you know anything about that?'

'No, of course not. I'm sorry; I really don't know anything about Hugo or his dodgy dealings. We hadn't seen each other for years.'

'Do you know about any of his associates?'

She wrapped her arms around herself defensively. 'No. I'm sorry,' she repeated. 'As I said, I haven't seen him for years, and even when we did see each other I couldn't have told you who his friends were. I don't think he had any.'

'Did he know Derek and Arlo?'

'The satyrs?' she asked, surprised. 'No. Not as far as I know. Why?'

'They were killed the same way.'

'No, the satyrs were beaten to death. The detective told me my brother was bludgeoned to death.'

'Essentially that means the same thing,' I said gently.

She coloured. 'Oh. But ... Hugo was in Liverpool, wasn't he?'

'He was, yes,' I confirmed.

'But you think the deaths are linked?' She frowned in confusion.

'I think it's likely.'

Becky stared at me hopelessly. 'I really have no idea if Hugo knew Derek or Arlo. I can't imagine them in the same circles but it's not impossible, I suppose.'

'Thanks, you've been a great help.' *Lie.* I agreed with my lie detector. This had been a great big waste of time, right when I absolutely shouldn't have left the castle.

We said our goodbyes and went back to the car park with the brethren following not so discreetly behind. On our way through the village, we saw Izzy the ice-cream parlour owner. She waved hello, though she raised her eyebrows at the army of men following me.

I was trying to ignore them. The whole situation felt ludicrous, but I was doing my best to grit my teeth and bear it. The brethren needed to feel useful; they needed to know that I accepted them in my life, and that I trusted them to guard me. I didn't, but that was beside the point.

'Hi Jinx. Have you found Andrea yet?' Izzy asked.

It took me a moment to place who she was talking about. Andrea Lyons: the waitress who had moved away after Derek and Arlo had hit on her.

'No, sorry. I haven't got to her yet.' I smiled apologetically. I had retrieved a magical artefact, had my car bombed, fought a mad dragon and found two dead bodies, so I hadn't been resting on my laurels. 'Sorry,' I repeated. 'I'll make her my next priority.'

Izzy nodded, but she looked disappointed and I felt bad. 'I promise,' I said.

'Sure,' she responded evenly. *Lie.* Ugh. Now I felt *really* bad. We waved goodbye. 'Hey, Shirdal, can you drive?' I asked.

'Of course,' he said, sounding superior and looking smugly at Reynard.

'I'll bloody well get to it.' Reynard shrugged. 'I've had more important shit to deal with.'

Shirdal opened his mouth and I held up my hands. 'Let's not argue.' I felt like I was accompanying a pair of toddlers. I bit back a sigh. 'Just get in the car. Shirdal, take us to Caernarfon, please. I want to work on my laptop in the back.'

I slid into the back seat and pulled out my laptop, fired up my search engine for Andrea Lyons and waited to see what it would spit out. While that was running, I dug into my emails. Suddenly I saw the one Sean Hardman had sent, back when we were in Smuggler's Cove. Fuck. I'd dropped the ball. The car bomb had distracted me. He had sent me a file with all the complaints he'd investigated against Derek and Arlo and I hadn't even opened it. I did a mental head thunk.

I downloaded the zipped file then extracted the data. I was dismayed at the number of files in the folder; there were a *lot* of complaints to comb through.

I opened the files; needless to say, they didn't make pleasant reading. The complaints ranged from inappropriate jokes to inappropriate touching to full-blown rape allegations. It was one of the latter that gave me pause. Each file included a small picture of the victims, easy enough to grab from social media these days, and one or two of the faces looked achingly familiar. I'd seen them before – and recently – but I couldn't place where.

We were nearly at Caernarfon when my laptop search engines spluttered out the results for Andrea Lyons. What was interesting was that there hadn't been a single entry on her credit card or debit card history since she'd arrived in Liverpool about three years ago. Neither had she paid taxes. It was like she'd stopped existing. I double-checked whether a death certificate had been filed for her, but the only Andrea Lyons I'd found had died back in 1892. It was as if my Andrea had been wiped off the face of the earth.

Something clicked loudly in my brain. Oh shit. I brought up the files of the two victims that had set alarm bells ringing. I was right: I had seen them before – at The Other Circus.

When I looked at an image of Andrea Lyons on social media, I went cold. I'd seen her at the circus, too. That was three people whose lives could now be restored to them because of Derek and Arlo's deaths. And the circus was in Portmeirion around the time of those deaths.

I plugged Juan Ramirez and Maria Ramirez into the system and waited impatiently. The results didn't take long to come back because there wasn't much there. Like Andrea, they hadn't paid taxes, claimed benefits or used a debit or credit card in years. Either they were dead, or, like Andrea, they were in the circus.

Social media hadn't been a thing when they had disappeared, so it took some trawling to find a copy of Mr Ramirez's driving license. When I saw it, I recognised him straight away. He was in the circus, too; he was the dryad who had helped me fight off Bentley Bronx and his men.

I'd found the common denominator. All of the murder victims had wronged people, and the people they had wronged had been so scared by them that they'd gone into hiding in the circus.

To my knowledge, there was only one man who knew everyone in the circus's true back-stories: Farrier. That was why the victims had been bludgeoned to death. Farrier had killed them while he was still in the Common realm, but he'd still had a little extra werewolf strength to make them resemble burger patties. Damn.

I hesitated about my next steps. Elvira had helped me, she'd passed me files and information and I wouldn't be so far forward if it hadn't been for her help, but I didn't trust the Connection and I couldn't expose the circus. It had helped hundreds of people escape the Other realm. I couldn't tell Elvira about it, and without that context the deaths didn't make any sense. It wasn't that I didn't trust Elvira, but telling her would put her in an invidious position. She couldn't close the file officially; she'd have to lie to Bland and the officers around her... No. It wasn't fair on her to tell her the truth, much as I wanted to. I couldn't risk the circus being exposed to the Connection.

Like Farrier had done, I was going to have to deal with this vigilante style. I wished Gato was with me because I always felt better with him riding shotgun. I looked at Shirdal and Reynard. They'd have to do.

Chapter 31

I did a quick Google to find out where The Other Circus was currently located. It was on the Wirral, near Ellesmere Port, not too far from my home. Not that I'd spent much time there recently.

I felt a pang. I missed my home. Castles are nice, but they're not homey and there are people everywhere. Brethren, dragon circles, Elders ... Emory and I had barely had a hot minute together. For a moment I wished for everything to go back to the way it had been, just me and him, hanging out and having takeout. But we couldn't go back; the only way was forward, and if I was going to become Emory's true mate I had to accept all of the trappings that came with that role.

'Turn the car around,' I ordered.

'What?' Shirdal protested. 'But we're nearly back at the castle.'

'We have a new destination.'

'Where?' Reynard asked.

'Ellesmere Port, on the Wirral. We need to go and face the bludgeoning killer,' I explained.

'And that is?' Reynard enquired.

I sighed. 'Farrier.'

Shirdal stared at me. 'You sure?'

'Pretty sure.' I blew out a breath.

'Who is fucking Farrier?' Reynard asked, frowning.

'Clarke Farrier—' Shirdal started.

'The werewolf-rights activist?' Reynard interjected. 'He went missing years ago.'

'He went underground,' I stated. 'He runs a circus that helps people who want to leave the Other.'

'So if they want to leave magic behind, they have to become a sodding trapeze artist?' Reynard asked.

'No, not all of them stay with the circus. He re-homes some of them and helps them start a new life somewhere else. The circus moves up and down the country, helping people as they go.'

'That seems like good work,' Reynard pointed out.

'It is,' I agreed glumly. 'That's why I don't know what to do about Farrier. He's gone a step too far. I think he's killing the threats that sent some of the refugees underground in the first place, so they can return to their old lives.' A thought occurred to me. 'Damn it, I probably inspired the whole thing when I rescued Alfie and Bella. If I hadn't saved Alfie, maybe this whole vigilante-killing thing would never have occurred to him.'

Shirdal did a U-turn and the car following us did the same. 'Off to the circus we go.'

My phone buzzed with a text from Elvira. *Derek Ives' new Will left all of his wealth to The Other Circus. What aren't you telling me about the circus?*

Motherfucker.

Elvira is a sharp investigator and she knew I was omitting. I hoped that she'd trust me enough to let it go. *Maybe he's always liked clowns?* I replied.

She didn't respond.

A show had just finished and the circus was teeming with people. We pulled into the car park and waited for the masses to depart before we hunted down Farrier. It was just past midday, so we had at least another couple of hours before the 3pm show.

I hopped out and knocked on the brethren's' car. 'I can't have you follow me in there.' The circus was full of people running away from the Other; having four big burly brethren men come in would start a panic. They were all dressed in the brethren uniform of black combats, black boots, black T-shirts; they were all muscle bound and moved like predators. No, I didn't want to scare the circus. 'To be clear, I'm ordering you to stay here. Got that?'

The leader nodded but tightened his hands on the steering wheel. 'Yes, Prima.' *True.* He wasn't happy, but he'd stay there.

When the circus was empty of civilians, Shirdal, Reynard and I strolled in.

'What are you doing here?' Stu asked glumly, kicking his legs against the popcorn counter that he was sitting on.

'Don't mind him,' Bella said, giving me a warm smile. 'He's grumpy because Alfie is back with the herd.' She was snuggled into Ike, her ogre boyfriend. Ike gave me a friendly nod and what passed for a smile for him. Stu folded his arms and glared harder at me.

'Sorry,' I offered. 'I need to see Farrier. Do you want to show me the way?'

'You know the way,' he muttered huffily, but he hopped down off the counter and started to lead me to Farrier's caravan.

I turned to Ike. 'Actually, I might need some help. You want to come?' I'd turned down the brethren, but we might still need some more muscle. Ike was the circus strong man. I knew that Shirdal and Reynard could handle Farrier, but hopefully a familiar presence would put him more at ease.

Stu led us through the circle of carefully parked caravans. Farrier's black van was parked in the centre, as clean and shiny as always. I hoped it would stay in one piece after we'd managed to talk with him. I gave a robust knock on the flimsy door and Farrier called, 'Enter!'

I led Shirdal and Reynard in, with Ike trailing behind us. Maybe it was a good thing there were so many of us; there was barely space to stand, let alone fight.

'Jinx,' Farrier greeted me evenly. He looked suspiciously at Shirdal and Reynard, but he stayed seated, fiddling with his hands in his lap.

'Farrier,' I responded coolly. 'You've been a busy boy.'

He looked at me questioningly, but I didn't buy the polite confusion he painted on his face. I was testy and emotionally drained and I wanted to be home with Emory, so I went straight to the heart of the matter. 'You killed them. Why? Why risk bringing the Connection's attention to the circus like that? It's madness.'

He didn't even deny it. 'You inspired me,' he said proudly. 'When you faked Bella's death, you made me realise that there *was* a way that we could return safely to the Other realm. Death was the key – not Bella's, but her husband Bronx's. If I could kill off the people who had forced members of my troupe into hiding, they could return to normal society. They would no longer be forced to hide who and what they are. It's obvious really.' He frowned. 'I'm not sure why I didn't figure it out before.'

His eyes were feverish and his hands were jittery. My stomach lurched as I recognised the signs. If I was right, then Farrier wasn't doing this alone: he had been influenced by a daemon, just like Sean Hardman and Darius.

I wasn't sure if daemon influence was contagious, so I summoned the IR and willed Farrier to be held still. He started to yell so I silenced him, too. Then I hauled out my phone and called Amber.

'Hi, Jinx,' she answered cheerfully.

'Hi Amber. Listen, I have an issue,' I said urgently.

All merriment dropped out of her voice. 'Of course you do. No one ever rings me for a chat,' she grumped.

'Sorry.' I paused. 'How are you?' I enquired awkwardly.

She sighed. 'It's no good now I already know there's a problem. Just spill it.'

'I have a guy here who I think has been influenced by a daemon, but he's in the Common realm. Is that possible?'

'Yes,' she confirmed grimly. 'There's a reason why the elves and I worked our socks off to get those thirteen daemons locked up. They can cause havoc in both realms.'

'How can I tell if he's influenced?' I asked.

'You can't. You need a witch to rune it out of him.'

Dammit. 'I know you're too far away, so who do you recommend that's local to Liverpool?'

She thought about it. 'I'm on my way to Caernarfon, so you'd better use Kass Scholes. She's the coven mother in Liverpool. She'll have enough power to get out the daemon's influence,' she admitted reluctantly. 'She'll be able to help you.'

'Oh! I've met her already. She was the one that runed out the last daemon-influenced guy I met,' I said triumphantly.

'Oh, have you?' Amber muttered, sounding annoyed.

Uh-oh. I'd inadvertently stirred up some ill feeling. 'Is that … okay?'

'She's the only other viable candidate for the position of Symposium member. But this is too important to be petty about such things. You need to root out the daemon's influence, and then you need to find the daemon that's spreading ill intent. This isn't an accident – there's a daemon out there sowing seeds of discord. You need to find him.'

'Me? Why me?'

'You're a PI. Who else is going to do it?' Amber demanded impatiently. 'We can't just leave a daemon running around influencing people to do dastardly acts.'

'Great. And how do I find a daemon?' I challenged her.

'That's your problem, not mine. You're the one that finds people. Find the host and you'll be laughing.'

Wonderful. 'Can you give me Kass's number?'

'Text me your address and I'll send it to Kassandra and tell her to get there ASAP. See you later.' Amber hung up.

It was telling that Amber didn't want to give me Kass's number. Did she think that I would find her less indispensable if I had another witch on call? I wouldn't; Amber was my go-to witch these days.

I texted Amber the address and got a thumbs-up emoji. I hoped that Kass wouldn't be too long because I was starting to feel itchy. The Common realm was calling my name, and if I didn't answer it would drag me kicking and screaming out of the Other, leaving me wholly vulnerable to Farrier with the daemon's influence still clinging to him.

Marvellous.

Chapter 32

Once I'd hung up from Amber, I removed the magical gag from Farrier. I regretted it immediately. 'Hey!' he yelled in outrage. He was trying to move his body around but it was immobile, bar his head, which bobbed as he tried to thrash around. 'What have you done? Let me go!'

'Sorry, but I can't risk you spreading the daemon influence to anyone else,' I explained.

'The what?' He paused in his flailing.

'You've been influenced by a daemon. That's why you suddenly thought running around and murdering people was a good idea.'

'I've always thought running around and murdering people was a good idea,' Farrier growled back. 'Hugo

Arnold forced the Ramirez family to leave everything they've ever loved. Emily has grown up moving from town to town and her education has suffered. She hasn't seen her grandparents in years, all because Hugo wanted to push drugs and Juan wouldn't stand for it. It's not right,' he snarled. *True.*

Frankly, I agreed with him. 'No, it's not, but the world isn't fair and you can't go around bludgeoning people to death – even if they're bad people.'

'Hugo had it coming. I watched him for days. He was a horrible wanker. I saw him hit a waitress because she spilled his drink.'

'That doesn't make your actions right. The Connection should have dealt with him,' I argued.

'So tell me, next time a dragon steps out of line is your darling Emory going to summon the Connection?' he sneered at me.

I thought of Darius and my blood ran cold. That was different – wasn't it? 'And Sands?' I asked instead of answering.

'Clarissa Sands was a bitch, a thieving, conniving, blackmailing bitch. Victoria – Victorine, as she was then – was friends with Clarissa before she started down her dark path. Victoria could see that path would lead to Clarissa's death and tried to convince her to change her ways, but instead Clarissa blackmailed her. She'd found out that Victoria likes women. Victoria's mum is old fashioned, and if she'd found out that Victoria was a lesbian she would have disowned her and stopped her from seeing her siblings. So Victoria ran away and joined us here.'

'Maybe her mum would have surprised Victoria and accepted her as she is,' I offered. I often saw the darker parts of society, but most people I encountered strived for good.

Farrier snorted. 'And maybe there really is gold at the end of a rainbow.'

'And Derek and Arlo?' I asked. 'What about them?'

'Those scumbags deaths were nothing short of a gift to society. They were rapists. I watched them for one weekend, and they both tried to spike girls' drinks. I sabotaged them, of course, spilling the drinks and warning the girls off. But that was it. Death warrants signed. Do you know, three of their victims are here in the circus, running away from them? None of them trusted the Connection. None of them.'

I thought of Elvira. 'There are good people in the organisation. If people worked with the Connection more, scumbags like Derek and Arlo wouldn't get away with shit for so long.'

'Juan reported Hugo to the Connection,' Farrier scoffed. 'Do you know what they did? Nothing. Absolutely nothing. They were being threatened, and the Connection did nothing. "Dryad politics," they said. Not their problem. The Connection washed their hands of them and then Hugo came knocking and threatened them all. So John – Juan – and his family packed up their lives and here they are. And now, because of me, they can go home. I'm doing great work.'

'You're whackadoodle,' Ike interrupted angrily. 'You risked the whole circus's anonymity. We've all cut off contact with family and friends to be safe and you risked it all.'

'To save us. To save us all. Forever.' Farrier was pleading for understanding.

'You can't kill every single person that's threatened us,' Ike snarled back.

'Why not?' Farrier asked, genuinely confused. 'Why can't I kill them all? I will cleanse the Other realm of these filth so that we can go home. Don't you want to go back? Don't you want to be welcomed with open arms?'

'Every day. But the only thing Kreig will greet me with is a mace. He'll pulverise me, and I don't blame him,' Ike said firmly.

'Why?' Farrier asked. 'What did you do?' Curiosity lit in his feverish eyes.

'Don't you know?' I asked in surprise.

'Not everyone has told me their story. Some people weren't comfortable sharing that information with me, though I would have got it out of them eventually. But once they all knew about my killing plan, they would have told me their stories so I could kill their aggressors.' He sounded very confident.

Ike laughed. 'If you think you'd survive a fight with Krieg when you're in the Common realm, you're absolutely crazy.'

'I survived a fight with a fire elemental, didn't I?' Farrier snarled.

'You bludgeoned her to death while she was sleeping,' I pointed out.

'Krieg sleeps too,' he countered.

'In a cottage full of ogres.' Ike shook his head. 'You're mad. This isn't you.'

'He's been influenced by a daemon,' I explained.

'So I gathered.' Ike sighed.

'How long has he been acting out of character?'

'I don't know. He's been withdrawn, keeping to his caravan for a few weeks at least.'

I frowned suddenly. Farrier's hand had been shaking after we had fought off Bronx and his men. At the time I'd assumed it was an adrenaline come down, but maybe it was the daemon even then.

'That's what I said when I was out hunting,' Farrier said proudly. 'I'd tape up a sign saying "do not disturb" and run off to kill the miscreants. It worked a treat until you came along.' He gave me an unfriendly glare.

'Sorry to ruin your fun,' I said flatly. *Lie.*

There was a knock on the door. I opened it, and in swept Kass Scholes. She had an electric-blue bag on one shoulder and her yellow lizard on the other. The lizard hissed loudly as he spied Farrier. 'Oh hush, Jax,' she muttered. 'We all know about the daemon.'

'Hello again.' I gave her an awkward wave. 'Thank you for coming.'

'You're going around finding daemon spawn, are you?' she asked briskly.

'Not intentionally. Can you rid him of the influence?'

'Of course.'

'Can I let him go?' My skin was itching like mad and I wasn't sure how much more magic I had left.

'Hold him a little longer, please,' Kass instructed.

'Is he contagious?' I asked, concerned that I might be too close to Farrier.

'No, nothing like that. The daemon's influence is only on the targets that he chooses, but it tends to make them lash out and try and stop you from painting rune ona them. I don't fancy getting punched in the face right now.'

'Oh. In that case, Shirdal, Reynard – can you hold him still? I don't have much IR left.'

Both of them seized Farrier. When they were holding him securely, I let go of the IR with a sigh of relief. The itching lessened; I would need to leave the Other realm soon, but at least I wasn't in imminent danger of being booted out.

Kass eyed Reynard. 'And what are you?' she asked bluntly, her eyes sweeping over his black wings.

'I'm one of the black-winged,' he said proudly.

'Never heard of you.'

'We're new.'

She blinked. 'Do we *do* new things?'

'It looks like it,' Shirdal interjected.

'Well, now. And what can you do, Mr Black Winged?' Kass asked.

'Mostly I can fly.' Reynard was being evasive and I guessed he didn't want the hand-claw thing to be common knowledge. If you weren't keeping secrets were you *really* part of the Other?

'Not too handy.' The witch dismissed his flying skills.

'We're still working out the rest of the shit,' Reynard admitted. *True.*

'Right you are. Keep to yourself until you find some more advantages to work with.' *True.* 'You don't want to be weak in this realm.'

Reynard snorted. 'Don't you worry your pretty little sodding head. We're going to be top dog.'

'He was subject to a curse,' I explained hastily. 'His language is peppered with expletives but it's not his fault.'

'It might not have been once, but it fucking is now,' Reynard said confrontationally. 'I like my curse words, the more inventive the better. Did you hear the one about the gonorrhoea-ridden whore?' I shot him a warning look, which he blithely ignored.

Kass was on board with the ignoring Reynard plan. She took off her backpack and started pulling out jars of potions. The lizard skittered down her arm onto the table. 'Um. What's with the gecko?' I asked.

'He's not a gecko, he's a bearded dragon.' She flashed a suddenly mischievous smile. 'I like having a pet dragon.' She winked.

She set out her potions and brushes methodically, pulled on disposable gloves and started painting. Farrier immediately started to scream and writhe. It wasn't pleasant, and Ike decided he'd best jump into the action. He moved behind Farrier and held him still.

The screaming didn't seem to bother Kass and she calmly continued painting. 'His shirt, please,' she instructed Ike with an impatient gesture. He obligingly ripped the shirt off Farrier's back. Farrier's screams reached fever pitch.

Stu pounded on the door. 'Boss, is everything okay in there?'

I popped my head through the doorway. 'Everything is fine. Farrier will be better soon. You know how he's been holing himself up?'

'Yes?' Stu replied cautiously.

'He's not been feeling too well and the witch is here to heal him. She'll do the job, but it's not nice.'

'Help me!' Farrier screamed. 'Kill them, Stuart.'

I smiled reassuringly. 'He'll be fine in a minute.'

Stu hesitated. 'You're sure?'

'Kill them, Stu! Kill the bitches! Kill them all!'

If anything, Farrier's refrain reassured Stu that Farrier didn't need his help. 'I'll be out here,' he reiterated.

'No problem,' I smiled winningly. 'You do that.' I shut the door firmly.

Farrier's screams had descended into sobs; it wasn't nice to watch.

'There,' Kass said finally with satisfaction. She put down her paintbrushes, murmured something I couldn't hear, and Farrier stopped sobbing just as suddenly as he'd started.

He blinked several times and looked around as if he'd just woken up. He frowned. 'What the fuck?'

'You were influenced by a daemon for a couple of weeks,' I explained helpfully.

He licked parched lips.

'Can we let him go now?' I asked Kass.

She nodded and the men released Farrier. Ike walked to the tiny sink and ran him a glass of tap water. Farrier took it with trembling hands and gratefully downed the water. 'Thanks.' He chucked the glass back to Ike. Ike caught it, picked up three others and casually stood there juggling, like you do.

I guess in the circus that's what you did.

Chapter 33

Kass packed up her gloop and paintbrushes into her handy blue backpack. She held out a hand to Jax and he ran obligingly up her arm, settling behind her neck under a cascade of her brown hair. Even knowing he was there, I couldn't see him at all. Sneaky.

'I'll send my invoice to the Prime Elite's residence,' Kass said primly.

'That'll be fine.' Damn; I guessed that this time casting out daemons wasn't free. The witches' invoices were always steep. No good deed shall go unpunished, I thought glumly – but she'd given me a freebie in Smuggler's Cove so I really couldn't complain.

'Wonderful. Thank you for thinking of me. The Liverpool Coven is honoured to assist you.' Kass touched her hand to her heart and gave me a little bow.

I reciprocated. 'I appreciate the assist.'

'No problem. You'll want to try and find the daemon that's spreading discord. He seems to be focused on you.'

'What makes you say that?' I frowned.

Kass's eyebrows rose. 'Well, for one thing, that's twice you've called me to cast out daemon influence. The common denominator is you.'

Wonderful. And she didn't even know about Darius.

'*Ciao.*' She waved goodbye and let herself out of the caravan.

Stu ducked in his head and looked anxiously at Farrier. 'I'm okay,' Farrier reassured him in a gravelly voice. 'You did the right thing. Go on now, I need to talk to these people some more.' Stu darted back out and shut the door.

Farrier steepled his fingers; he was back in control of himself. 'What are you going to do about this?' His eyes were steely.

'Are you planning on killing any more people?' I asked drily.

'No.' *True.* 'It was a stupid idea.' *True.*

'It was. The Connection hasn't made the – well, the connection between the deaths and the circus. If you keep your head down and the killings stop, they'll become just some more cold cases.'

'You're not going to report me?' Farrier sounded surprised.

'And expose every single person in this circus to the Other realm?' I tugged on my messy bun. 'No. I'm not that much of a bitch. And it helps that the people you killed were all douche bags.'

Farrier grimaced. 'They'll still have mothers, brothers – families who'll miss them.'

I didn't know how many of his actions were his and how many were the daemon's, but it was done now and there didn't seem to be much point in him lugging around a bunch of guilt forever.

'Not really,' I admitted. 'Hugo's mum is dead and his sister always disliked him. Clarissa was an orphan. Arlo had a cousin, but he doesn't seem cut up by his loss. They were the dregs of society. I'm not absolving you, but you didn't kill upstanding citizens.'

'No.' Farrier scrubbed a hand across his face. 'The last few weeks are all hazy.' He frowned. 'I forged a document. A Will?'

I put two and two together. 'You drew up a Will for Derek Ives, leaving all of his estate to the circus.'

He grimaced. 'I remember spilling a spiked drink that Derek was going to give to a young girl. She looked too young to be in the club. It makes you sick, what they were up to.'

'Yeah, it does,' I agreed. 'Maybe the head horn can reach out to the victims he knows about and let their relatives know they've died. Maybe it will give them some closure.'

'That sounds good.' Farrier licked his lips. 'Sorry about the car bomb.'

I couldn't help my glare. I'd *loved* that car. 'You owe me big time for that. That was a present from Emory. And the note was creepy, too – you must have spent ages cutting out the letters.'

'I got the circus kids to do it,' Farrier admitted. 'Practising with scissors is important. We home educate the kids here in the mornings and on off days.'

'You do good work here – but no more murders,' I instructed firmly.

'No, I swear it.' *True.*

'Or car bombs,' I tacked on.

'No, ma'am.' *True.*

A thought occurred to me. 'Could you speak with the head horn, Sean Hardman? Maybe between the two of you, you can give me a lead as to who the daemon's host might be.'

He stared at me. 'I'm not averse to giving it a try, but all it takes is a bump in a crowd. It'll be virtually impossible to trace.'

Nevertheless, I wrote down Sean's number. 'Give him a call. If you remember anything helpful, please let me know.'

'Sure,' Farrier agreed though I could see he thought it was a waste of time.

'Do you need anything? Anyone?' I asked.

'Could you send in Victoria, please?' He rubbed a hand across tired eyes.

'The seer?'

'Yes.'

'Sure. We'll find her.' Awkwardly, I picked up the pieces of Farrier's shirt that Ike had literally ripped off of him. 'There you go.'

'Thanks,' he responded flatly. Ike was getting him another glass of water as we left.

Victoria was still in her fortune-telling tent, eating a sandwich with her turban resting over her crystal ball. 'Hi.' I gave her a wave.

'Jinx Wisewords,' she greeted me.

I blinked. 'Um, yes. Farrier would like to see you.'

'Is his turmoil resolved?'

'Hopefully.' The daemon stuff was resolved, but the turmoil in Farrier's soul might be harder to settle.

'Good. I will visit with him.' She pushed back from the table.

'About Clarissa…' I started, before she could walk away.

Victoria's eyes softened. 'She was a damned fool. I told her what the outcome would be, but she didn't listen.'

'I'm sorry she blackmailed you. Will you go home now?' I asked.

'No, not yet. I'm not here because of the blackmail.'

Huh. 'Why are you here then?'

'Because of the future if I did not stay here.' She studied me. 'You have seer magic within you but it is largely untapped. You've locked it up tight. If you ever want to access it, come and talk with me.' She swept out of her tent.

Why anyone would want to know the future, or the possible future, was beyond me. I could barely cope with the life that I had, let alone envisaging a hundred more stretching out before me. No, ignorance was bliss. The seer magic could stay locked up within me, thank you very much. The only future I wanted to know about was what was for dinner.

I was still itchy. 'While we're here, we'd best take me to a portal. I need to recharge in Common and I don't want to have to force Gato to send me there right now.' He'd looked so tired when I'd last seen him; the battle with Darius had taken it out of him.

'No problem,' Shirdal agreed lightly.

The three of us returned to our car; the brethren visibly relaxed when they saw us climbing into our vehicle. With Shirdal driving, I could relax in the back. I pulled my phone out and gave Lucy a call. I needed a moment's sanity with my bestie. She anchored me.

'Hey, Jess,' she answered the phone happily.

'Hey! How are you doing?' I asked.

'I'm okay. How are you?'

'I've solved four murders!' I said triumphantly. Jackie and Dave's killers were still loose, but I had them in my crosshairs. They were on borrowed time before I brought them down – they just didn't know it yet. I pushed them out of my mind; they were tomorrow-Jinx's problem.

Today-Jinx had solved a crime. My mum had taught me a bunch of mental-health techniques and one of them was mindfulness, being present in the here and now and celebrating today's victories no matter how small.

'Wow – and it's just after lunchtime! You've been busy.'

'Well, it's taken more than this morning. I've been juggling a few things.' I took a deep breath and admitted the truth to her. 'I'm worried about Emory. It was an easy decision to save the gargoyles at the time, but now the Elders are here... If Emory loses his Primeship, it's going to destroy him.'

'No, it won't. He's stronger than that – you're stronger than that. Together you will be unbeatable, no matter what phase of life you find yourselves in.'

Something in me relaxed. 'You're right. Of course you are. It might be rocky, but we'll get through it.'

'What's a little turbulence? It's nothing you can't ride out. Hell, you skydive – you probably live for this shit. Jess, you've got this.'

'Thanks. I miss you,' I admitted.

'That's handy,' she said mischievously.

'Huh?'

Lucy laughed and hung up. I stared at the phone in confusion. People were being weird today. I shook it off and called Emory on the off-chance that he was free.

'Jessica Sharp,' he greeted me lightly, but I could feel his underlying worry.

'Emory Elite,' I teased back. 'How are you?'

'I'm okay,' he paused. 'I've been better.'

'How are things at the castle?'

'I've notified Dave's and Jackie's families. That was horrible.'

'I bet – it must have been tough. Anything more on their killers?'

'Not yet.' He said grimly, 'But this is the final straw. The Anti-Crea have been attacking the creatures more and more, but to bring the fight to our door like that? To kill innocent brethren? The stakes have changed. The masses are calling for blood, and I'm hard pressed to deny them.' His voice was dark, but then he cleared his throat and tried to lighten the mood. 'How are you?' he asked.

I let him change the subject – for now. 'We found the murderer. He's agreed to stop murdering.'

'And he was telling the truth?' Emory asked cynically.

'Yup,' I confirmed.

'There's a reason you don't want to bring him in?'

'Yeah. It's Farrier from the circus. He was trying to help more of his people get home – like Alfie,' I explained.

'That's some fucked-up logic,' Emory said drily.

'Yeah. But here's the kicker – he was influenced by a daemon like Sean was, and maybe Darius was too. Farrier is going to ring Sean and see if they can come up with any mutual contacts they might have been influenced by.'

'That's a needle in a haystack,' Emory cautioned.

'How else are we going to find this daemon?' I asked with frustration zinging through me.

'I've no idea. Look for some flashes of red in people's eyes?'

'That's even more needles in the haystack!'

'Are you on your way back to the castle now?' Emory's tone was light, too light. Hmm. He sounded like he should be whistling.

'No, we're popping to the portal. I need to head to the Common realm for a little recharge, and I don't want to use Gato,' I explained.

'You could use Indy.'

'She doesn't really know what she's doing yet. I'll wait until Gato has shown her the ropes a few more times. Hopefully Gato will be rested enough to pop me to the Other later, or I'll head to a Welsh portal somewhere.'

'There's one in Bangor,' Emory suggested. 'You could go there. It's only about twenty minutes from Caernarfon.'

'That's doable, if we need to.'

'Exactly.' He paused. 'Don't get home too late. You're supposed to be doing something.'

'O–kay.' My bullshit-ometer had been tingling all day; something was up. 'Is this a good surprise or a bad surprise?'

He laughed. 'A good one.'

'Have we got time for this? We've got the Elders visiting, we've just been attacked and—'

'We've got to live our lives. This has taken a lot of hard work by someone you love, so we've got time. Don't be late.' He hung up.

I frowned at the phone. 'Bye-bye. I love you,' I muttered at it.

Reynard gave me a tight smile. 'I'm sure the phone loves you too.'

I thought back to my conversation with Lucy and winced. I hadn't been exactly sensitive to Reynard's presence. 'Hey, I'm sorry if what I said to Lucy—'

'Don't be silly,' he interrupted. 'It's not like we gargoyles are not already aware that we're a fucking inconvenience. We've made Emory's life harder and we feel awful about that because we just want to *help* him. A few others suggested we kill the Elders but I didn't think that would please Emory.'

'No,' I agreed hastily. 'That would make Emory upset and angry.'

Reynard's shoulders slumped. 'I thought so.' He pulled his phone out of his jeans' pocket and dialled. 'Tamsin? It's definitely a no-go on the Elder plan. It will upset Emory. We'll think of something else.' He hung up.

Oh my days! Thank goodness we'd had that conversation. I wasn't thrilled about the Elders, especially Geneve, but even so massacring them was *not* the answer.

Shirdal parked the car and we slid out. This time, we waited for our brethren back-up. Shirdal shifted onto four legs and turned to Reynard. 'If Jinx is in the Common realm, she's vulnerable. It is up to us to see her safely to and from the portal and back to the castle. I don't know what other tricks you've got up your sleeves, but at the very least try to look tough.' His tone was doubtful.

'I'm a tough motherfucker,' Reynard growled. 'I've been a sodding gargoyle for as long as you've lived, and before that I was an alpha werewolf. I can and will protect the Prima to my last breath.'

Shirdal inclined his eagle head in satisfaction. 'Let's go and terrify the masses then.'

Reynard grinned. 'Let's.'

Chapter 34

The portal Shirdal took me to was in another café. Called Tococo's, it was off the main shopping street in Liverpool. We had to climb up some narrow steps before popping out at the top. The café sprawled across several rooms, and the décor was far more luxurious than Rosie's. The main room overlooked Lord Street so you could people-watch in safety.

Virtually every person in the café was Other. A handful of water elementals sat in one corner flicking their watery locks everywhere. Two wizards were discussing something animatedly. A bushel of dryads sat in another corner near the plants. Six perfect vampyrs were sipping coffees – I always found it funny to see them drinking something other than blood. Nate said they didn't get any nutrition from coffee, but they could still enjoy the taste.

As always, it struck me as sad that each species sat separately. Hopefully Emory's academy would change that. It would take time, but change always did. I wondered what would happen to the academy if Emory lost his primeship. I still hadn't found the right time to bring it up with him – I'd been hoping he'd tell me of his own volition, but so far he was keeping schtum.

Shirdal was making a show of himself in the café. Rather than leaping up the stairs, he had flown up them, and even now he was hovering near the ceiling. He was there to be seen. 'Come down,' I hissed to him in annoyed embarrassment.

The whole café had frozen; the hubbub paused as everyone stared at the deadly griffin, wondering if the assassin was there for them.

Shirdal landed beside me. 'As you wish, Prima,' he said loudly. The murmuring began once more and this time all eyes turned to me. Wonderful.

'The dragon queen,' someone stage-whispered.

Not yet, not by a long shot. Maybe not ever, if we couldn't convince the Elders to do the right thing and keep Emory as Prime.

Reynard was busy posturing too, his black wings extended around him, taking up a huge space and looking menacing. 'What are you?' a dryad child asked him curiously.

His mother hushed him, panic in her eyes. 'I'm sorry, he didn't mean any offence.'

'I am a black wing,' Reynard proclaimed loudly.

'An angel!' the child called.

Reynard grimaced. 'No, I'm not an—'

'Seraphim!' someone else called.

'No,' Reynard said firmly. 'We're the black-winged.'

'Angel,' the crowd whispered among themselves, pointing at Reynard.

I turned to the waitress, a fire elemental, before this circus became a total shitshow. 'Your portal?'

'Follow me, your majesty.' She gave a curtsy. Bloody hell. I followed her as she took me to a door that simply had a triangle on it, rather like a warning sign. I opened the door and stepped in. And immediately stepped back out.

The waitress's flames were gone. Everyone looked ordinary, even Shirdal; I *knew* he was on four legs in griffin form, but all I could see was all his usual hobo glory. Reynard looked ordinary too; without his wings, I could study the man a little more. He was actually more handsome than I'd initially thought. His hair was such a pale blond as to be almost white, but his skin was tanned and warm. He was wearing a T-shirt, yet I *knew* he was shirtless in the Other. How far the Other realm went to protect itself – it even painted T-shirts in my mind. If it wasn't so amazing, it would be terrifying.

'Let's go,' I said curtly to the men. I suddenly wanted home. I felt vulnerable and I hated that. I hated that being in the world I'd lived in for twenty-five years suddenly gave me an itch between my shoulder blades.

The vampyrs were still sipping their coffees. They weren't interested in me, but everything in me was ready for fight or flight, even if I couldn't see the danger coming. Right now, it would be better for everyone if I opted for flight.

We headed quickly out of the building. Outside, baby-blue skies were shining down on us, and I wished blue didn't equal weakness now. I could still feel the magic inside me, but it was a whisper to its usual roar. How quickly I'd become reliant on it.

We marched hastily to the multi-storey car park. I was relieved that the brethren were there, skulking behind us as extra back-up. There was safety in numbers; even the vampyrs would think twice about attacking us all.

Shirdal paid the parking ticket. I tried to imagine him pushing the buttons with deadly claws, but all I could see were his hands. I let out an explosive breath as we reached the relative safety of the car. It was a relief to be on the move again.

Reynard gave me a side-eyed glance. 'What?' I finally snapped.

'You should rest, Prima. You are anxious. Relax and your recharge will go faster,' he advised sagely.

He wasn't wrong, so I closed my eyes and tried to get comfy. Thoughts kept plaguing me, and the window wasn't very comfortable as a headrest because I could feel the vibration of the road through the glass. Then I heard a click – Reynard had unfastened my seat belt. He reached over and gently tugged me so I was lying down, resting my head on his thigh. 'Rest, Prima. We will protect you.'

I closed my eyes as Reynard began to hum a soft tune and I let the sounds of his gentle music soothe me to sleep.

'Wake up, Prima.'

My mind was foggy and sluggish but I opened my eyes. I pushed myself up from Reynard with a yawn. 'Thank you for being my cushion,' I said, fighting a blush. I can be such a dweeb.

'You're welcome. Emory will be pleased with me for helping you.'

I grimaced internally but I kept my smile in place. 'He will,' I agreed. The nap had rejuvenated me in more ways than one; I felt sharper and ready to tackle whatever was coming.

The sky was still blue and for the first time I missed the lilac. It was different being in the Common realm, not knowing how or when I'd get back to the Other. I had been spoiled by Gato and now I was experiencing what the human half of the Other realm faced all the time. It wasn't nice, so no wonder they were jealous of the creatures that didn't *need* to visit the Common realm unless they wanted to go out of choice. Frankly, I couldn't imagine being like the Other Circus – like Ike and Bella – and choosing to live a vulnerable life in the Common realm. It was incredible and scary how integral magic had become to my existence in only a matter of months.

Shirdal parked in the employees' car park at the castle. We bypassed the turnstiles and used a staff entrance secured with a code and a thumb-print scanner. The staff entrance took us straight into the kitchens. 'Hi, Mrs Jones,' I called as we walked in.

'Prima Jinx, what a pleasure to see you home, and in plenty of time too. I've been distracting myself from Dave and Jackie...' She sniffed, rubbing at red, watery eyes. 'I've done a lot of baking. I have a few cakes for you to try.'

'For what?'

'For your wedding cake, of course.' She rested a hand on her hip and gave me an exasperated look.

'Oh, right. Of course.' The wedding. How could I forget that?

'Come and sit over here.' She moved me to a table out of the way and pulled a chair back for me to sit down. Shirdal and Reynard fanned out on either side of me, still in bodyguard mode even in the castle. The brethren guard had melted away; presumably they had fulfilled their brief.

'I'll make you a brew to go with the cake. Just give me a moment.' Mrs Jones bustled around and I was quite happy to be fussed over for five minutes. She slid a mug full of joy towards me and handed me a plate full of cake samples.

I tried the chocolate cake first. It was absolutely delicious, with the tiniest hint of chilli. 'That's amazing,' I enthused. 'You're wonderful. That's the one, for sure.'

She smiled then pushed another bit of cake towards me. 'Try this one. Cleanse your palate with tea first.'

I'm not sure whether tea works as a palate cleanser but I wasn't fool enough to argue with her. I took a happy sip before trying the next cake, a sumptuous lemon drizzle with a hint of something I couldn't identify. 'What else is in this?' I asked around another hasty mouthful. 'Lemon and what else?'

'Lavender.'

'Wow. It's amazing. This is *definitely* the one.'

Mrs Jones looked pleased, but then she pushed the last piece of cake towards me. It was carrot cake, so I knew I'd love it. She gestured to the tea and I hastily took an obliging palate-cleansing gulp before I dived in. The cake was moist, full of sultanas and carrot, and had a perfect blend of spices. It was enough to make me wish I could cook myself. 'Wow. This is amazing. This one is *definitely* the one.'

Shirdal snorted at me. 'You are shit at this.'

'I am not!' I protested.

'You're supposed to be picking a cake. So far all three of them are "definitely" the one.'

'Exactly. I definitely choose all three,' I said defiantly. I turned to Mrs Jones. 'Can we do that? Three tiers?' I asked hopefully.

She smiled indulgently. 'Of course, Prima.'

I smiled smugly at Shirdal and resisted the urge to stick my tongue out at him. Sticking your tongue out is not Prima behaviour – Summer had already told me that. She'd made me a list. It was like she didn't trust me to behave all by myself, which was ludicrous because I hadn't even taunted NotLeo recently.

Chapter 35

I tried to shake off Shirdal and Reynard, but they stuck to me like glue so I blithely ignored them and went to find Emory. He wasn't in our rooms so I headed to his office. As usual, Summer was ensconced at a desk outside his rooms. She smiled brightly when she saw me, which frankly unnerved me a little. 'Hi, Summer,' I greeted her.

'Hi!' She beamed at me. 'One last question about the chair covers...'

I groaned. 'Summer, I just don't care. If they are cream or green, then I'm happy.'

'Cream with a forest-green sash around them, tied in a bow?' she proposed.

'Yes. Perfect. Thank you.'

She made a note in a leather journal. 'Great. I'll confirm. And have you spoken with Mrs Jones about the menu?'

'No,' I admitted. 'But we have ages yet. Weeks.'

'Weeks are not long to plan a wedding, Jinx,' she said reproachfully. 'And Mrs Jones needs to order in enough supplies for all the guests. The king of the dragons doesn't marry often – this is going to be *the* event of the year. Century, even! I've already got my dress and booked my hairdresser.'

Huh. Maybe that was something I needed to do too. 'Um ... do I have a hairdresser?'

'I've lined you up with Jules. She'll do your hair and makeup – she's a siren.'

I'd met a few sirens; one had worked at the Connection's headquarters in Liverpool. She had thick, pencilled-on eyebrows and filler-filled lips. 'Erm, she'll do my make-up naturally, right? Not clown-like?' I asked dubiously.

'She's very good, I promise. I've booked her in a for a trial the week before, so you can specify what you want then.'

That sounded doable and I relaxed a little. 'Great. Thank you so much, Summer. It's been amazing having your help.' *True.* I would have been completely swamped planning the wedding on my own. And this no ordinary wedding; because of Emory's status, invites would soon be winging out to the who's who of the paranormal world. It was nerve wracking. I tried to focus on the fact that I was marrying Emory and everything else was window dressing.

'I've loved it,' Summer admitted, clasping her leather journal to her ample chest. 'I've always wanted to be a wedding planner.'

'What happened?' I asked curiously.

'It turns out the brethren don't really need wedding planners. We're not fancy folk, and dragons get married once in a blue moon.'

'You could have worked as a wedding planner in the Common realm,' I pointed out.

'I could have but ... I'm brethren. I need to help the dragons – that's just a part of who we are.' It sounded a bit like brainwashing to me – but wasn't that the whole problem with the gargoyle made-brethren, too? Their fanaticism? Okay, so Reynard was a bit over the top at times, but was that so different to how Summer felt? I wasn't so sure.

'Is he free?' I pointed to the door.

'He is, but he's got a meeting with the Elders in an hour or so,' Summer cautioned me.

I bit back the sigh that wanted to escape. Couldn't we get more than a handful of snatched minutes together? 'Thanks. You two stay here,' I ordered Shirdal and Reynard.

'You got it, sweetheart,' Shirdal said as he sprawled on the sofa in by the fire.

'We'll keep a damned good guard here,' Reynard promised.

'You're basically a chocolate teapot for all the help you'd be,' Shirdal groused at him. 'But I'll keep watch, Prima,' he assured me.

'You're as much use as a chocolate fireguard,' Reynard countered.

'That's really original, bouncing off my comment like that.'

I tuned out their bickering and knocked on Emory's office door then let myself in without waiting to be invited. He was sitting behind his desk and for a moment my heart stuttered that he was all mine. His emerald eyes were tired but warm, and a rush of love rolled down our bond as he saw me. I knew he was feeling the same from me.

'It's good to see you, love.' He pushed up from the desk, closed the distance between us and touched his head to my forehead.

'Hey,' I said softly. 'Are you okay?'

He sighed. 'Not really. Notifying Dave and Jackie's families of their deaths was horrible. After Scott and Jane… This has been a real shit week.'

'I'm so sorry,' I said inadequately.

He pulled away and rubbed the back of his neck. 'Everyone was already baying for Anti-Crea blood. It's hard to disagree with that attitude when we're burying more of our own.'

'Scott and Jane's deaths are squarely on Darius,' I pointed out.

'Or a daemon,' Emory countered.

'Maybe. We don't know that for sure.'

He frowned. 'It fits.'

'Maybe,' I repeated. 'What are you going to do about the Anti-Crea?'

'I reached out to Eliot Randall to see if we could sit down and talk. He told me to fuck off.' He shook his head. 'The dragons are furious. Unless we can de-escalate this, it's going to get bloody – and fast.'

'Bloodier,' I corrected, still remembering Jackie's blood spread around her like a grim halo.

'Exactly. The truth is, I want retribution too. I'm sick of being the voice of reason, sick of calming it down.

Sometimes the Other realm demands violence, and if Randall isn't careful that's what he'll get.' Emory shook his head. 'But soon it may not be my problem.'

'Hey! Don't talk like that. It's going to be fine.' *Lie.*

He smiled at me. 'Your lie detector just pinged, didn't it?'

Smartass. I didn't answer; instead I pulled him into my arms and we shared a leisurely kiss that woke me up from my head to my toes. It was slow and loving. Soothing. I decided a change of topic was in order. 'So I caught a killer. Yay for me.'

He shot me an amused glance. 'You also let the killer go.'

'Well ... he was really sorry,' I said lamely.

He laughed. 'I love your kind spirit.'

'I love spirits,' I said mock-seriously. 'Shall we drink gin and do some grinding and dancing?'

'As delightful as that invite is – and it really is – I have to work tonight. And you have a prior engagement.'

'I do?'

'You do,' he confirmed firmly.

'Lucy's throwing me a surprise hen do, huh?'

His eyes narrowed. 'Getting anything past you is really hard. How did you know?'

'A few things,' I admitted with a grin. 'Mostly it was the way people kept saying, "See you later" and "thanks for inviting me". Plus Lucy hung up on me, and she only does that when she doesn't want to lie to me. So ... hen do.'

'Remind me never to plan you a surprise anything,' Emory teased.

'Talking of surprises, Mrs Jones made three amazing cakes for our wedding. I couldn't decide so I said all three. Is that okay with you?'

'You can have a hundred cakes if you want.'

'No, that's excessive. Three is fine,' I said happily.

He grinned. 'Then have your three.' His eyes darkened and his voice deepened. 'I'm more than happy to give you three.'

I licked my lips. 'Are we still talking about cake?' I asked, suddenly breathless.

'No.' He leaned in and kissed me, pulling me up against his hard body. His hands went for the snap of my jeans. 'This is number one,' he whispered against my lips.

Suddenly, I forgot how to count.

I would never think of Emory's office in quite the same way again. I blushed a little as I looked at his desk. He smirked as he watched the colour rise up my cheeks. 'I'm never changing desks,' he said.

'You're incorrigible.' My blush deepened.

'You love it.'

'I do,' I admitted easily.

'Go and see Gato. He might be able to send you back to the Other now,' Emory suggested.

'I've not been in Common very long,' I pointed out.

'You don't seem to need long to recharge,' he noted. 'If not, you have time to head to Bangor before the hen do starts. I have to go and meet the Elders.'

I was suddenly glad that we'd christened his office together because it made me feel weirdly territorial that he was about to hang out with Geneve. Some sort of primal instinct was happy that he was relaxed and content before meeting with her.

I gave him a long kiss goodbye and left him to do some last-minute prep while I hunted down Gato. I didn't have to hunt for long: he was in the room adjoining Emory's suite, lying in front of another roaring fire. He lifted his great head up to greet me; although he didn't get up, he tapped his tail with happiness. Indy leapt around the room – she had the zoomies. She needed a walk and I needed a break from my gargoyle watchdog.

'Reynard,' I called out. 'Can you take Indy out for some exercise?'

The gargoyle puffed out his chest and shot a smug look at Shirdal. 'Of course, Prima. It would be my honour.'

'You're a glorified dog walker now,' Shirdal snarked.

Reynard ignored him,. 'Come on, Indy, let's go.'

Indy looked at me and I nodded. 'Go on.' She followed Reynard out. Poor bastard.

I put my hands on my hips. 'Shirdal, do you *have* to irritate Reynard?'

He considered. 'Why, yes. Yes, I do.'

I sighed and went to kneel by Gato. 'Hey, boy. How are you feeling?'

I called up the ocean in my mind and let the sounds of the waves recede. I reached out to Gato with my magic and felt a crushing grief rush up and overwhelm me. Dad was missing Mum. Tears sprang to my eyes.

'I miss her too,' I admitted. And I did. It was harder some days than others, but for me having her back had been a blip. For me, she'd been dead and gone for years and my grief was an ever-present shroud around my shoulders. Some days the grief lost its sharp edges; some days it didn't.

She'd been gone for seven achingly long years then suddenly she was alive again and it had been amazing and miraculous, but we hadn't been able to *talk*. She couldn't hug me or wipe away my tears like I'd dreamed of a million times. She was there but also not there, not the way I remembered her, needed her. But it had been better than nothing, and it was reassuring to think that she'd been with me all those years even if I hadn't known it.

For Dad it was different. They'd been together that whole time I'd thought them both dead, and they'd been tied even more intricately than Emory and me. I couldn't even begin to imagine the loss Dad was going through. To lose your mum is truly awful, but at least it's the natural way of things. To lose your life partner is different. In life, it's a Russian roulette which of you pops your clogs first, and nobody is ever prepared to be the one left standing.

I concentrated and tried to probe around the crushing grief to see what else Dad was feeling. Love and pride; he was proud of me.

Gato lifted his head and, before I could object, touched his nose to my forehead and sent me back into the Other realm. Then he dropped his head back down, spent. 'Hey!' I objected. 'You didn't need to do that. I was going to go to the hall in Bangor.'

Gato gave a derisory snort. He didn't want me going to a hall.

'I went to a hall in Liverpool, Tococo's,' I told him. 'But I didn't enjoy it as much as I enjoyed Rosie's. You've spoiled me. I felt vulnerable the whole time I was in Common. I can see why people try to stay in the Other as much as possible. Being without your magic isn't a nice feeling, particularly when you don't know exactly when you'll get it back.'

Gato's eyes were sliding shut and here I was, blathering on. I leaned over and kissed him. 'Go on, have a rest, big dog. I'll see you later when you're more yourself.'

I went quietly into Emory's bedroom and closed the adjoining door between us. 'Shirdal, can you find me the wizard who helped Gato? I want to have a word.'

'Of course, Prima.' He bobbed a little bow and walked away.

I turned to my wardrobe. What did one wear to a surprise hen do? I had no idea. Parties aren't really my thing. When I had arrived at the castle, I'd brought little more than an overnight bag but every day more and more clothes mysteriously appeared in my wardrobe. I wasn't sure whether Emory or Summer was to blame, but either way I had a full range of outfits.

I hopped in the shower for a quick freshen up, then dressed in clean jeans and a fresh T-shirt. Nothing fancy, but it was me.

I towel dried my sodden hair and was tying it back in a messy bun when there was a knock on the door. 'The wizard, Robert Chive, ma'am,' Shirdal called in a respectful voice.

I opened the door. Robert was in his sixties, portly and with a sizeable grey beard. His eyes twinkled from behind wire-framed glasses; put him in red suit and he'd make a killing playing Santa. All he needed was a sack and some black boots and he'd be good to go – although the three triangles on his forehead would need covering up.

'Prima.' He touched his hand to his chest. 'My honour to meet you.'

I parroted the phrase then moved impatiently to business. 'My hellhound, he's not well even with the healing. I don't understand. It was just a dragon hurting his ribs. Why is he still so weak?'

'He has expended his energy, Prima. I'm a bit of an expert when it comes to hellhounds.' He took his glasses off and cleaned the lenses. 'It seems to me that Gato is constantly straining his magical energies. Did he take you to the Third recently?'

I nodded.

'That may well be it. Hellhounds protect their bonded when they go to the Third. Without the bond, the Third realm takes its toll on you.' Once again I thought uneasily of Leo Harfen, an elf more present in the past than the moment. 'With the bond, the hellhound bears the brunt of the trip to the Third because they are better able to handle it. With time, the effects will dissipate. For now, Gato needs rest.'

'Thanks for coming by again. You're sure he'll be fine after some rest?' I asked anxiously. Fear was curling in my gut. I couldn't lose Dad too, I just couldn't.

'Yes, ma'am.' *True.*

'Thank you. I appreciate your time.' I shook his hand without even thinking about it and felt his happiness in looking after a hellhound. I released his hand quickly before I invaded his privacy any further.

'It's no problem, ma'am. I'm happy to have had the opportunity to examine another hell hound up close and personal.' He smiled warmly.

There was a brief knock at the door before it swung open to reveal Summer. She was beautiful on any day of the week, but now she was dressed in a red cocktail dress and matching heels that complemented her skin tone.

'Jinx, Mrs Jones has sent up some more cake samples for you to taste. They're in one of the private libraries. I'll show you the way.' *True.* Hmm.

'See Mr Chive out, won't you, Shirdal?' I asked.

'Sure thing, sweetheart. I'm all over it.' He winked: *there* was the scoundrel I knew and loved.

I let Summer lead me through the castle to an old wooden door. She knocked once and swung it open.

'SURPRISE!' everyone yelled.

I grinned. 'Oh my goodness. What a shock!' *Lie.*

Lucy huffed. 'Damn it, you're not even slightly surprised! Who gave it away?' She glared around the room. My hen do consisted of Amber, Hes, Elvira, Summer, Audrey and Lucy, a mix of strong women I'd come to greatly admire.

I went to Audrey and gave her a hug. 'Thank you so much for coming, but doesn't Emory need you to deal with the Elders? I don't want to hog you – he needs you more than I do.'

She smiled. 'I've spoken to a few of them and showed my support. Honestly, he's in a bit of a pickle.' Audrey has always struck me as being largely unflappable, the sort who would call a hurricane a 'bit of a breeze'. 'Anyway, Cuth is with him. We'll see what can be done, but this night is about you. I'm just here for dinner and cake – when you ladies get rowdy I'll make myself scarce.'

I wondered if my mum would have done the same: supported me and showed her love but excused herself before the dildos came out? Probably. She wouldn't have wanted to inhibit the atmosphere. Despite the sudden rock in my throat, I managed a bright smile at Audrey. She wasn't my mum but she *was* Emory's, so at least I had some sort of mother-figure with me. 'I'm glad you're here,' I said softly.

'I know, dear.' She took my hand. 'None of that sadness now. This is a happy occasion. Bottle it up for another day.'

'I'm not sure that's healthy advice,' I said with a little laugh.

'Maybe not, but smile. Today is your day.'

'And what's tomorrow?' I asked, still feeling maudlin.

'Another day.' She gave me a squeeze and went to the cake-laden table. Mrs Jones had indeed baked up a storm.

'Test wedding cakes,' Summer announced. 'Help yourselves.'

Elvira powered over to the cakes and grabbed a slice. She'd had a tough day; Emory had pulled her in after Jackie and Dave had been killed and she was being run ragged, yet she'd still come. I truly appreciated it.

'Who wants a drink?' Lucy asked. Everyone put their hands up.

'Music?' Hes suggested.

'Go for it,' I agreed.

She pulled out her phone, connected it to a speaker and started playing some tunes. Suddenly we had a party atmosphere going. For a moment, I struggled not to feel disrespectful about having fun with all that was happening, but life goes on and being miserable doesn't help anyone. Life is just too damned short; you have to seize it or it will pass you by entirely. Seize the moment and make it great.

Lucy started pouring out glasses of Prosecco and I let myself relax. My hen do was officially under way. When we'd had our fill of cake, Lucy and Hes started moving the tables and seats to clear an area. 'Um, what's going on?' I asked.

'Ha!' Lucy spat out triumphantly. 'At least one thing will be a surprise.'

'That you've suddenly gone minimalist?' I asked, frowning.

'We have a surprise guest,' she said happily. Uh-oh.

The door opened and in walked a lady dressed right out of *Moulin Rouge*. On cue, Hes changed the music to the film's soundtrack.

'This is Madame Rouge and she is here to teach us burlesque dancing!' Lucy announced loudly.

Hes let out a whoop. She'd already downed one glass of Prosecco.

Madame Rouge was dressed head to toe in red, with the notable exception of her black top hat. She wore a red corset with a red burlesque bustle skirt, and the whole outfit was completed by a red feather boa tossed around her neck. She was a woman whose curves had curves and she exuded confidence. 'Jessica Sharp, it's time for your transformation,' she said with a glimmer of mischief in her eye.

Oh boy.

Chapter 36

I found myself dressed in a white corset, white skirt and white feather boa. I even had a white top hat. Everyone else was dressed in black, even Audrey. My kind-of mum-in-law was rocking fishnets. Life was weird.

Madame Rouge made us stand in a semi-circle while she showed us some moves we had to copy. First she made us stand 'like dancers', one foot forward at right angles to the other, then she made us bounce on the spot. Next she taught us the 'shimmy', which I can only describe as shaking our tits about. That was more effective for Summer and Elvira than it was for me and Lucy, since we're not overly blessed in that area. Even so, we giggled as we jiggled. Lucy kept the Prosecco flowing and we drank it in between the steps that Madame Rouge taught us.

After we'd shimmied our tits off, it was time to do some sexy hip grinding. I would never be able to remove the image of my 500-year-old mum-in-law grinding from my mind. I'd try, but I was pretty certain it was ingrained in my mind forever.

Another glass of Prosecco later and we were all laughing our asses off as we took turns doing hair flips and sexy walks across the library. I'd never look at Amber again in quite the same way.

Madame Rouge was hilarious and shameless. She told us that our greatest assets were our smiles and our confidence, then she gave us some air kisses and left us to get truly raucous. Audrey embraced me. 'You're happy,' she smiled.

'I really am,' I beamed. I was also a little drunk. Lucy is the best; the evening had been a total blast, lifting my spirits right when I'd needed it most. There is no problem in this world that time with good friends can't solve – except maybe climate change.

'Good. Emory loves you with all of his heart.' Audrey tucked some stray hair behind my ear.

'I love him too. So much,' I babbled.

She gave me a gentle kiss on the forehead. 'I know, dear. You love him like I love Cuth. Your love will span your whole lives, and long may they be. There will be good times and bad. You may be moving into the latter now, but your love will strengthen you and see you through. Then, when the good times come again, you'll appreciate them all the more. Thank you for inviting me today. It was very special.'

'It was.' I focused on standing still. 'Thank you so much for coming.'

'Bye, ladies,' Audrey called to the room. 'Don't do anything I wouldn't do.'

'Is that restrictive?' Elvira asked curiously.

Audrey flashed a grin. 'Not in the slightest. I was young once.' She winked then sashayed away, still rocking the burlesque clothes. She was awesome. I wanted to be just like her when I grew up.

'You heard the lady,' Lucy cheered. 'Anything goes. It's time for shots!'

Audrey had excused herself some time ago, back when the world wasn't spinning quite so fast. I was sitting in the middle of a prim and proper library wearing a white sash that proudly proclaimed me a hen. The others were wearing black sashes that confirmed they were on the hen do. The sashes seemed otiose, given that we hadn't left the library, let alone the castle. Plus, we were all still dressed in our burlesque clothes.

Hes was busy snoring in the corner. Amber snorted. 'The youth of today have no stamina!' Her words were only slightly slurred, so she was winning.

My face was numb. I knew enough to recognise that meant I was probably shitfaced; plus my legs weren't walking too well. I was drunker than Bambi.

Elvira and Summer had built what they called 'a makeshift pole' consisting of a huge stack of books that they were dancing around, putting their burlesque moves into practice. I laughed every time one of them got too close and bumped the 'pole' so that they had to stop their sexy seduction to do some desperate 'pole' reconstruction.

'I'm pretending it's Mike,' Sumer said as she gyrated around the book-pole. Ha! I knew she had a thing for Mike Carter. I wondered if he knew? I tried to make a mental note to tease him in the future but my mental book was swaying too much to write in.

Lucy bust a gut laughing as the pole toppled over for the third time in as many minutes.

'Mike's a lucky man,' she commented. 'You've got a great thrusting action.'

Summer winked, 'So has he.'

We all cackled a bit. 'Stop abusing the books and come and play a game,' Lucy commanded.

'You're getting good at the queen lark,' I commented. 'You're all imperious now.'

'No business talk allowed.' She glared at me. 'This is a cock-based chat area. You may discuss anything, as long as it is cock-based. Or pussy-based. I'm an equal opportunities smut talker.'

'Lucy!' I giggled. I'd already had way too many Proseccos. 'Don't say cock and pussy in front of Amber! You know she doesn't swear.'

'I'm not going to call it my flower,' Lucy said firmly.

'We really don't have to call it anything,' Elvira muttered.

'That's your problem right there,' Lucy said. 'You need to get some.'

'I could get some if I wanted,' Elvira protested.

'You could,' I agreed. 'Inspector Tasty wants you.'

'He what?' She looked at me in genuine surprise.

'Who is tasty?' Lucy asked, waggling her eyebrows.

'Elvira's partner. His name is Gordon Bland but he's really quite dishy.'

'The nineties called, they want their terminology back,' Summer giggled.

'What's wrong with dishy?' I protested.

'Nothing, if you're sixty,' Hes muttered from her place on the floor.

'I thought you were unconscious,' I slurred.

'No. I was just temporarily not conscious.' She sat up and crawled over to us. 'I think I drank too much.'

'Thank you, Captain Obvious,' Amber said drily.

'Hang on,' said Elvira. 'Can we get back to me? How do you know Gordon wants to get it on?'

Summer rolled her eyes. 'Truth seeker, remember?'

Elvira froze. 'What?'

'Oh shit. I'm so sorry.' Summer's eyes were wide and panicked as she realised what she'd done.

'It's okay,' I assured her. *Lie.* 'It's no big deal.' *Lie.* Stupid lie detector. I met Elvira's eyes. 'I'm a truth seeker and an empath.'

'And a wizard,' she muttered.

'And she can control fire and water,' Lucy added. 'She's a kick-ass mutha who could take over the world if she wanted to. But she doesn't want to. She has all this morality in the way.'

'Yes, thank you, Lucy.' I pinched the bridge of my nose, wishing I was more sober for this conversation. 'It's no big deal.'

'It is. It's a huge deal. Do you know what good you could do with that power?' Elvira said earnestly.

'She already does good stuff,' Hes piped up. 'She finds killers and things!'

'Not the latest one.' Elvira rolled her eyes. I grimaced a little. She caught it and turned to me, eyes wide. 'You did! You found them. Who is it?' she demanded.

'I can't tell you.'

'Can't or won't?' she snarled.

'Can't,' I pleaded.

'You can't let a murderer run around free because you like them.' Elvira's voice was hard.

'It's not like that. It's complicated.' I was begging her to understand.

'They were daemon influenced,' Amber chimed in.

'Do all of you know who it is?' Elvira looked around. 'Am I the ignorant bitch here?'

'You're not being ignorant,' I pleaded. 'It's not a big deal.'

'It is to me.' She stood up. 'Thanks for having me. It's been enlightening,' she said as she stormed out.

Summer was upset. 'I'm so sorry. This is all my fault.'

'It is,' Lucy agreed flatly, glaring at her.

'Lucy! It's not. It's just … tempers are high when there are drinks involved sometimes.'

'Games,' said Hes desperately. 'Aren't we supposed to play games? We haven't done games. This is my first hen do.'

'Of course it is,' Amber snorted. 'You're a little chick. Cheep-cheep.'

'Hey,' I slurred at Amber. 'Do you use face potions or something? You don't look old.'

'I'm not old! I'm forty-one.' She glared at me. I noted she didn't answer the skincare question.

'Games!' Lucy said hastily. 'Jess, answer these questions!' She pulled out some cards. 'Who takes more time getting ready? You or Emory?'

'Emory,' I replied, staring at the door where Elvira had exited.

Lucy turned over the card. 'Emory said the same! Who is the better driver?'

I laughed. 'Given that he doesn't even have a licence ... me!'

'Correct!' She applauded me. 'Who has the most shoes?'

I pictured Emory's wardrobe. 'Emory! Definitely Emory.'

'Correct! He has seventy-six pairs to your four.'

'How can you only have four pairs of shoes?' Amber spluttered.

'Trainers for running in, short ankle boots, long knee-high boots and sandals,' I listed. 'Why would you need anything else?'

'Glitzy heels to go dancing in,' Summer interjected in a 'well-duh' voice.

'That's what the boots are for!' I argued.

'What if it's hot?' Summer asked.

'The sandals.'

'You are impossible,' she laughed.

Lucy was grinning. 'She borrows my shoes.'

'I do,' I confessed. 'Good thing we're the same size!'

'More questions!' Hes shouted.

Lucy slid her a sidelong glance and replaced her Prosecco with a glass of water. 'Who is the more romantic one?'

'Emory,' the room said as one.

'Hey!' I protested. 'I can be romantic. One time I got him bacon roses.'

'Technically *I* got him the roses,' Amber interjected.

'You organised the roses for me! That's not the same thing,' I objected.

'Semantics.' She rolled her eyes then reached out a steadying hand. Rolling your eyes when you're drunk makes your brain spin.

'Next question!' Hes yelled.

'Who is the better cook?' Lucy read.

I shrugged. 'Christ. We both suck.'

'I hope *you* do!' Lucy said with a leer, giving me a nudge and a wink.

'Lucy!' I blushed bright red.

'What? If you're getting married, you need to know how to keep your man happy. Or your dragon. Whatever he is.'

'I know how to keep him happy.' I folded my arms.

'Butt sex,' Summer said sagely. 'And slutty outfits.'

I blinked. Maybe I didn't know how to keep him happy, though he'd never made any complaints.

'I love this song!' Hes screamed as 'Love Shack' came on.

We abandoned the questions in favour of some shots and a spot of 'pole' dancing. We knocked the pole over twice, but we were laughing our asses off so I guess it didn't really matter. The thing with Elvira wasn't great, but I tried to put it out of my mind. This was my hen do, dammit, and I wasn't going to get morose. I was going to get drunk. More drunk. Way more drunk.

Chapter 37

'I love you.'

'So you keep saying.' Emory's voice was amused. 'Let's get you into bed.'

'Wahoo! And then someone can be a cowboy! I don't mind being a cowboy. Unless you want to be a cowboy?'

There was a pause while Emory tried to work out what to say. 'Bedtime. To sleep.'

'Pffft. I don't want to sleep. I have all this energy. Look!' I ran down the corridor. The corridor must have been slanted, though, because I fell into a wall and I slid along it.

'Come on, Usain Bolt,' Emory teased me. 'Let's pour you into bed.'

'You can't pour me. I am meat, not liquid. Look at all this meat.' I waggled my breasts in his face using Madame Rouge's tit shimmy and he flashed a huge grin at me.

'You are going to be *so* hungover,' he warned me.

'I'll be fine. No hangovers is a super power of mine.' *Lie.* Dammit lie detector, shut up.

We made it to our room. 'I'll take her from here,' Emory said to our escorts, Mike and Shirdal, who were both grinning.

'I don't know why you're all chuckling.' I rolled my eyes and my head spun even more. Ugh.

'It's a mystery,' said Shirdal with laughter in his voice.

'I'm good at solving mysteries. I'm like Nancy Drew. But sexy.'

'You're very sexy,' Emory agreed. 'Come on, Nancy, say night-night to the nice guards.'

I made a show of looking around. 'I don't see any *nice* guards.'

'Burn,' Mike chuckled.

Emory tugged me into our rooms and shut the door firmly. 'Let's get you undressed.'

'Yes,' I purred. 'Let's.' I stripped off as quickly as I could but I fell over when my bustle skirt caught around my ankles.

Emory didn't seem to mind. 'I love you,' he murmured. 'Even when you're shitfaced.'

'That's nice.' I beamed. 'I love you too. I don't think I've ever seen you shitfaced.'

'After a couple of centuries, maybe I've learned my limit.'

Oooh, he was good at wordsmithing. '*Or* dragons don't get drunk or high, no matter how hard they try,' I pointed out.

He laughed. 'Yeah, it's mostly that. Damn metabolism.'

'Don't curse it. It lets you eat like a horse and still be ripped like you are. With all those muscles. Have I told you how much I love those muscles?'

'You've mentioned it a time or two,' he confirmed, still smiling. I was amusing him.

'Should I mention it more? Just because you're so pretty, it doesn't mean you don't feel insecure sometimes. Should I compliment you more? You are very pretty.'

'I think you're supposed to call me ruggedly handsome.'

'I like pretty things. I can't take my eyes off you. Come here, and then I won't take my hands off you either,' I promised.

'You slip into bed, and I'll join you soon,' he assured me. When I'd climbed under the covers, he passed me a pint of water and two paracetamols. 'Here, have these.'

'I'm okay. I'll be fine. I don't think I'm rat-faced.'

He laughed. 'The phrase is rat-arsed or shitfaced, love.'

'I like rat-faced,' I said stubbornly.

'Well, you're definitely not rat-faced,' he agreed. 'Take the water and meds.' I huffed but did as he bade. 'Snuggle down.' He pulled the covers up around me.

'Wait, aren't we going to have sex? I'm totally ready for it. I'm sure I could find a sexy outfit somewhere.' I started to push myself back up.

Emory gently laid me back down and kissed my forehead. 'If you're conscious when I come back, then we can talk,' he promised.

'I don't want to talk. I want to play cows.'

He snorted. 'Cowboys.'

'That's what I said,' I replied petulantly.

'You're such a funny drunk. I love you so much, Jessica Sharp.' He kissed me again and went into the bathroom.

I snuggled down under the warm duvet, wrapping it around me like I was doner in a kebab. I was actually very tired; my eyes were gritty, plus the room was spinning quite a lot. I decided to rest my eyes for a minute while I waited for Emory to come back.

'Wake up, sleeping beauty,' Emory said, softly stroking my hair.

I swatted him away and pried my eyes open. Oof. Too bright. I flung my arm over my eyes. 'Shut the curtains!' I ordered.

'It's 10am. You need to wake up,' he insisted.

'I don't want to,' I moaned. 'Shut the curtains.'

'You've got to. The trial starts in an hour and you said you didn't want to miss it. You'll be mad at me if you do.'

Fuck. He was right. I didn't want to miss it. I sat up reluctantly and my stomach lurched. 'I don't feel so good,' I admitted.

Emory was all false sympathy. 'You got wrecked.'

'Ugh.'

'It was fun. You suggested sexy outfits.'

I groaned louder.

'And you kept talking about cows and cowboys. You're a fun drunk.'

'I'm hungover. Help me,' I begged.

'I've asked Mrs Jones to make you a full English. It will either cure you or make you vomit.'

'I don't like the second option.'

'Let's hope for the first, then. Hop in the shower. Food will be here when you get out.' He passed me two more paracetamol, which I swallowed gratefully with another pint of water. I was *thirsty*.

Feeling a little more able to face the world, I pulled back the covers and lurched into the bathroom. The room was still spinning more than it should, my tummy was revolting and my hands were shaking. A hen do before a trial was a damned stupid idea. Stupid Lucy with her stupid surprise plans – but God, I loved her. She is the best bestie ever. Our lives are insanely busy but she'd organised a hen do for me. She is the best.

I stood under the hot water and let it blister my skin. As I dried off, I felt fractionally more human. Emory had laid out clothes for me – suit trousers and a black blouse; I guessed we were going for court-appropriate attire. I dressed and tied back my damp hair. The food smells wafted in and my tummy gave an audible rumble.

Mrs Jones had gone all out and my full-English breakfast had everything I could want, including hash browns and black pudding. She hadn't skimped on the bacon or eggs, either, and she'd given me a dragon-size portion. I wasn't complaining.

Emory was sitting at the table scanning the newspapers, and Gato and Indy were sitting beside him. 'Hey! How are you feeling boy?' I asked Gato.

He gave a happy tap-tap and a lick. 'I'm so happy to see you're feeling better, pup.' I flicked my gaze to Indy. 'Indy – no!' She paused mid-chew and carefully spit out my shoe. I sighed. 'Can't you teach her not to chew?' I complained to Gato.

He looked at me and very deliberately shook his huge head. Marvellous.

I sat opposite Emory and started shovelling in the food. Emory poured me a can of Coke. I sipped it cautiously and, when my stomach didn't freak out, I sipped a little more. Gradually the shakes settled and the pounding behind my eyes eased. 'I think I'm going to live,' I said optimistically.

Emory smiled. 'Of course you are. If that hadn't worked, I had the wizard on standby. We can't have you throwing up during the trial.'

I was tempted to summon the wizard anyway, but I soldiered on through the food and the can of Coke instead. 'And you – how are you feeling?' I asked Emory. I reached out to the bond between us expecting to feel anxiety, but instead there was only calm acceptance. 'You think they're going to replace you,' I accused.

'Yes,' he said simply.

'That's so wrong!' I snarled.

'I broke the law. It was the right thing to do, and I'd do it again if I had to. I'll miss being Prime, but it'll give me more time to focus on our business ventures.'

I liked how he said 'our'. 'I'm sorry,' I said miserably. 'I've cost you everything.'

'Don't be ridiculous. I have you and we have a future. One day we'll have a family. The title comes with a lot of trappings. How often have we been able to see each other lately? I'm always fielding the dryads' complaints or settling a dispute between brethren or dragons. Or helping the mermen stay off of the Connection's radar... '

'You make it sound like you don't love it, but I know that you do.'

'I do. It's been – validating. You know where I came from, where I started in life. Being at the pinnacle of dragon society appeased something in me, but I find that I don't need it anymore, not in the way that I used to. I'll still be Emory even if I lose the Elite.'

'You'll always be the Elite to me.' I took his hand and squeezed it.

I felt a shot of uncertainty from him. 'And you still want to marry me, even if I'm no longer king of the dragons?'

'Of course I do! To be honest, the king and queen thing has always been tricky for me to get my head around. Someone is always on my heels – Shirdal or Reynard or Mike. Living with guards, under the microscope ... it's not something I wanted. But I wanted you – however you came. I still want you, whether you have a title or not. It's you that I love, Emory.'

He lifted my hand up and kissed the back of it, a surprisingly intimate kiss. 'I love you, Jessica Sharp. We're going to be fine, whatever the ruling is.'

'We are,' I said firmly and was pleased when it rang *true*.

'We may not be having Summer's huge wedding, though,' he warned me. 'No one will want to come to the wedding of a disgraced dragon.'

I snorted. 'You couldn't be disgraced even if you tried.'

'If I streaked naked across the castle shouting "down with the dragons", I reckon they wouldn't be pleased.'

I grinned. 'Now that's a visual I'll keep, thank you very much.'

He snorted with laughter. Yeah, we'd be okay, no matter what happened.

We ate until our plates were empty and I drained the Coke. I used the bathroom, applied some basic make up, slung on a leather jacket and put Glimmer on my hip. When I walked back into our room, Emory had put on his suit jacket. The man radiated sexiness, even when he wasn't trying.

'Looking fine, my dragon.' I had a sudden flash of myself telling him he was super pretty. Ugh. At times, I am such a doofus.

'I have one last thing to tell you,' Emory confessed. 'I was planning it to be a surprise for our wedding day, but I'm not sure if it will come out today in the trial and I want to tell you myself.'

'What is it?' I asked, even though I had a pretty firm idea.

'I've been organising an academy for the dragons and the other children of the Other realm. Somewhere they can mix. Hopefully, if we start with the kids it will close the gap between the factions.'

'Indoctrinate them young.' I winked.

He sighed. 'You don't seem surprised.'

'Evan told me,' I admitted. 'He was excited about it.'

'Well, I'm glad for that at least. I don't think I'm ever going to surprise you, am I?'

'Surprises are overrated.' I closed the distance between us. 'It's an amazing thing that you're doing. I'm very proud of you.'

'My legacy,' he murmured, resting his forehead against mine. 'My last act as Prime.'

I pulled back to look into his eyes. 'We don't know it'll be your last act. Not for sure.'

'We haven't found a loophole, Jess, not a single one. The only reason they'll let me stay as Prime is because they like me.'

'That's perfectly acceptable,' I argued.

'Even the Prime can't be above the law. It's okay – *I'm* okay. Do you want to be my witness when I sign the papers for the academy?'

'Sure, but you'd better collar someone else too, just in case anyone tries to say I'm not impartial,' I suggested.

Emory called Mike in, and he and I both countersigned as Emory signed The Other Academy into existence. His last order made it compulsory for each species he ruled to attend the academy for a minimum two-year term, to be extended to a maximum of six years depending on the age of the pupil. The academy would house centaurs, dryads, gnomes, mer, griffins, satyrs, dragons and brethren; whether any other creatures, or the human side like the wizards, witches, werewolves, seers or sirens, would choose to join was anybody's guess.

Emory had set aside funding for the teachers' wages, pupils' uniforms, accommodation, heating, lighting and food costs for a minimum of twenty years, and he'd factored in inflation. It would cost the pupils nothing to attend; finances wouldn't be a barrier to this venture's success. And the accommodation itself? He had bought Alnwick Castle for a cool £35million. From his own wealth.

Come what may, Emory owned The Other Academy.

Chapter 38

I don't know what I'd expected of a dragon trial, but I hadn't expected Emory to be ushered in with magic-cancelling cuffs. At least they'd had the decency to cuff him in front of his body, but even so I was furious. 'How dare they drag you in, like this? Like a common criminal? You're their king and you saved LIVES.' I spat. '*Hundreds* of lives. This is outrageous!'

Emory was calm, Ying to my Yang. He sent soothing waves down our bond, but I didn't want to be calmed or soothed. I wanted to be furious. This whole thing was a travesty and the cuffs were the last straw. He couldn't shift into his dragon form – but they didn't need to keep him from flying away from the law. He was there willingly.

Ludicrous: the whole thing was a farce and I was spitting fury. The only saving grace was the brethren lining the hallways, all in smart black trousers, black shirts and shiny black shoes. They saluted as Mike led us to the gathering hall where the trial would take place. Emory smiled, nodding at the soldiers as we went – because that's what they were. They had been his soldiers for ten years, and man and woman alike jumped to attention as we passed.

Another day it might have made me teary, but instead it fuelled my fury. None of the brethren wanted him to go. They loved and respected him as a leader. This whole thing was wrong.

Mike paused at the entrance and turned to face Emory. He knelt down on one knee and hit a clasped fist to his heart. 'Prime Elite!' he called. Down the hall, the men and women knelt like a Mexican wave. 'Prime Elite!' they roared back.

'Elite!' Mike called as he hit his chest, like the beat of a thumping heart.

'Elite!' the gathered soldiers called back.

'Elite!' Mike shouted again, hitting his chest.

'Elite!' the roaring echo came.

And then silence fell. Mike stood and bowed to Emory; when he straightened, Emory grasped his forearm. 'Thank you, Mike. Thank you all. Thank you for your service. I am honoured to have led you. You are all the very best of men and women that the Other realm has to offer, and I am proud to have served as your Prime Elite.'

I hated this, hated that it was a goodbye. Why was everyone acting like it was a foregone conclusion? Surely something else could be done? I had never seen Emory lose, not once, but now he was doing it with a grace that I simply could not muster. I would not give up hope until the gavel hit the bench.

Mike turned and knocked three times before swinging the huge door open. Tom Smith, Emory's right-hand man and number two, stood on the other side. Like me, he was battling his emotions. 'The Prime Elite,' Mike murmured the introduction.

Tom turned to the assembled crowd, raised his voice and hollered, 'The Prime Elite.' The crowd thumped their fists to their chests. 'The Prime Elite!' they called back, then fell silent in hushed anticipation.

Someone had turned the hall into a courtroom. The five dragon Elders were sitting on a raised dais. Of the so-called Elders, I had only met Geneve in passing, but she was sitting in the centre of the four men like some sort of queen bee. Before her, on its own pedestal, was the Eye of Ebrel.

On Geneve's left were Alfred and Benedict, and on her right were Conan and Darwin.

Darius had been Darwin's brother. He glared at me and I glared right back. *I'll put you down too if I need to.* I barely kept my snarl silent.

On a lower dais to the right was Emory's circle including Elizabeth, Leonard, Fabian and Veronica, all dressed as if they were going to a ball rather than a trial. I struggled not to glare at them; all nine of them held Emory's fate in their hands and I did not trust them with it.

The hall was full, full of brethren and dragons and dryads and mermaids and former gargoyles. Jesus, was that a gnome? Despite the huge gathering, it was absolutely silent.

The pricks had set up a dock for Emory to stand in. What a farce. He turned and strode at a measured pace towards his fate. Fuck that. I caught up to him and looped my arm through his, then I smiled up at him as I made him hustle to the dock. We weren't going to make this more of a show than necessary.

Geneve turned up her head and breathed fire towards the cavernous ceilings. It was a nifty trick for someone in human form, not one I'd seen done before. 'Let the trial commence.' She spoke with her honeyed tones into the silence, like she wasn't about to condemn her former lover. Maybe she wasn't. Maybe there was still hope. But my gut didn't believe it, not for one moment.

I battled despair; Emory didn't need to feel that from me even though I was despairing for him, not myself. He was about to lose everything he'd worked for for so long. And it was *wrong*.

Alfred stood. 'We, the assembled Elders, have questioned the people that were formerly known as the gargoyles.'

Reynard flapped his black wings and rose up above the assembled row of black wings. 'We will be known as the dark seraph.' Dark angels? They'd be avenging angels if the Elders weren't careful.

Alfred's jaw clenched at the interruption but he inclined his head in acknowledgement. 'The dark seraph have been questioned,' he continued as if he hadn't been interrupted. 'It is clear from speaking with them that the made-brethren have undue affection for Emory Elite.'

'Who is to say what is undue?' I asked loudly. Emory shot me a quelling look. I ignored it. My question was valid.

'It is a question for this court,' Alfred responded coolly. 'One which we have discussed at length.'

'For the two whole days you've been here,' I muttered.

'In times gone by, a made-brethren was killed because it was assessed as a threat to all other brethren. But times have changed and we are a modern court.' I felt a stirring of hope. 'In discussions with Emory Elite, it has been agreed that, should Emory be removed as Prime, the dark seraph will remain with him under his protection and as his ongoing responsibility.'

Emory nodded once and the dark seraph in the hall erupted into cheers.

'Order!' Darwin shouted. 'Order in this courtroom.' He had watched too many courtroom dramas. The assembled crowd ignored him.

Emory cleared his throat. 'Settle down now,' he ordered. The room fell silent.

Take that, Darwin. You may be old, but your people's respect for you has long since waned.

Geneve stepped forward. 'With the fate of the dark seraph decided, the only outstanding issue for this court to consider is the fate of our Prime, Emory. Emory, your word is your honour and we expect all answers to be truthful and to not omit essential truths. Do you confirm?'

'I do. My word is my honour. I will give truthful answers. I will not omit essential truths,' Emory swore.

'Excellent. Explain to this court how the dark seraph came to be,' Geneve demanded. Would it kill her to say please? Manners cost nothing. Though Elizabeth Manners might cost Emory everything.

Emory cleared his throat.

The door burst open and in walked Lucy. 'I'm the reason Emory is in this mess,' she declared loudly. 'I am Lucy Barratt, Queen of the Werewolves. I am here to be a witness for Emory Elite.'

Love, fierce and strong, roared in my heart. Never had I loved my bestie more. She was wearing black sunglasses, which was one of her signs she was battling a hangover – an impressive achievement for a werewolf – but nonetheless she sauntered in like she owned the place. She wore jeans, a white top and a pink blazer. She was blithely ignoring the Other realm's black dress code.

'You are not welcome in this court,' Geneve snarled, nostrils flaring.

'Tough shit. Try and throw me out. Start a war with the werewolves. Or let me say my piece and then I'll leave,' Lucy threatened.

Geneve turned to the other Elders and they murmured among themselves.

'You may approach the court,' Conan confirmed grudgingly.

As if they had a choice. They had the Anti-Crea to deal with so they couldn't afford a war with the wolves as well. I wanted to stand up and cheer for Lucy but I held it in.

She came to stand next to Emory. 'I was in a pickle. I was being attacked by another werewolf pack, but it wasn't just werewolf politics at play. A black witch was pulling the strings and, as part of that, she was trying to destroy werewolves forever. You are very old,' she said guilelessly to Geneve. 'You must remember the Great Pack?'

Geneve gave an abrupt nod.

'The Great Pack was ripped from us by a curse the witches laid centuries ago. Any werewolves that spent too long in their wolf form became feral and golden-eyed. With time, they became twisted and grey and became gargoyles. The black witch thought the original curse didn't go far enough – she wanted the Great Pack destroyed. Instead, another witch helped us to break the curse. In breaking the curse, we changed the course of the gargoyles' fate. As you all know, Emory is king of the gargoyles. They had knelt to him as their Elite and in exchange he had offered them his protection. When they knelt to him, he swore to them that he would protect them. If he had failed to act that day, not only would the gargoyles be dead, but Emory Elite would be foresworn. An oath-breaker.'

An oath-breaker is one of the worst insults you can throw in the Other realm. To have a Prime who is an oath-breaker would have had huge ramifications for dragon society. Their word would no longer be trusted. Emory had had no choice but to act – surely the Elders could see that? I felt another surge of hope. This wasn't over yet.

Chapter 39

Silence reigned after Lucy's testimony. The Elders conferred among themselves for an achingly long twenty minutes.

'We thank you for your attendance.' Conan said finally to Lucy as if they'd had a choice in the matter. 'You may now leave.'

What shithouses they were; they'd left her standing there for twenty minutes for no reason. Dragons and their powerplays.

Lucy shot me an apologetic glance, squeezed Emory's wrist, and then she left.

'As I was saying... ' Geneve said drily. 'Prime, please explain the series of events that led to the gargoyles becoming the dark seraph.'

'As Lucy Barratt has already described those events, I do not intend to re-visit them.' Emory didn't want to be questioned on Lucy's secrets. 'Following the release of the old curse, it became clear that the gargoyles were dying. A huge magic was being sucked from them. As you know, gargoyles are immortal. Something in the curse had unnaturally sustained their life force, and when the curse ended so did the extension of their lives. Had I not acted, all of them would have died, every single gargoyle the world over. I had given my oath to protect them, so I did so. I made them brethren, tying them to me in a bond of magic big enough to replace the magic that had been taken from them. That stabilised the magical forces within them and saved their lives.' Emory's voice was loud and clear. The room burst into whispers.

'Order!' Darwin called, slamming his gavel repeatedly. Emory shot the occupants of the hall a quelling look and silence fell.

'Were you aware that it is illegal to make brethren?' Geneve demanded.

'I was.'

'Do you accept that you broke the law?' she asked.

'I do,' Emory responded simply.

'To save lives!' I interjected loudly.

'Laws are laws,' Geneve snarled. 'They are sacrosanct.'

'Extenuating circumstances are *extenuating*,' I insisted. 'If he hadn't saved their lives, you'd have him hauled up here as an oath-breaker. No matter what he chose, you would have fucked him over.'

This whole thing had been brewing for a while. Emory was too much of a peacemaker for some of the dragons' tastes, and the escalation of Anti-Crea sentiment had worsened matters. My tummy sank like a stone. This had never been about the gargoyles.

'Jessica.' Emory shook his head at me, taking my hand in his cuffed ones.

Was I not allowed to speak in his defence? He had let Lucy speak, so I would not be silenced either. 'This isn't a trial! Where are the advocates to speak in Emory's favour? Where are the arguments and speeches? Only a threat of war made you let Lucy speak. This is a kangaroo court.' I scowled at the Elders.

The hall burst became noisy again as everyone started talking among themselves. 'There will be order in this court!' Darwin shouted. They blithely ignored him and continued talking and arguing. There was some pushing and shoving; the atmosphere was turning ugly.

'Quiet.' Emory spoke softly but everyone in the hall obeyed instantly and turned their eyes back to their king.

'It is time for the Eye,' Alfred said. 'Take the Eye of Ebrel,' he ordered Emory.

I saw Elizabeth lean forward, eager to see what was coming next. Bitch.

Mike stepped closer to Emory and unfastened the magical cuffs around his wrists. Emory didn't make a show of his newfound freedom; instead he simply walked to the jewel where it nestled once more in its pillow on a pedestal as if it had never been missing. I was glad I'd managed to find the damned thing before all this; it would have been awkward in the extreme if Emory had lost it. Accusations would have flown – even more accusations.

He hesitated for the barest of seconds in front of the stone and I sent a wave of encouragement down our bond. *You can do it,* I reassured him. Though honestly, I had no idea what he was about to do.

As Emory reached out and lifted the twinkling yellow diamond into the air, the tension drained out of his shoulders. And then something happened within the Eye, a shimmer, a light. What the hell? The room seemed to hold its breath, then the Eye flashed red. Sinister blood-red. And red it remained.

Elizabeth's mouth dropped open. She hadn't expected that. I didn't know whether that was a good thing or a bad thing.

'The Eye has judged,' Darwin called out triumphantly. Oh fuck. Red is *never* a good colour; it's second only to Disney's evil green.

Darwin sent a smirk in my direction and I wanted to punch the smug smile off his face. 'And it finds Emory Elite guilty. The Elders will now convene to determine what sentence should be imposed.'

What the fuck? How could a damned diamond judge all this crap? 'This is bullshit,' I muttered.

Emory laid the jewel back on the pillow and returned to my side. Mike surreptitiously forgot to place the cuffs on him again. I hugged Emory and I was glad when he hugged me back. I guessed he was okay with PDAs if he wasn't the Prime Elite. 'Stupid fucking jewel,' I muttered into his neck.

'I hoped for a moment.' He sighed.

'I'm sorry. This is so shit.'

'It is what it is.'

'What it is, is shit.'

The Elders wasted no time in returning with their judgement. Couldn't they have at least *pretended* to be weighing things up?

Emory's sense of resignation hummed down our bond. Audrey and Cuthbert had discreetly made their way to us and were now flanking us. Emory sent them a grateful look. Moments later, Evan joined us and stood silently next to him. I flashed the brave boy a small smile.

Geneve stood. 'The Elders have made their decision but let us hear first from the circle. The circle's vote would usually only be required in the event that the Elders vote is a tie, but as Darius is … no longer with us, it is only a formality. Nevertheless, it is right that we observe the procedures. Elizabeth Manners, is Emory your Prime? Yay or nay.'

Elizabeth stood and met Emory's eyes as she coolly responded, 'Nay.' Backstabbing bitch.

'Fabian Sheldrake, is Emory your Prime? Yay or nay.'

Fabian swallowed hard and studied his feet as he proclaimed, 'Nay.'

'Leonard Caruso, is Emory your Prime? Yay or nay.'

Not-Leo smiled at me as he replied, 'Nay.' Bastard. I'd get him back for this; I'd get all of them.

'Veronica Forest, is Emory your Prime? Yay or nay?'

She lifted her chin high and said in a clear ringing voice, 'Yay.' The crowd burst into cheers.

'Silence! Silence in the hall,' Geneve shouted. Everyone ignored her. Emory held up a hand, and hush descended again. 'Let us go around the Elders. Alfred?'

'Nay.'

'Benedict?'

Benedict was snoring. Alfred surreptitiously kicked him and he snorted as he jerked awake. 'What?'

'Yay or nay?' Geneve asked tightly, glaring at the elderly man.

'Um ... yay?' Cheers erupted again and we had wait for things to calm down. This time, Emory didn't help the Elders regain control of the room. It was already apparent that crowd control wouldn't be a part of his role for much longer.

Geneve huffed when silence finally fell. 'Conan?'

'Yay.' The crowd whooped again.

'Darwin?'

'Nay.'

The tension in the room ramped up. It was only the Elders' votes that really counted; the circle's vote had been window dressing. It was equal votes, possibly because

Benedict hadn't known what he was voting for; now it was all on Geneve. She had the deciding vote.

'For myself, then. Is Emory Elite my prime?' She paused dramatically, drawing out the moment. 'Nay.' She smiled spitefully at Emory. 'Three Elder votes nay, and two Elder votes yay. They nays have it. Emory Elite is no longer the Prime of the dragons.'

The hall exploded into noise.

Fuck.

What's Next?

Revival of the Court

Well, what did you think of *Betrayal of the Court?* I hope you enjoyed it. I really loved writing this one! If you're desperate for more, then never fear! I never leave you waiting for long. The next book in this series is *Revival of the Court* coming out in June 2023. Have you read Lucy's trilogy yet? For *maximal* reader enjoyment I thoroughly recommend reading Lucy's trilogy first, which starts with *Protection of the Pack.*If you would like two free books in the meantime, then please subscribe to my newsletter! My newsletter comes out twice a month, with a third in release months. You can subscribe through my website: www.heathergharris.com/subscribe.

Reviews

As always, I appreciate reviews SO much. I really do read them all. One of them recently said they hate the use of the word "whilst" in my writing as it seems old fashioned. I have used "while" this time, just for you dear reviewer. So please do review, I promise I listen to them. The really nice ones make me beam for hours.

Please review on Amazon, Bookbub and Goodreads if you can! I'd also appreciate a mention on genre appropriate Facebook groups if you can.

Reviews and positive buzz from readers makes a huge amount of difference to us little Indie Authors and I really can't thank you enough for taking the time to review for me, wherever you can.

Patreon

If you'd like to support me *even more* then you can join me on Patreon! I have a wide array of memberships, ranging from £1 per month – £300 per month. No one has taken me up on the biggest tier yet but a girl can dream!

I give my patrons advance access to a bunch of stuff including advance chapters, cover reveals, art and behind the scenes glimpses into what goes on into making my books a reality.

About the Author

About Heather

Heather is an urban fantasy writer and mum. She was born and raised near Windsor, which gave her the misguided impression that she was close to royalty in some way. She is not, though she once got a letter from Queen Elizabeth II's lady-in-waiting.

Heather went to university in Liverpool, where she took up skydiving and met her future husband. When she's not running around after her children, she's plotting her next book and daydreaming about vampires, dragons and kick-ass heroines.

Heather is a book lover who grew up reading Brian Jacques and Anne McCaffrey. She loves to travel and once spent a month in Thailand. She vows to return.

Want to learn more about Heather? Subscribe to her newsletter for behind-the-scenes scoops, free bonus material and a cheeky peek into her world. Her subscribers will always get the heads up about the best deals on her books.

Subscribe to her Newsletter at her website www.heathergharris.com/subscribe. As a welcome gift, you also get two free novellas for subscribing!

Too impatient to wait for Heather's next book? Join her (very small!) army of supportive patrons at Patreon.

Contact Info: www.heathergharris.com

Email: HeatherGHarrisAuthor@gmail.com

Social Media

Heather can also be found on a host of social medias including Facebook, Instagram and Tiktok. She has a Bookbub and Goodreads page and would love a follow on Amazon.

Glossary - The Jinx Files

Jinx's Other Log – An aide memoire

Amber - A feisty red-headed witch. Business-like, money minded, she lost her partner Jake who was coaxed to death by Bastion (see below). She's one of the contenders to become the next Coven leader.

Bastion – paramount griffin assassin. Laconic and deadly. He can coax (make someone take a course of action that they're already considering). He thinks of me like an niece, and although he kills people, I still think he's a good man under his kill count. Has a daughter, Charlize.

Chris – Emory's brethren pilot. Always on standby with a helicopter.

Emory – yum yum dragon shifter king. King of a bunch of creatures. So far I've ascertained that he's the Elite of the following creatures: centaurs, dryads, gnomes, mer, gargoyles, griffins, satyr.

Elvira – Inspector Elvira Garcia. She used to be kind of betrothed to Stone, and she loved him. She's prickly but I think she's warming to me. I think she's an honest person, underneath the prickles.

Elizabeth Manners – Greg Manners' mum, member of Emory's dragon circle.

Fabian – member of Emory's dragon circle. Saw him once at Ronan's ball raising money for making more Boost. Query his motives for being there.

Gato – my Great Dane turned out to be a fricking hell hound. He can grow huge with massive spikes and he can play with time like it's his favourite ball. He can send me between the realms for a magical re-charge. He also houses my father's soul. He used to have Mum too but she died closing the daemon portal.

Glimmer – A sentient magical blade, created by Leo Harfen, the elf. It can take magic from someone Other, and be used to make someone Common become magical.

Or, make someone magical have an even bigger skillset. The transference of power always changes the magical gift somehow, in unknown ways.

Greg Manners - brethren soldier. I used to turn his hair pink to get a rise out of him but lately the only one getting a rise out of him is Lucy. He's her second in command and all round enforcer of all things Lucy, so nowadays I don't pink his hair.

Hes – my once-Common assistant. I rescued her from Mrs H's clutches, but Glimmer made her magical, she's a vampyr that doesn't need blood.

Lucy – my bestie! I turned her into a werewolf using Glimmer. Now she's accidentally a werewolf alpha, with her kick-ass wolf Esme.

Nate – Nathaniel Volderiss is the son and heir of Lord Volderiss. He also has a master/slave bond with me. We can sense each other and he has to obey me. I need to be so careful in how I phrase things so I don't accidentally force him into an action he doesn't want. He used to date Hes but when she betrayed his trust he dumped her to the kerb.

Reynard – He was once a squat, grey-skinned little gargoyle but the Other Realm waved a wand and now he's something else. Something new. The Other realm doesn't like new. Watch this space.

Roscoe – Head fire elemental, used to run Rosie's Hall where I got introduced to the Other Realm. Partner to **Maxwell Alessandro** (see Lucy's files).

Shirdal – head honcho of the griffins. He appears to have a drinking problem but everything is deceptive when it comes to this man. Always dressed in rumpled, mismatched clothing I once saw him kill thirty men without breaking a sweat, yet I trust him …

Stone – Inspector Zachary Stone, he died in a hellish fiery portal, closing the daemon portal to the daemon realm. He was raised Anti-Crea but despite his father's best efforts, he ended up being a good man.

Tom Smith – Emory's right hand man (brethren). He's loyal, taciturn and loves to hide in bushes.

Printed in Great Britain
by Amazon

38082475R00218